THE SECRET

D1060042

ALSO BY K.L. SLATER

THE SECRET

K.L. SLATER

bookouture

Published by Bookouture in 2018

An imprint of StoryFire Ltd.

Carmelite House
50 Victoria Embankment
London EC4Y 0DZ

www.bookouture.com

ISBN: 978-1-78681-576-7
eBook ISBN: 978-1-78681-575-0

For Francesca Kim & Moo xx

Three things cannot long stay hidden: the sun, the moon and the truth.

Buddha

PROLOGUE

Archie

Eighteen months earlier

My favourite place isn't real and that's why it's called a virtual world. It is a place that is far away from real life. Headphones on, volume up high. I can screen everything out when I'm inside a game.

You look as if you're just sitting there, but it feels like you're actually leaving your body where it is and setting your mind free in a completely different world. A place where bad stuff only happens to the people on the screen.

Best of all, you can't hear the real-life shouting.

I take off my headphones and listen. There are no raised voices, no slamming doors, so I get up to go to the bathroom.

Everything is quiet, as if I'm completely alone. I don't feel scared, I like the silence. I like it better than the sound of adults fighting.

The door opposite the bathroom is open a little and I hear a noise coming from behind it. A sort of puffing, scratching sound.

I take a couple of steps closer and peer through the crack.

For a moment, it feels like I'm still in the game world. Where things aren't real, where nothing that's in front of your eyes makes any sense.

Before I can stop it, my breath catches in my throat. My hand flies up to my mouth but it's too late. The gasp is already out and I know I have been heard.

I turn to run, but I hear shouting and I feel a hand clamp down on my shoulder.

'I won't tell,' I cry out. 'I promise I won't tell.'

PRESENT DAY

My teacher, Mrs Booth, speaks to us a lot in class about secrets. She always says the same thing, but does it in lots of different ways.

Last week she said, 'Some secrets are fun and *safe* to keep. Like, if your dad is going to throw a surprise party for your mum, for instance.' I looked over at Matthew Brown, who hasn't even got a mum. 'You wouldn't want to tell a secret like that, as it would spoil the surprise.'

The class started to buzz with everyone telling their own stories of good, safe secrets, but then Mrs Booth clapped her hands once and started to count, 'ONE, TWO…'

The rule is, if she gets to three and we're still noisy, we might have to forfeit our break time.

So everyone stopped talking right away and the classroom was so quiet you could hear a pin drop. Except that's just a saying because it's virtually impossible to hear a pin drop. You'd have to have what's called *ultrasonic hearing*, which I'd like but haven't got.

'But we have to remember that some secrets are not good to keep,' Mrs Booth continued. 'Some secrets are *not safe* to keep. If something makes you sad or afraid, or if you, or someone else, could get hurt by keeping a secret, then what should you do?'

'Tell a trusted adult,' we all say, in unison.

Despite what Mrs Booth says, I used to think that secrets were mostly exciting, something to look forward to.

I used to think that telling a secret, at the right time, was a joyful thing to do. Like ages ago, when Dad surprised Mum with her new car and she cried and hugged us both and didn't get her frowny face for days.

But now I know that there are some secrets that can lie on your chest like a sheet of lead, or seethe at the bottom of your stomach like a knot of poisonous snakes.

I could get top marks in literacy if I wrote a story like that, but it doesn't feel as good when it happens to you in real life.

There's a sort of secret that grows bigger and bigger in your mind like a tumour and it stops you feeling any happiness at all.

Mrs Booth doesn't realise that if you tell a trusted adult a big enough secret, it can get you into serious trouble.

Worst of all, telling a secret like that can hurt the people you love the most.

CHAPTER 1

Alice

'Be a good boy for Auntie Alice,' Louise says, and gently pushes my reluctant nephew towards me.

She hands me an overstuffed plastic sack and places Archie's school bag and coat behind the door.

It has been precisely five days since my sister deposited the poor kid on my doorstep for an impromptu overnight stay. It seems to be happening more and more.

At least this time it's just for the evening, I console myself.

'It's boring here.' Archie plants his feet and folds his arms. 'There's never anything to do.'

I'm the first to admit, I haven't anything in the flat that would be remotely interesting to an eight-year-old. Apart from Magnus, that is, my big white tom, who detests Archie with a vengeance.

'I'm sorry, poppet,' Louise tells him, and ruffles his hair. She looks at me and pulls her lips and eyes into a squinty face. 'Sorry he's here again. His Xbox is in the bag, so he shouldn't be too much trouble.'

Her phone beeps and she reads the text message, staring at the screen. Looking up at last, she gives me a tight smile and heads for the door.

'Hang on, when are you picking him up?'

'I'll be back soon as I can get away from the meeting. It shouldn't be too long after nine.' She backtracks a few steps. 'That's all right, isn't it?'

I brush down the front of my old grey fleece. It must be obvious I'm not going anywhere, but that's hardly the point.

Despite the fact that she's been at work all day, my sister's make-up looks fresh, and she's wearing tailored black trousers with high heels and a stylish mixed-tweed jacket. Her perfume fills the hallway, a fusion of sharp citrus notes softened by delicate florals.

Louise is the kind of woman who wears a different perfume on each day of the week. Not for her a signature scent.

There was a time I wore my Miss Dior fragrance like a piece of essential clothing. Wrapped myself every day in its comforting cloak of Italian mandarin, jasmine and patchouli.

When I wore it, I walked a little taller, spoke a little easier… I thought then that the scent helped to show others who I was, when in actual fact it became clear that it merely helped to cover up the fault line I hadn't yet recognised in myself.

Too shallow, too impulsive, too shy, too selfish.

What I did to Jack proves it beyond doubt.

Louise is staring at me.

'Where is it you're going again?' I say vaguely. I can't remember if she's actually told me or not.

'Just a last-minute work thing,' she says briskly. 'Tedious but necessary, I'm afraid.'

Three months ago, Louise was promoted to the position of senior marketing manager at the Nottingham-based PR company she's worked at for the last three years. At the time, she hinted she'd benefited from a very good salary hike, but I've noticed they now seem to expect a great deal more of her. Over recent weeks, there have been frequent late evenings and even the odd overnight stay in London.

It doesn't help matters that Darren, Louise's husband and Archie's stepdad, also works very long hours.

Consequently, when Louise finds herself in a childcare fix with Archie, I'm usually her first port of call. I'm happy to help out, of course. I'd like to do more, if only it didn't take so much out of me.

'They ought to make allowances at work; they know you've got a child.' I look at Archie's glum face. 'It's hardly fair, just landing stuff on you like this.'

Louise gives a mirthless laugh.

'Welcome to my world. I don't mean to be unkind, but we don't all get to watch daytime TV and stare out of the window for hours on end at some bloke on the tram we fancy, you know.' She ruffles Archie's hair as she heads for the door again. 'See you soon, pudding.'

I swallow hard but say nothing. Louise has always engaged her tongue before her brain, but I wish now I'd never told her about my man on the tram.

I wouldn't have thought it possible to feel a connection with someone you've never met, but that's what has happened. It became harder to keep it to myself, so one day I told my sister about him in passing. Louise being Louise, she wanted the lowdown on him, of course. But there was very little to tell, although the date has seared itself into my memory.

Friday 26 February. It was the first time I saw him and a day that also happened to be my thirtieth birthday.

I was standing right by the front window, opening my single birthday card, from my sister. I set it on the windowsill, its bright metallic greeting and colours incongruous against the scudding grey sky.

Sounds dramatic, but the bleak outlook from the window seemed to pretty much sum up how my day, and most probably my life, was likely to pan out, and I'd already started to turn away when I happened to glance down to street level.

The 8.16 tram had just arrived at the busy hub that sat right outside my apartment block.

This was just a regular street when Mum first bought the flat; not a busy high street dotted with shops, not a quiet back road with residential parking only, but somewhere in between mainly used by traffic rather than people.

Before she got too ill, she would sit by the window in her nightie and slippers, watching the starlings and sparrows that perched on the rooftops of the houses across the road. When they flew past, she'd press her fingertips to the glass and get this expression of longing on her face that made me look away.

But since the city council's much-lauded tram scheme was completed, the road and the stretch outside the apartment block have been transformed into a buzzing hive of activity at all hours of the day. I don't see Mum's birds as much now.

That morning, as usual, there were so many different faces and moving bodies to watch. Everyone seemed lost in their thoughts and plans for the day ahead. I found it fascinating and comforting, watching others.

Popular advice online for single people with few friends is to join clubs, walk a dog, do their food shopping at the same time every evening, I assume in the hope of casing the aisles to spot a potential suitable mate who is perhaps browsing the cook-chill meals or queuing at the deli counter.

That may all work splendidly. I wouldn't know, I haven't tried it. What I have discovered, however, is that it's sometimes surprising how little it takes to make one feel a bit less lonely.

I turned back to the window again and watched the numerous passengers boarding and alighting. It was done as nothing more than a welcome distraction from the empty day that stretched out endlessly in front of me.

A few seconds before the tram pulled away, passengers rushed down the aisle to get a seat and my eyes were drawn to a pocket of stillness in the middle of the second carriage… to *him*.

He sat there amongst the chaos, all calm and together, fully absorbed in a book. I reached for Mum's small bird-spotting binoculars I'd not yet had the heart to move and twisted the lenses to focus in on the tram window.

My breath caught in my throat when the striking cover of *The Old Man and the Sea* by Ernest Hemingway filled the viewer. It was the exact same edition as the slim volume I had in my bedside drawer. The one that had remained my favourite book of all time after I first read it at school.

It felt like some kind of a sign. At that point, I hadn't even realised his physical resemblance to Jack.

In that moment, if I'd known the extent that seeing him would rattle me and unearth the memories I'd worked so hard to bury, I'd have turned away.

But I didn't turn away. I couldn't.

CHAPTER 2

Some time ago, I read a convincing article in a magazine about cosmic ordering. It gave examples of celebrities who subscribed to this method of thinking and had subsequently applied it to their lives with great success. I spent the months leading up to my thirtieth birthday silently beseeching the universe to send me a sign.

The morning of my thirtieth birthday, I thought that maybe, just maybe, this was it.

'Hello, earth to Alice, you still with us?' Louise's glossy red manicured fingernails wiggle in front of my eyes.

'Yes.' I snap back to attention. 'Sorry.'

'See you later, then…' She turns before stepping out of the door and onto the communal landing. 'If I don't break my neck going back downstairs, that is. I don't know how you stick it here. The lifts are never working and the foyer always looks in need of a good clean. My colleague has just moved to a nice new flat in Cinderhill and it's immaculately maintained.'

She's exaggerating. This is not the poshest apartment block in town, but it's far from the worst. The valuations of the flats here have really shot up in the last couple of years.

We're no longer stuck on the outskirts of the city at the mercy of a scant and unreliable bus service. It's just a fifteen-minute tram ride into town and there are plenty of young professional buyers with good salaries that it seems to suit perfectly.

When Mum became ill and I stopped work, we sold the family home to buy a more manageable place and to pay for regular home help, which wasn't available on the NHS.

Mum hated it at first, missed her garden terribly, but I quickly discovered I rather liked apartment living. The way that up here you feel sort of safely tucked away from the street and from other people.

Although when Mum was still alive, her companionship made it a cosier place that felt more like home. I didn't realise how empty and soulless the apartment would feel without her.

I close and lock the door behind Louise and walk back into the lounge. A sullen Archie flops down on the sofa and swings his legs up.

'Just slip your shoes off, please, Archie,' I say lightly.

With the opposite foot, he forces each shoe off, scattering small lumps of dried mud over the carpet.

'You might want to take your fleece off too,' I suggest.

I'm terrible for feeling the cold and I know the flat is too warm for most people's tastes.

'I'm OK, thanks, Auntie Alice.' He zips up the fleece as though I might tear it off him. 'Can you set up my Xbox?'

'*Please*,' I chide him.

'Please.'

I suppose that's my planned soap-viewing scuppered for the evening. Thank goodness for catch-up TV.

I pick up his shoes and head for the kitchen.

'What's that noise?' Archie says, cocking his head and looking up at the ceiling.

'Just upstairs. They can be noisy sometimes.'

'It sounds as though someone is throwing furniture around.' Archie frowns.

'I'll sort your game out in five minutes. I'll put your tea on first,' I call distractedly as I leave the room.

'Not hungry,' Archie shouts back just as I turn on the oven. 'Mum bought me a McDonald's on the way here.'

I turn the oven off again with a sigh. I bought some healthy breaded chicken pieces especially for Archie. Not much use to me, as a vegetarian.

More worrying is the fact that my nephew is piling on weight. It's logical to assume that if I've noticed, surely Louise must have done too. I know only too well how cruel other kids can be about that sort of thing.

As I start to fill the kettle, a terrible yowling noise comes from the lounge.

I drop the kettle in the sink and tear into the other room.

'Stop it!'

Archie releases Magnus from a bear hug and the cat scoots away.

'I only wanted to cuddle him.' He looks upset. 'I want him to be my friend.'

'You can't force animals to like you, Archie,' I explain. 'You have to relax around them so they learn to trust you.'

'I always do the wrong thing.' He sighs and flops back onto the sofa again. 'I'm just a stupid fat lump.'

'Hey! I don't want to hear you talking that way about yourself. Has someone called you that?'

'No, but that's what they all think.' He shrugs and looks down. 'I'm bored.'

I take a deep breath and try to look at it from his point of view. He's had his evening plans ruined just as I have.

'Look, let's not start our time together like this. I'll set your Xbox up right now on one condition.'

He raises an eyebrow in anticipation.

'Are we friends?' I say, beseechingly.

Archie gives me a half-hearted high five and I set about sorting out the tangle of wires, trying to work out what goes where.

CHAPTER 3

In the end, the struggle is worth it… almost. For the next two hours at least, Archie doesn't complain about being bored.

Instead he is engrossed in yet another virtual world that has been designed for streetwise teenagers over the age of fifteen, most certainly not for impressionable eight-year-old boys.

I really need to point out the age classification to Louise. She leads such a busy life and probably hasn't realised that most of the games in his carrier bag have an age restriction.

Archie reluctantly pauses the game so he can visit the bathroom. It's scary, how rapt he becomes while playing.

I sit for a moment, relishing the silence.

My eyes are drawn towards the window. I don't feel the need to draw the curtains, being on the third floor. It's another benefit of apartment living, having nobody overlooking me.

The tram stop below is well illuminated and the light permeates up, giving a soft glow, so it's never really fully dark outside. I find that reassuring rather than irritating.

The day after I first spotted my man on the tram, I impulsively pushed the tiny square table from the kitchen over to the front room window. I decided I'd now start each day by taking my morning coffee and toast there, eating my breakfast while I listened to the morning show on BBC Radio Nottingham.

That change, although slight and seemingly insignificant, seemed a fitting way to begin my thirty-first year. Any change was better than nothing.

And after that, every weekday morning, on the 8.16 tram that I knew terminated at Old Market Square, he was there. Always sitting in the exact same kerbside seat.

I couldn't see much detail up here on the third floor, yet it was still close enough to garner an impression of him. Such as how his short brown hair was shot through with gold when the weak sun shone through the glass.

In some ways, he looked nothing like Jack. It was more to do with his mannerisms, the way he held himself. He had a pale complexion and he always looked clean-shaven. His outerwear seemed to alternate between an unremarkable beige raincoat and a more casual black Puffa jacket, which I noticed he would don on the days the temperature dropped a little.

He seemed to gravitate from reading to staring blankly out of the window. Increasingly, as the tram slowed each morning, he'd look down and swipe rapidly through his brightly lit phone. Often he seemed quite absorbed in tapping away.

He always looked so… I don't know, *lost*, I suppose.

There was something about him that touched a part of me I kept well hidden from everyone. I didn't always acknowledge it, even to myself.

Such observations about someone you've never actually met sound crazy, I know. I'm just saying that's how it was at first.

Archie reappears, back from his visit to the bathroom.

'Only ten more minutes.' I check my watch as he slumps into the chair without answering.

'Die! Die!' he screams, pummelling the console.

I wish I could build a bit of rapport with my nephew.

Despite trying to entice him – unsuccessfully – to play a board game or watch a film with me, I've spent most of the time looking up from my Kindle, lurching between horror and disbelief at the amount of blood and gore – not to mention bad language – on the television screen.

I issue a second ten-minute warning, which falls on deaf ears. My hearts sinks as I realise certain warfare looms ahead.

My third warning is futile.

Finally, I've had enough. I turn off the television at the mains.

'No, Auntie Alice, please… I'd nearly finished that level!' Archie launches the joystick at the wall. It hits the framed photograph of Mum and knocks it off the coffee table. I rush over and snatch it up.

Three years earlier

The day I took the picture, Mum was heading out of the door to get to the pre-booked cab that would take her to her regular ladies' group meet-up. That week it was afternoon tea at the local garden centre.

She'd curled her hair and put a little eyeshadow and lipstick on. She seemed to be lit up from the inside.

'You look lovely, Mum,' I told her. 'Bright and energised.'

'You sound surprised.' She laughed. 'There's still life in the old dog yet, you know.'

I knew she found great pleasure in the freedom of choice she had. Getting out to events, deciding what to have for tea, watching what she wanted on television. Things that most people wouldn't give a second thought to, but that were massively important to her.

Even this long after Dad had gone, the novelty of living her life for just her remained fresh.

'Smile for *Candid Camera*.' I grinned as I picked up her camera from the side.

She rolled her eyes and stood still at the door for me. I could tell she was flattered, despite her objections.

That photo that Archie knocked to the floor as though it were nothing was taken just two weeks before she collapsed.

Present day

I use my sweater to dust it off and place it back on the table as I give Archie a look.

'That's enough.' I try to affect a firm but calm tone, even though I'm shocked at his sudden angry outburst. 'You've been playing now for two and a half hours. That's far too long.'

'I'm nine soon. I'm not a baby.'

'You need to be at least fifteen to play some of these games,' I try to reason with him.

'*Please* put it on again, Auntie Alice,' he whines.

'I think you've had enough, Archie. How long does your mum allow you to play?'

'She lets me play all night if I want to.'

I know Louise has been distracted by work just lately, but I doubt very much that's the case. At least I *hope* it's not.

Archie seems to be running on an adrenalin high after his marathon gaming session and doesn't look remotely ready to settle down. If Louise doesn't get here until after nine, it'll be at least ten o'clock before they get home and Archie sees his bed.

By anyone's estimation, that's far too late for a boy of eight who's got school in the morning. But as Louise has often let me know in no uncertain terms, she knows what she's doing when it comes to her son.

Archie throws himself off the sofa and thrashes around, banging his heels into the floor, coordinating each blow perfectly with his yells.

'I – WANT – IT – BACK – ON – NOW!'

I spring up and grasp his hand firmly.

'Right, that's enough.' I pull him back onto the couch, praying that the tenants downstairs are out for the evening. 'Sit there, and when you're quiet, I might think about getting you a glass of milk and a biscuit.'

'When's my dad back home?'

Despite my inflamed temper, I instantly feel guilty. I know that Archie sees very little of Darren during the week. Archie's biological father, Martyn, Louise's first husband, is never mentioned, and it's become an unspoken understanding that we don't talk about him.

Archie was five when Louise remarried. Me and Mum were so impressed when Darren insisted he should formally adopt Archie, and as far as I know, Archie has always thought of him as his father. He's a good stepdad, although I suspect he's a bit of a pushover when it comes to my headstrong sister. As we all are, I suppose.

Darren's job as a regional sales manager for a pharmaceuticals company takes him all over the Midlands, and often he's travelling until very late in the evening. Louise told me that by the time he gets home, Archie is often already in bed. He's bound to miss him.

I return from the kitchen with a glass of milk and a plate bearing two Jaffa Cakes by way of a peace offering.

'Thanks, Auntie Alice,' Archie says meekly. 'Sorry I got angry, I didn't mean to.'

'Don't worry, Archie,' I tell him. 'But instead of you kicking off, I'd rather we had a conversation about something if you're not happy.'

He nods and takes a sip of milk.

I watch him, thinking how his flash of anger over turning off the game was so sudden and powerful, as if it had been simmering under the surface all along. I wonder briefly if something is bothering him.

Magnus, having smelled the milk, sidles up to him. I smile and nod, encouraging Archie to relax around him, but he reaches out and tries to press Magnus closer to him.

The cat springs away, upending Archie's glass.

There's milk everywhere. On the sofa, on the carpet, all over Archie's clothes. Magnus ventures over and starts lapping at a small puddle of it.

Archie screeches and tries to push Magnus away. His fingers only just touch the cat, but he isn't fast enough to evade Magnus's retaliation. Extended claws rake down his arm.

Magnus stalks regally from the room against the backdrop of Archie's wailing.

CHAPTER 4

'I'm sorry about Archie's arm,' I tell Louise when she eventually arrives to pick him up at nine thirty. 'I've bathed it with antiseptic. The scratches aren't very deep and should heal quickly enough.'

'Do you think he'll need a tetanus injection?' Louise peers at his arm, frowning.

'I'm sure that won't be necessary.'

She jabs a finger at the cat. 'You ought to sort that vicious old fleabag out.'

Magnus glares, unrepentant, from the lounge doorway.

'Archie isn't used to handling animals. You can't really blame the cat; they act on instinct.'

'Go and put your shoes on,' she tells Archie curtly. When he's left the room, she shakes her head. 'I don't know what's got into him lately. He's either withdrawn or losing his temper at the slightest thing.'

'He got angry because I called time on his Xbox,' I tell her. 'Some of those games are really unsuitable, Louise. Have you actually watched them?'

'I don't have time for that!' She turns, muttering to herself. 'I'm doing my best, OK? I can do without more criticism being sent my way.'

I sit down and lean my head back against the seat cushion as a wave of exhaustion washes over me. I love my sister and nephew dearly, but they're both hard work at times.

'What's the matter?'

'I'm just… exhausted.' My voice sounds thin and insubstantial.

'You want to try working a twelve-hour day and see how you feel then.' She studies me and her face softens a touch. 'How come you're so tired?'

'I took my tablets before I knew Archie was coming, and I've had to clean up the milk he spilled all over the—'

'You should be careful with those prescription drugs. It's very easy to become addicted, you know.'

I'm over the worst of the ME now – my symptoms are classed as mild unless I overdo it – but there are still some people, my sister being one of them, who don't really consider it a proper illness. So she can't really understand why I still take medication and get a bit flaky at times.

With difficulty, I hoist myself up to standing and move towards the doorway. It takes a real effort now the fatigue has got a hold.

'You spend too long stuck in the house. You're seizing up, that's the problem. What the hell was *that*?'

We both look up as something heavy thumps to the floor in the apartment above. Then a few moments of muted yelling and pacing around.

'Oh, it's the people upstairs, I hear it a lot lately. I don't know what's happening up there.'

Louise's gaze sweeps around the hallway. 'This place is far too big for you to manage, Alice. You don't need three bedrooms any more and you can do without inconsiderate neighbours like that.' She rolls her eyes up to the ceiling. 'We really need to discuss selling again, for your own good.'

She pauses and tips her head while watching me, trying to gauge my reaction, but I can't face going over it all again, not now. I'm not ready to move yet and I won't be bullied into it.

When I stare blankly back at her, her lips tighten in barely concealed frustration.

'Fine. But at some point soon, I would like to discuss it. I think that's only fair and reasonable.'

I hold the front door open without comment.

'Bye, Archie.'

'Bye, Auntie Alice, I'm sorry about the milk.'

'Don't worry about it, sweetheart. Bye, Louise.'

'See you later.' Her voice sounds flat. 'Thanks for having him.'

She sweeps past me, and I don't know if it's the poor light, but her face looks drawn with worry.

I lean back against the closed door, feeling the relief flood over me. These interactions always leave their mark on me. After everything that's happened, my sister still has the power to make me feel guilty for thinking the worst of her.

Back in the living room, I stare at the semi-dark window. Throughout our childhood we were close, and left to our own devices, we might have remained so. But Mum, although I'm sure she never intended to, somehow periodically managed to set us against each other.

We lived out of the city in those days, in a modest but large semi-detached house on a busy road. A short walk away were fields and a small wood. We weren't allowed to go far on our own, but very occasionally, we'd walk there as a family, perhaps for a picnic in the warmer months.

Twenty years earlier

One day, right at the end of the summer holidays, Dad promised to take us blackberry-picking when he came home from work after lunch. It looked very miserable out there, as if the rain was here to stay, and I voiced my concerns to our mother.

'He'll have to take you another day,' she said briskly as she wiped down the kitchen counters for the umpteenth time.

But blackberry season didn't last long, everyone knew that. Dad had taught us that the nicest berries were prey to a number of pests. So although there would be plenty on the bushes for a while yet, they'd all be grubby and half-eaten.

Plus, as Mum was always reminding us, Dad was a very busy man and most days wasn't even home from the bank by the time Louise and I went up to bed.

Dad letting us down was nothing new. The trip to the zoo, the sleepover in our bedrooms with friends, the pizza party in the garden – blackberry-picking in the woods was about to join the list.

I was just ten years old but I remember that day because it was the first time I'd recognised a pattern, and I felt a real sense of injustice.

'I'm going to tell Dad he has to stick to his word and take us out,' I said firmly, planting my bare feet on the cool kitchen tiles. 'You said people should stick by their promises, didn't you, Mum?'

Mum's face paled. 'Yes, but… you mustn't repeat that.'

'Why not?' I folded my arms and waited.

'Because it's not fair. He works so hard and does his best for us.' Mum rubbed harder at the pristine work surface, but she wouldn't look at me.

'You've already cleaned that bit,' I said peevishly.

Louise watched us silently, her mouth set in a mean line.

'Alice, just leave it!' Mum closed her eyes for a second before she opened them again. They were so big and blue in her pale, startled face. 'Please don't go on about it. Dad will take you both out another time.'

He wouldn't. We all knew it, but I understood there was no use going on about it.

'The fruit will be full of maggots by the time he can take us again,' I said glumly, letting my arms fall to my sides.

'Ugh, shut up… She's making me feel sick, Mum.' Louise pulled a face and stuck out her tongue. 'You're gross, Alice. I'm glad we can't go into the woods, it's boring.'

'That's enough, girls. There are plenty of other things you can find to do today, I'm sure.'

'We'll play hospitals,' Louise announced, handing me a nurse's hat. 'I'll be the head surgeon again and you must do as I tell you at all times.'

I watched as Louise grabbed Big Ted and placed him on a towel on the kitchen table, which served as our operating theatre.

'Can't we play something else?' I asked without much hope.

'It's my favourite game,' Louise replied firmly as she selected the most exciting-looking implements from the medical play case she'd received years ago but still insisted on using like a big baby.

'Louise, remember what we talked about,' Mum said gently, stroking her long light-brown hair. 'It can't always be your choice. It's Alice's turn to choose today.'

'But she always chooses boring things.' Louise scowled, stamping a foot.

'What would you like to play, Alice?' Mum asked me.

I thought for a moment. 'I'd like to paint,' I said, brightening at the thought of it.

'Oh great,' Louise huffed. 'I told you it would be dull. Everybody at school thinks she's boring too.'

'They don't!'

'They do!' She smirked, her eyes narrowing. 'That's why nobody ever picks you for their netball side and why you always have to stand on your own in the playground after lunch.'

Present day

Louise has always known how to put me down.

I turn now and walk out of the lounge, towards my bedroom.

I don't know where that memory came from, but I know that in twenty years, the feeling hasn't changed.

In my sister's eyes, I will never quite measure up.

CHAPTER 5

Louise

As she bundled Archie and his bags out of the apartment block, Louise reflected that it had been one hell of a day.

The new Hilton Hotel campaign was taking so much of her time and yet she still had to somehow pull in the draft marketing plan for New Pages Press, the small publishing press the CEO's daughter had just created, hot on the heels of her wedding planning business that had started up and then folded within a record eight-month period.

It was high pressure and almost impossible to do well in the time available. And yet Louise had to admit she'd been attracted to go for the promotion to senior marketing manager for precisely that reason.

Her job as assistant marketing manager had become laborious. She wasn't utilising her innovation skills at all, and that was largely due to Meryl Corner, her boss, refusing to delegate or allow her any space to breathe in her own role. Every day was a drag and dampened any creativity.

Happily, when Meryl had reluctantly retired three months ago at the age of sixty-seven, Louise felt her chance had finally come. She'd put everything she had into the application, and the CEO had finally given her the opportunity to shine.

But right now, that well-known cautionary phrase, 'Be careful what you wish for' came to mind.

Louise was struggling, and it wasn't just the job. But she wouldn't, and couldn't, let anyone know that.

She'd find a way to get through the bad times and emerge calm and capable. That was how she'd always dealt with her problems, and this would be no exception.

Of course, it would be far easier to focus on the job in hand if everything else didn't seem to be disintegrating around her ears.

Archie's deteriorating behaviour was really beginning to get out of hand, and she felt increasingly ill equipped to cope with him. At times, he seemed to actively seek to wind her up to snapping point. To her shame, he had succeeded on one or two recent occasions.

She had to admit that Alice, whom she'd written off as an irredeemable shadow of her former self, had been a star since Louise had accepted the new job. She'd stepped in at the eleventh hour on a number of occasions to mind Archie while Louise had to work… at least that was what Louise had told her when she had to be elsewhere for reasons she intended to keep to herself. For now.

It was a battle to get Archie up to the apartment, though; he always kicked back against going.

'It's boring there. She doesn't know anything about gaming and there's nothing else to talk about,' he'd said before tonight's visit.

'Auntie Alice, not *she*,' Louise corrected him.

Archie had a point, though, Alice was out of touch with young people. She'd often make caustic comments about the amount of time Archie spent on the computer, or piously point out that he ate too much junk food. This, from someone who barely went out and whose only friend was a cat.

It was easy for Alice to get on her soapbox and pass judgement; she wasn't desperately trying to keep her head above water.

Louise considered the Xbox and fast food a godsend when it came to juggling her son and all her other, increasingly demanding hats.

Professional working woman, mother, wife, sister… the list went on. She knew she wasn't alone; it was what was expected these days, wasn't it? A sign of women taking back power by being bloody fantastic at everything and having it all.

Except it wasn't working… for her, at least.

Sometimes, probably like half the female population, she dreamed about leaving the house one morning, getting on a train and then a plane and never coming back. That was how bad things felt right now.

She would never admit it to anyone else, but for the past twelve months, it had felt as if she and Darren were wading through knee-high mud. And not holding hands, either.

She supposed lots of couples could say the same, but it was a complete reversal of how it had felt when they'd first married. That was only four years ago, but back then they'd had far less money and less impressive careers and yet every day had felt as if they were skipping through life and making time to smell the roses and just be a family.

Since then, life had somehow beaten them down, slowly turned them into different people altogether, until now she didn't recognise the man who'd inspired and excited her at all.

It was sad and troubling and she wasn't quite sure what to do about it. Louise acknowledged she probably wasn't dealing with it in the right way, but she was a living, breathing woman with her own needs. And if he wasn't meeting them, then he deserved everything he got.

When Alice complained about her low energy because of some condition Louise couldn't even remember the name of, or simply the fact that she had to leave the flat to do an errand, it made Louise's blood boil.

She tried hard not to show it, tried not to take her own frustrations out on her sister, but then the occasional caustic comment would slip out of her mouth before she could bite it back.

It was certainly true that Alice had shouldered the brunt of their mother's care during the last eighteen months of Lily's life. Louise had been grateful for that, and had told her sister so. She couldn't claim she'd nursed Mum with care like Alice had, but she'd done the best she could at the time.

Alice could be a bit of a martyr at times, and often failed to acknowledge that she'd been more than happy to hide herself away from the world. After all, closeted away up there on the third floor, there was no one to answer to about what she had done to Jack.

And now, over a year after their mother had passed away, Alice was still clinging onto the flat and, subsequently, Louise's half of the inheritance.

Worse still, she'd told Louise that she'd taken a shine to some guy who caught the tram past her apartment block each morning. She'd gone on and on about him, as though she was fostering some kind of weird and ridiculous obsession about what might happen between them in the future. Louise suspected this might mean her digging her heels in even harder about moving to a smaller property.

But things had changed. Louise had no choice but to make Alice see sense now and sell up, because her own options were fast running out.

She was entitled to that money, and somehow she had to get her hands on it quickly.

Whatever it took, she had vowed to herself that she would somehow make it happen, because the alternative was unthinkable.

CHAPTER 6

Alice

On Monday morning, I open my eyes and a sober realisation hits me. These days, I seem to have just one reason to get out of bed, and pathetically, that is to get myself to the lounge window in time for the 8.16 tram.

Technically, the man on the tram is still a stranger. But a few weeks after my initial sighting, something happened that I definitely counted as progress.

That morning, when the tram stopped, he slipped his phone in his pocket and stared directly up at my window. It wasn't an accidental thing, like he'd been looking around and settled on my face. It was a definite, bold stare that immediately grabbed me.

I took a sharp intake of breath when my eyes met his and that's when the similarity to Jack hit me.

I immediately dodged behind the curtain, heart pounding, and stayed there until the tram moved off again.

It's not him, I kept telling myself. It's not Jack.

Of course, on a logical level I knew full well that that was the case, but that didn't stop it raking up and magnifying all the emotions I felt about Jack. The clutching, desperate hope in my throat that it *was* him and the terrible crushing guilt in my chest of knowing it couldn't be. What I'd done had made sure of that.

The rest of that day, I fretted terribly. Illogically.

Had the man on the tram seen me at the window before and wondered why I was staring at him like that?

What if he'd seen me dart away behind the curtain and thought me unfriendly?

Surely he couldn't know I'd been watching him every morning for weeks. He certainly hadn't given any sign he'd noticed.

Anyway, even if he had spotted me, he couldn't be certain it was him I was looking at. There were so many other people around, I might just be watching out for a friend each morning, or waving someone off.

Perhaps I'd imagined the whole thing and he wasn't staring at me at all.

But then the next morning, as soon as the tram arrived, he quite deliberately twisted in his seat and looked directly up at my window again with no hesitation at all.

This time, I didn't dash behind the curtain. I forced myself to stay put.

I felt my cheeks burning like red-hot coals, but I reasoned he was far enough away that he wouldn't spot the extent of my embarrassment.

I considered my impression of his face. His features were softer than I'd imagined from his more angular profile, which had such a resemblance to Jack's.

He wore a striped wool scarf in a trendy fashion, tied like a student might. He pulled at it until it loosened, and I caught a glimpse of something beneath it: the dark knot of a tie nestling on a white collar.

A professional job, then.

I held his gaze, saw the ghost of a smile that played on his lips, but I couldn't bring myself to respond with a similar gesture. My features felt frozen in place.

When all the remaining passengers had boarded and the tram moved off at last, I felt a curious mixture of relief and disappointment.

I leaned back in the chair, relaxed my shoulders and gulped in air. I hadn't even realised I'd been holding my breath.

Here I was, just turned thirty years old, and trapped in a monotonous life that had sapped me of any energy or enthusiasm. Worse still, there was no sign of anything changing.

I'd quietly accepted my lot for so long, but now I wondered, did this always have to be the case? Was a normal life still within my grasp?

I felt a sudden longing for the person I used to be... bright and confident. I knew what I wanted and felt well able to achieve it. When I'd first met Jack, I honestly thought there was a strong chance we'd settle down, have kids, the whole shebang.

But life had had something else in store for me, something I had no chance of controlling.

Added to this, the time looking after Mum had taken its toll, and when I finally emerged on the other side, it felt like all that I had left to work with was the husk of the woman I used to be.

So on my birthday, seeing this guy who looked so much like Jack, who just happened to be absorbed in one of my favourite books of all time... it might sound crazy, but it was as if someone had lit a touch paper, and I felt a warm glow inside me again despite everything I'd promised myself.

This was my chance.

Had the universe smiled on me and given me a way out if I was brave enough to take it? Call me desperate, deluded or just plain stupid, but that was how it felt and that was what I chose to believe.

I couldn't just let the opportunity to get to know him pass me by.

I knew then that I had to work out a way I could find out more about him.

Easing my legs out of bed, I press my bare feet into the fluffy rug that I bought to cover the worn, flattened carpet. I close my eyes, but if anything, it makes my thumping head feel even worse.

I'm not a great sleeper at the best of times, but last night I had help in staying awake.

Between one and three a.m., an infuriating buzz sounded periodically above my head. At first, I thought it was a trapped wasp or a bee, but then I realised it was a phone.

Buzz, buzz, buzz. It seemed like every few minutes, then a pacing around, right above my head.

Someone was obviously picking it up on occasion and dropping it back onto the floor again, evidenced by a regular single thud.

If you want to take calls and texts all night long, I thought, seething at the blatant selfishness, at least turn the ruddy vibration off.

I stretch my neck side to side in an effort to ease the tension. It doesn't work.

A short burst of weak sunlight filters through the dusty glass of the bedroom window, and I close my eyes, willing it to warm my face for a few seconds before it fades.

Even when I'm not kept up half the night, on mornings like this, when my energy dips low, sometimes I haven't even got the strength to negotiate the shower.

I wash my face and hands at the sink. As I brush my hair and watch myself in the mirror, I wonder how it is a person can slip so far in so short a time. I used to actually have a *life*.

I get dressed in stretchy garments that slide over my neglected body with the minimum of effort, and manage to get everything done to enable me to be in position with my coffee and cereal by the window in good time.

I sit down at the small wooden table and look up across the rooftops. The clouds are heavy and grey this morning. The earlier sparse rays of sunlight are probably the last I'll see today. The flat feels cool but the heating makes me snuffly and a bit irritable.

I push away the bowl of cornflakes and pull the mug of coffee towards me.

Today, I count twelve people waiting at the tram stop. They are all strangers to each other this morning, no friends or colleagues chatting together. Some stare expectantly down the road, watching for the flash of the metal, the searing electrical glide, the squeaking brakes. Others flick through their phones, stamp their feet, while their breath putters out in frosty clouds.

I sip my coffee and wonder what it feels like to be one of those souls: miserable to be going to work, but leaving in the full knowledge that your partner, your kids... *your life*... will be there when you return home later.

I put down my mug and notice that my forearms prickle as the tram approaches and slows to a halt. One or two people get off, and then the line begins to shuffle forward.

My eyes flutter along to the second carriage and stop at the beige mac, the glare of a phone screen and a sandy-haired head bent over it.

And then he looks up.

He looks right at me.

CHAPTER 7

I stare out of the window, unblinking. My lips morph into a soft line that's not quite a smile but is friendlier than a straightforward stare.

We hold a look for a beat or two, and then the light on his phone screen dims and he leans over to one side to put it in his pocket. My heart is racing, *boom, boom, boom*.

Tentatively, he smiles. Then he raises one arm and waves, and before I even register what I'm doing, I wave right back at him.

Time stands still for a second or two before the tram pulls away again, and then I sit staring at the dull, empty tracks that I know can gleam like chrome brushstrokes on the charcoal asphalt when the light changes.

My heart rate slows, the black cloud moves back over my head and the spell is broken.

It will be a full twenty-four hours before I see him again. Another day of trying to convince myself that my life will somehow improve though I have nowhere to go, nothing to do.

The acknowledgement of this settles on my chest like a millstone.

I don't know how many minutes pass while I'm steeped in my own misery, but suddenly I lurch from my seat as a shrill and unexpected ringing starts up next to me. My phone shudders, vibrating on the spot as the screen announces Louise as the caller.

Usually, I might ignore it, call her back when I feel up to it, but it's almost like she knows what I've been doing, smiling and waving at a complete stranger, and I snatch the handset up and answer it like a guilty party.

'Alice? It's me, have you got a moment?'

I look down at the spot the tram was in just a few minutes earlier. He was right there, with his muscular jaw and dark eyes, looking up here at plain, ordinary *me*.

'Alice?' Louise says again.

'Yes,' I say quickly. 'I'm here.'

'Sorry, have I caught you in the middle of something?'

'No, no. It's fine, I was just making my breakfast.'

'Alice…' My ears prick up. It's not very often that Louise hesitates. 'I… need a favour.'

Another one?

'I'm sorry to have to ask,' she continues, back to her brisk self now. 'You know I wouldn't ask unless I really needed to, right?'

I ignore her rhetorical question. 'What is it?'

She takes a sharp breath at the end of the line and then pushes out all the words, one after the other, without any punctuating gaps.

'I know you don't like going out unless absolutely necessary these days but I really need you to take Archie to school. It's just for a few mornings.' She clears her throat. 'But he has to be there early, I'm afraid, for the start of his breakfast club. I have to book and pay for a place in advance, you see.'

I close my eyes and move the phone away from my ear a touch as if that might put a little more space between us. My silence doesn't deter her.

'I could drop him off at yours at seven each morning, and school's only about a fifteen-minute walk from your place… I can't tell you how grateful I'd be.'

I want to help her out, but this is a big commitment to ask of someone who barely leaves the house, and at the very time of day I can do without it, too.

I pick up my mug and take a swig of coffee to alleviate the dryness in my mouth. It's cold, and I wince. 'Can't Darren do it?'

I'm not putting up much of a fight asking a question that I already know the answer to, but the thought of taking on this massive task is currently eclipsing all other thoughts in my head.

'How can Darren do it? You know he works away for half the week, and when he is home, he's always gone before six.'

'I'm not so good in the morning these days, Louise,' I say slowly. 'It takes me time to come round, and—'

'Please, Alice. You know I wouldn't ask unless I was desperate. I've always been there for you, haven't I? After the accident, when you were in hospital.'

She visited a couple of times, and drove me home when they discharged me.

'That's what sisters do,' she continues. 'Remember how I took time off work so you didn't have to sort Mum's stuff out on your own?'

When Mum died, she took a day off to lay claim to most of her jewellery and the antique dresser in the front room that had been in the family for over a hundred years. It took me weeks to go through the rest of Mum's belongings.

I think about the past and how I was there for Louise when it all kicked off with Martyn. But I don't bring that up.

'Alice?'

'Yes, I'm listening,' I tell her. 'Why is it that you can't take Archie to school yourself?'

'There are some early meetings that have been scheduled last minute that I just can't get out of.' She sounds offended. 'Do you honestly think I'd ask unless I—'

'OK, I'll do it,' I say, finally beaten.

'You're an angel! I won't forget this, I promise.'

'How long will it be for?' I ask. 'That I have to take Archie to school, I mean?'

'Oh, only a few days, probably not even the whole week.' I can almost see her waving me away, moving on to her next diary entry. 'Tomorrow, then. See you at seven or just before, yeah?'

'Yes, but—' I can google the quickest route to Archie's school from here, but I need to find out from Louise what the procedure is when I get him there, so I can at least rehearse it in my mind. If I have no choice but to leave the flat, then I want to be prepared. I don't want anything to go wrong.

But Louise calls goodbye over my words and ends the call.

CHAPTER 8

Tuesday morning, the shrill call of the alarm rouses me from sleep.

I've had another restless night, waking for no apparent reason at two a.m. and lying awake long enough to see the glaring red digits of my alarm clock click past four.

My heart sinks when I remember the reason for setting the alarm. It's 6.45, and Archie will be arriving in just a few minutes' time.

I slide my legs over the side of the bed and press the soles of my feet into the slippers that I always place strategically on the rug. I pull my dressing gown towards me from the bottom of the bed and shrug it on as I stand up, just as the noise starts.

Banging on the door. Muffled voices.

I sigh and open the bedroom door, and Magnus swishes around my lower legs, yowling in protest. I usually let him lie on the bed with me, but I felt so tired the previous evening, I obviously didn't think to leave the door ajar.

Magnus will not enjoy Archie being here for the next few mornings. And who can blame him? My nephew's particular brand of forcing a cuddle is any cat's worst nightmare.

'You're not going to speak to me for a week, but it can't be helped,' I tell Magnus as he stares up at me petulantly.

Cue more banging on the door.

'Alice… are you awake? *Alice?*' Louise's voice calls out as she continues to hammer.

It isn't seven yet and I spare a thought for my neighbours. Mr Jephson, who works nights and gets in at six in the morning. He's probably just managed to get to sleep. Donna, across the hall, who doesn't have to leave for work until nine and won't be up yet.

'I'm coming, hold on!' I call back, hoping to avoid more of her impatient hammering.

I slip back the deadbolt and turn the lock. Louise pushes the door open wider and charges in, Archie trailing gloomily in her wake.

'Thank goodness for that. I thought you weren't going to answer.' She frowns at my dressing gown. 'I hope Archie isn't going to be late for school.'

It's a shame her bedside manner has deteriorated so badly from her pleading call to me yesterday.

'You said you'd be here at seven,' I remind her, at the same time wondering how she's managed to achieve a full face of make-up, immaculate hair and a stylish navy shift dress with matching box jacket at this unearthly hour.

'I can't be held to the minute.' She rolls her eyes. 'It's *nearly* seven. Do you want us to go out and come back in again?'

'Morning, Archie,' I say brightly. There is no winning with Louise when she's in this mood.

Louise gives him a prod. 'Say hello to Auntie Alice.'

'Morning,' he mumbles.

He looks just about as happy to be here as I am to have him. But I don't want to become his enemy.

'I wanted to ask what the procedure is when we get to school,' I say to Louise.

'Just take him to the main reception and they'll buzz you through.' She waves her hand dismissively. 'Archie knows what to do, don't you, pudding?'

'I've got a belly ache,' Archie grumbles, rubbing his soft stomach.

'He always says that when there's something he doesn't want to do.' Louise frowns.

'I have got a belly ache, though!' Archie protests, his face reddening. 'And I don't want to stay here again… The cat doesn't like me.'

Magnus glares back at him.

'We'll be fine, and I'll put Magnus in the bedroom. I've told you, Archie, you just need to be a bit gentler with him.' I manage a little smile, hoping to defuse the telling-off that, judging by the look on Louise's face, Archie is about to receive. The best thing I can do is get her out of here, get Archie sat in front of the TV and earn myself a few more minutes to get ready. 'I'll call you if I have any problems.'

'Well, I'm in a meeting from seven thirty onwards, but I'm sure you'll be fine.'

I see Louise to the door and Magnus disappears back into the bedroom. I hand Archie the remote control.

'I'm going to get ready,' I tell him. 'It takes me a while, I'm afraid.'

'Why?' He frowns up at me.

'Sometimes I'm in a bit of pain in the mornings,' I say. 'It slows me down.'

He nods and turns back to the TV.

After a quick wash, I dress in the clothes I got ready last night. It's easy-wear stuff again. Black leggings and a loose patterned tunic top. I rake a hairbrush through my dull mousy bob, smear on some moisturiser and a lick of tinted lip balm.

I scribble a few things down on my notepad and rip off the piece of paper to take with me, then take my socks into the living room so I can sit in the low chair to put them on. I bend forward slowly, trying to ignore the throbbing that immediately starts up at the bottom of my spine.

Archie turns from the television and watches me as I take a breath and push myself a little further until I can hook my toes into the sock.

The pain is banging now, all through my back, shoulders and neck. I'm faintly aware of Archie leaving the room as eventually I manage to get one sock completely on.

Cartoons blare from the television, far too colourful and loud.

I reach for the other sock just as Archie walks back in and stands in front of me.

'I brought you these,' he says, holding up the flat black ankle boots I set by the door ready for our walk to school.

'Oh!' I close my mouth quickly to cover my surprise. 'Thank you, Archie. That's really kind.'

He bends down, taking the remaining sock from me.

'And I can help you with this too, Auntie Alice.' He pats his knee. 'Foot up.'

CHAPTER 9

Louise

She'd been sitting in gridlocked traffic for at least four minutes now without moving an inch. Four minutes didn't sound long, but to Louise it felt like an age.

She could feel the tension building inside her again like a pressure cooker, but she couldn't lose focus, not now. It had to be done.

She'd made some decisions and she couldn't back out. Thank goodness she'd been able to rope Alice in to look after Archie. The two of them hadn't been really close for a long time now, but her sister was proving to be invaluable. Fortunately, she didn't ask too many questions.

Sometimes Louise felt so envious of Alice, and sometimes, she admitted, slightly irritated. When Alice had opened the door of her flat this morning in her dressing gown, obviously just having woken up, she couldn't help but compare that to the fact that she herself had been awake since five, risen before six, taken a shower, styled her hair and put on her make-up and clothes – her disguise that would get her through the day.

Nobody knew the real Louise. Not Darren, Archie or her colleagues at work, and certainly not her sister. But there was a cost to maintaining an effective facade. Several times lately she'd come close to losing it, unleashing the anger and pain on someone close. Such instances felt like a tear in the invisible fabric that held her together.

She'd need to curb her cynical comments to Alice and keep her temper in check until she could get help. But help was a long way ahead yet.

She reached forward and turned on Smooth Radio, hoping for some chill-out tunes to settle her, but as soon as the music started, she immediately regretted doing so.

The dulcet tones of Adele filled the car, transporting her back to when she'd first set eyes on Martyn Hardy.

Ten years earlier

It had been a balmy late-August evening and Louise had organised a night out with Lucy, her oldest friend from school, who was back in town after completing a four-year teaching degree at Newcastle University.

'I can't get over how fab you look,' Lucy gushed as soon as Louise got off the bus. 'I feel so pasty compared to you. I suppose that's what happens when you become stuck in a textbook for too long.'

Louise laughed, but secretly she felt pleased at Lucy's compliment. She'd managed to get a nice tan thanks to a good week weather-wise and spending afternoons revising in the garden at home.

She'd managed to swing a job as an assistant events organiser in a small hotel in town, and they were supporting her in a college course to gain a hospitality qualification.

This was her designated college week, so she'd been in class each morning and then back home studying for her end-of-week examination in the afternoon.

She'd taken the exam yesterday, and although she'd have to wait a week for her official mark, she knew she'd done well because she hadn't struggled with any of the questions at all.

Tonight, she'd worn her white mini skirt and a tight white T-shirt to show off her tan and her lithe figure. Life was good, and Lucy noticing and commenting on her appearance had given her an extra boost.

Arm in arm, the girls clip-clopped up the street in their heels, chattering non-stop, each desperate to update the other on her news. The doorman, looking appreciatively at Louise's toned legs, waved them both straight in, ahead of the queue, and they skipped gratefully inside the club, giggling at the irritated groans of the people left waiting outside.

Inside, the queue for drinks was four deep at the bar, but Louise didn't mind; they had all night, and Lucy was recounting hilarious and entertaining stories about her drunken exploits at uni.

Gradually, in that sixth-sense way she sometimes had if someone was staring, Louise became aware of someone watching her intently from across the bar. At an opportune moment, she allowed herself a quick glance away from Lucy's face.

He was tall and well built, his shoulders almost twice the width of those of the man standing next to him. He too was wearing a white T-shirt, the sleeves straining against his tanned, bulging biceps, and there was something else she found very attractive: he looked to be in his early thirties, probably about ten years older than her. A man in a club full of spotty boys her own age.

She pulled her attention back to Lucy's story but she knew she'd kept her eyes on him just a beat too long to pretend she wasn't interested. He'd already recognised this, and smiled and raised his glass to her.

Within thirty seconds, a barman had beckoned Louise forward, again eliciting annoyed glances from other waiting customers before her.

'What can I get you, love?' he called above the music and chatter.

'Ooh, thanks! Two white wine and sodas, please.'

She gave an impressed Lucy a thumbs-up and opened her handbag for her purse as the drinks appeared in front of her.

'No charge, sweetheart. Courtesy of Mr Hardy over there.'

The man across the bar winked and raised his glass again, and she mouthed a silent thank you as she moved back to Lucy.

'Blimey, you should wear that outfit more often,' Lucy joked when Louise explained what had happened. 'He's quite dishy, that fella, if a bit old. Do you reckon he's on steroids? His biceps are—'

Louise coughed, drowning out Lucy's words and letting her know that the man in question was now standing right behind her.

'Evening, ladies.' His voice was deep and smooth. 'I'm Martyn.'

'Louise.' She smiled coyly.

'I'm Lucy. Thanks ever so much for the drinks.'

'You're welcome. Hope you don't mind, seems a lot of girls object to a gentlemanly gesture these days.'

'Not us!' Lucy spluttered as she swigged back her wine. 'You can buy our drinks all night if you like.'

'Luce!' Louise rolled her eyes as she turned to him. 'Thanks, Martyn, it's much appreciated. I thought I might never get served at all.'

He looked at her properly then, with twinkling hazel eyes that seemed to be full of mischief, and she was grateful for the low lights as she felt her cheeks ignite. She couldn't tear her eyes away from his, as though she'd been hypnotised. That was the moment her favourite Adele song came on, 'Chasing Pavements'.

She closed her eyes and swayed to the music, the warmth of the wine moving through her. When she looked up, Martyn was still watching her, the faintest smile on his face, but it was a smile of admiration, not mocking at all.

Louise stood five foot nine in her four-inch heels, but she felt slight and vulnerable next to his six-foot-plus frame and broad shoulders. It was a nice feeling.

Lucy, who had already drained her wine glass and fallen quiet, spotted an old friend from school at the other side of the bar, and after throwing Louise a rather sour look, she melted away into the crowd.

'Luce!' Louise stepped forward after her, but Martyn's strong hand rested on her upper arm.

'Leave her, she'll be OK… I know it's selfish, but I'd like a bit of time with you. Your friend can see you any time.'

Louise sighed and nodded. Lucy had been the one who'd been away at uni all this time, after all. They'd have loads of time to catch up now that she'd finished her course.

Martyn turned to the bar and raised his index finger, and the barman immediately came over, serving him through the fidgeting throng of waiting customers. Louise couldn't help noticing that nobody uttered a word of complaint, seemingly silenced by Martyn's imposing stature and authoritative manner.

He handed her another glass of wine and then moved so close she could feel the heat of his body against her own. When he bent down to say something in her ear, she inhaled a heady, spicy scent that set her nerve endings alight.

'Sorry,' she told him. 'I didn't catch what you just said.'

'I said…' He leaned closer still. 'I love your beauty, your fire, your style.'

She smiled and felt her cheeks flush again. No man had ever said anything like that to her before.

Later, she often thought how ironic it was that those attributes were the very things he would come to despise in her.

CHAPTER 10

Alice

Finally I get my boots on with Archie's help, and we put on our coats and leave the flat.

As we walk up the corridor, I'm seeing my nephew in a new light. I've had an unexpected glimpse of a caring boy who had the empathy to see my frustration in carrying out a simple task this morning.

I press the button for the lift, and we listen as it clunks and whirrs into life on a floor somewhere above us.

'I can smell something.' Archie wrinkles his nose as we step inside. 'Is it wee?'

'I don't think so.' I smile. 'Smells more like cleaning fluid to me.'

Despite Louise's regular moans about the communal areas, which I'm sure Archie has overheard many times, they are cleaned and maintained, and the building is secure, too. Not the kind of place that undesirables can freely walk into and urinate in the lifts.

'It's raining,' Archie groans as we step out onto the street. 'I wish I was going to school in the car. I hate walking.'

'It's only drizzle.' I smile at him. 'The fresh air and exercise will do us both good. When we were little, your mum and I used to take turns standing outside in the rain as a dare.'

'Mum hates rain, she says it ruins her hair.'

'Well she didn't care about that back then.' I grin. 'We'd start with thirty seconds and graduate up to about five minutes. Apart from the time your mum locked me out for nearly fifteen minutes and I got the flu.'

'That's not a proper dare.' Archie seems unimpressed. 'It's not even scary.'

It's an effort, but I keep my face as normal as I can, because I too feel uncomfortable being outside. It's not the rain that's bothering me but the fact that I'm outside in the big wide world where I know things can go badly wrong. I fight a growing compulsion to rush back into the flat.

I haven't always been like this. It's somehow connected to the guilt I struggle with about the past. About Jack. I suppose I'm scared I'll inadvertently do something to ruin someone else's life, like I did his.

That day still seems like a blur to me, as if I took leave of my senses for a short time and became somebody else.

It doesn't make sense; it doesn't have to. Over time, the negative feelings have taken root and don't need any kind of logical explanation. Nothing can ever make what I did right.

As my therapist said at the time, until I learn to forgive myself, it's something that will continue to play out in my head. And I'm a hell of a long way from any sort of self-forgiveness.

I stopped seeing the therapist over two years ago. She might have gone now, but the raw emotions remain.

The main road is busy already, although there's still about twenty minutes to go to the official start of rush hour.

Shiny wet cars and buses whoosh past, too close and too loud. I wish I was watching from behind glass, up at my window on the third floor, where I'd feel calm and in control.

For a few minutes we walk in what I think is companionable silence; that is, until Archie suddenly turns to me.

'Auntie Alice, why are you acting so weird?' That good-natured boy who helped me with my socks and boots earlier seems to have his bite back.

I slow my pace and look at him. 'What do you mean, *weird*?'

'Well… you're walking too close to the fences and walls and you're sort of turned in a bit, as if you're scared of the traffic.'

'I don't think I am. It's just… I'm a bit cold, that's all.'

'Mum says you never go out any more.' Archie looks at me curiously. 'She says you're a *recluse*. That means you don't like mixing with people at all. Even with us.'

'That's not true.' But my own words sound empty and untruthful, and I sigh. 'I don't go out as much as I used to, and I suppose you just sort of get used to it, not having many friends.'

'Mum says you haven't got *any* friends any more.' He pats my arm. 'It's all right, you know, Auntie Alice. You get used to that too, after a bit.'

I wrestle with a swell of sympathy for Archie, but at the same time I'm thinking I really ought to pick my moment with Louise and ask her why she's saying such peevish things about me. Even as the thought occurs to me, I know I won't do it.

My sister has a short memory. There was a time when she was falling apart too. Her strong, fearless facade hasn't always been there.

I push away thoughts about the damage Martyn Hardy did to her. It was a long time ago now.

'Thanks, Archie, I'm fine, but it's nice to have a few friends if you can, you know. I'm sure there are people you get on with at school who could become your friends.'

He doesn't respond, and speeds up his pace a little so he's slightly in front of me. Probably time to change the subject.

'So, what lesson have you got first today?'

He shrugs and shoves his hands into his coat pockets.

'Literacy.' He scuffs his soles as he walks and I bite my tongue as the scraping sound agitates my ears. 'Some of the boys on our street play football at the bottom of the cul-de-sac after school. They talk about it in lessons.'

'Sounds fun. Do you join in?'

'I wouldn't want to play football. I don't like it,' he says, looking down at his feet. 'Even if they asked me to, I wouldn't.'

'That's a shame. Well, maybe you could just watch… or referee, even. Then you could still join in with the fun.'

He scowls. 'I don't care, anyway. I'm going to set up another game with some bigger boys from the academy who will beat them up if they try to join in.'

Archie is still at primary school, but in two years' time, when he's eleven, he'll move up to Wilford Academy.

He stops walking abruptly and kicks a large stone hard, from the edge of the pavement into the road and the path of an oncoming car. The driver slows and glares as he passes.

I decide to ignore his silent protest. He's obviously hurting.

'You know, I think, if you got talking to your classmates and they knew you were interested, they might invite you to join them.'

'I know you're trying to help, Auntie Alice,' he says wearily, sounding older than his years. 'But it doesn't really work like that. If people at school decide they don't like you, they hardly ever change their minds.'

'Have you spoken to your mum and dad about how you feel?' I'm sure Louise and Darren would be mortified if they knew how lonely and excluded Archie was feeling.

His face stretches into a grin that doesn't quite reach his eyes and he skips ahead.

'I know, I'll count blue cars, you count red, and when we get to school, the highest number wins!'

Clearly the moment for confidences has passed and he doesn't walk next to me again. We arrive at school at 7.58.

'See you tomorrow morning, then,' I say as he gives me a cursory peck on the cheek and heads into reception.

CHAPTER 11

I wait until I see the receptionist buzz Archie through the internal security doors and into the main building, and then I turn and walk back out of the school gates and onto the side road.

Once I'm out of sight of the school office window, I stop walking and lean against the fence for a moment, closing my eyes. There is no logical reason why my heart rate is up like this, why my mouth is dry and my hands a little shaky.

I've walked all the way here. I've managed to take good care of my nephew, and nobody has spoken to me, much less bothered me in any way.

Yet as soon as I step out of my front door, I feel vulnerable and afraid of what might happen to me, to other people around me.

I know there's nothing I can do about the past. Staying inside and avoiding contact with others might seem like a good plan, but actually, it can't change what's already happened.

Surely everyone must look back at something and wish with all their heart they could make a different decision at a crucial moment. It doesn't stop them living their lives and trying to make a future for themselves.

Yet on a physical level, my body remembers and panics and feels afraid. And what happened feels just as real today as it felt when Jack died.

I take a deep breath and will my feet to start moving again. In only fifteen minutes, I'll be home. Once I'm back, I can make a nice cup of tea and a slice of toast and calm down properly.

Taking Archie to school has forced me out of my comfort zone and I'm going to try and count that as a positive step forward in making some changes.

When I turn the corner onto the busy main road, my gaze is drawn to a crowd of people a bit further up. They're clustered together in a way that seems familiar from looking out of my window, and I realise it's a tram stop.

The 8.16 that I watch every morning will pick up passengers here and take in a couple of other stops before finally it reaches the hub outside my flat.

I glance at my watch. It's 8.10. At this time, I'm usually sitting comfortably by the window waiting for its arrival.

I wonder idly what my man on the tram will think of my absence this morning.

I'd hate for him to think that because he waved to me, I am purposely staying away from the window. I know we're strangers, but he's shown the first tentative signs that he's noticed me, and raising his hand like that... well, it counts as a greeting of sorts, doesn't it?

If the same thing had happened three years earlier, in the midst of my busy life, I would have barely noticed him, but lots has changed since then.

The fact is, a man smiling and waving, passing my home every morning... that counts as more contact than I've had with a new person for a long, long time.

There's something inside my recently-turned-thirty-year-old self that wants to grab him like a lifeline. However pathetic it might sound, at this very moment, the possibility of getting to know this guy – however much of a long shot that may be – feels like the only brightness in my life. At the same time, it terrifies me.

I stop walking when I get to the tram stop. I just need time to think, I suppose. To get my head around a crazy little idea that's just started sprouting in there. It's too crazy to articulate. In fact, it feels like a distinctly *bad* idea.

Part of me yearns for the calm safety of my apartment, but there's another, more insistent part that zings with excitement at the thought of doing something else… something impulsive and different.

I stand for a while watching as commuters rush past in their smart clothing, clutching takeaway coffees and talking on their phones. Nobody so much as glances my way. They're oblivious to the plain, shoddily dressed woman leaning against the wall of the newsagent's.

The earlier moderately busy road is now choked with grid-locked vehicles.

A frisson of anticipation shivers through the tram-stop crowd and they thin out and form a ragged queue. They're all looking over their shoulders, and when I too turn to glance behind me, I see the object of their sudden interest.

The tram is approaching, trundling past the stationary traffic on its tracks. At road level, the front of the driver's cab resembles a friendly face. It seems much larger and more imposing than from my usual view, looking down from the third floor.

My feet start to move. I'm walking, faster now, until I reach the end of the queue.

There's a screech of brakes, the whoosh of metal doors flying open. Voices, a beeping noise, the shuffling of feet.

My thoughts fuse together until I can't think straight at all, but then I let go of it all; I let go of the fear of getting close to other people.

The small crowd swallows me up and carries me forward.

And before I know it, I too am boarding the tram.

CHAPTER 12

The tram is busy, but everyone has a seat. I wait in line behind people who are still shuffling along the aisle, deciding where they want to sit.

Sometimes, when I watch the tram from my apartment window, I see that people are packed in and standing. They grip the long bright yellow poles that rise from the seats in an attempt to keep their balance, their expressions less than pleased.

I take the first empty seat I come to.

My man always has the same seat and he always sits in the second carriage along. That tells me he probably gets on at one of the earliest stops, which enables him to make the exact same selection each day.

Finally, the last person sits down, the tram doors close and we begin to move.

I stare at my hands, clasped in my lap. I'm willing my breathing to calm down.

Slowly in and out. In, out.

I did it. I actually boarded the tram, rather than just acting the thought out in my head. Rather than simply watching the world go by from my upstairs window.

When my breathing regulates a little, I allow myself to look up. I inch along, right to the edge of my seat so I can see through to the next carriage.

I spot him right away. He's looking out of the window, and from here, I can only see the back of his head and his partial profile. I recognise the short sandy-brown hair, the beige overcoat and the student scarf.

His head falls forward and I know he'll be looking at his phone. Although I can't fully see him, I imagine his angular jawline, slightly sharp nose. The full dark pink lips that remind me so much of Jack's.

The seat next to him is empty, as it always is, even when the tram looks busy. Perhaps he puts a bag on it to dissuade people from sitting down.

The chatter around me fades out as I imagine standing up and walking through into the next car. I often see people doing this when they're looking for a seat. Nobody would bat an eyelid if I got up to do it right now.

My breathing speeds up again and it feels like my heart is misfiring every few beats, giving me a horrible sickly feeling in my chest.

I push my hand into my pocket and pull out the piece of paper I put in there before leaving the house this morning. I read the list through, once, twice and a third time, until I start to feel calmer.

Wake up
Get dressed
Archie arrives
Breakfast, chat… keep him calm
Leave house
Walk to school
Drop Archie off and walk back

It was the lists that saved me back then. When the simplest everyday tasks threatened to overwhelm me, I would think through the steps of making a cup of tea or telephoning the benefits office and I'd write them down.

For months, I was virtually incapacitated. The physical injuries to my hips and the bottom of my spine weren't serious, but they impacted on my life and still continue to do so. But it was the anxiety that rendered me a nervous wreck, leaving me barely able to function on some days.

Yet someone had to look after Mum. Somehow we managed to get through that hellish time together. Although I struggled with the simplest tasks, I found I could write a list through the pain, extract straightforward steps that took the fire out of the constant burn of anxiety.

Even if I didn't follow the actions through, the act of writing the list made me feel as if I had achieved *something*.

Today's list has also served its purpose. I completed and actually surpassed the steps on there. Instead of walking back home as per the final step, I now find myself in the startling position of sitting in close proximity to a man I feel like I almost know… in a weird sort of way.

After glancing down my entries, I fold the list in half and push it back in my pocket.

I could reach his seat in approximately fifteen to eighteen steps. He wouldn't know I was even there until I sat down next to him. I can imagine it now… how surprised he'd be when he looked up and realised it was me. And then he'd probably smile.

He has the type of colouring that means his cheeks would flush quite easily. I know I would be exactly the same and we could laugh about our shared timidity.

I'm aware the tram is beginning to slow as we approach the next stop. A glut of faces appears at the window as passengers crowd towards the doors. This stop is busier than the last, even more so, I think, than the hub outside my apartment block.

This must be the stop where the tram really fills up.

Several people are already standing, waiting by the doors so they can be first off, and I take the opportunity to also stand up and move towards the second carriage. Then I'll be even nearer to him.

I look through into the next car to see that there are spare seats two rows behind him.

Impulsively, as the doors open and passengers alight, I rush through and sit down.

Now there are just two rows of seats between me and him.

There's a woman in front of me and a man sitting in front of her and directly behind my man. I curse him silently, wishing I could sit there, close enough to be able to smell his aftershave.

My man coughs. It's a polite, restrained cough that fits with what I perceive to be his quiet, friendly nature.

I wish his phone would ring so I can hear his voice. I'd guess he'll be well-spoken and intelligent; he looks confident and comfortable in his own skin. Just like Jack used to be.

I look out of the window, willing my heart to quit its hammering. Sitting behind him, watching him, feels sneaky… sly, somehow. Yet I'm only riding the tram like he and about a hundred other people are doing this morning.

Maybe we'll look back together and laugh at this, one day soon.

CHAPTER 13

I'm willing the passenger seated behind my man to get up, but annoyingly, he stays put in his seat.

There are more people on board now, some milling around in the aisle, getting in the way of my line of sight.

The tram sets off again, and its smooth electric wail fills my ears. I try to get my thoughts organised. Do I get off at 'my' stop? He'll see that I'm not at the window and never know I was so close to him all along.

There's a risk he'll spot me getting off and walking to the apartment building. Would I be forced to smile and wave to him from the kerbside… will he wonder why I didn't say hello?

I look down at my scruffy leggings and flat boots. I look a mess. It wasn't such a good idea, impulsively boarding the tram like this.

Annoyance bubbles in my chest as a woman adjusts her position and stands directly in front of me. I know it's illogical to get angry with an innocent stranger, but I feel like giving her a mighty push to get her out of the way.

The tram slows to stopping. It's time for me to decide whether to get off or not.

I stand up and take a couple of steps towards the exit door behind me before turning back again. Dithering. I can see the back of his head and a partial side view of his face from here, and he's looking up at the apartment building… *He's looking for me.*

I can't see my own window from this standing position and I can't see if there's disappointment on his face the moment he realises I'm not there for the first time in weeks.

The last passengers are now alighting. The woman blocking my view has found a seat. I could walk over to him right now, move the brown leather satchel I can now see lying on the seat next to him.

'I'm not up there, I'm right here,' I'd say to him, and we'd smile together…

The doors whoosh closed and I sit back down in my seat. His head turns away from the window and he looks down at his phone again.

I wonder if his heart feels as heavy as my own. Being so close and yet too scared to approach him feels like torture.

Staring out, I feel the *thump thump thump* of my heart on the wall of my chest. The houses and shops pass by in a confused blur, reflecting my unfocused thoughts back at me.

Panic has clenched its ugly fist inside me, and suddenly I feel alone and vulnerable.

Why did I act so impulsively, getting on the tram this morning? These days I always strive to stay calm, to think things through in order to protect myself from getting in precisely this situation. To avoid doing something that might impinge on other people's safety.

Now I'm travelling away from home at a speed of knots and I can feel a dull pain unfurling at the bottom of my spine. It's waited, picked its moment. Mine is an intelligent back pain, always striking at the worst possible time.

I think I'm going to have to get off at the next stop.

My breathing is becoming erratic; I can't seem to drag enough air into my lungs. An impending sense of doom gathers like a dense fog between my eyes.

It's a long time since I've had a full-blown panic attack, but I can still remember the sheer horror and force of how it feels. I can't afford to slide into that, not here, in front of… I purposely don't look at him again.

I focus instead on closing my eyes and getting my breathing under control. My back and hips are throbbing and all I can do is breathe through it, lifting my arms slightly to get some air circulating.

Breathe in, breathe out.

In. Out.

When the noise level around me suddenly ramps up, I open my eyes.

Shuffling, scraping, coughs and splutters pepper the hum of raised voices. Almost everyone is standing or getting out of their seats. I glance out of the window to see we've reached the Old Market Square, the tram's final destination point on this route.

My eyes dart to his seat. He is standing now, reaching down for his bag and a large brown envelope from the seat.

He's taller than I thought. Taller than Jack was.

He opens the flap of his satchel and pushes his phone in there before hoisting it over his shoulder and tucking the chunky envelope under his arm.

I want to stand up too, like everyone else, but I can't. My lower back is throbbing, as if the bottom half of my spine has completely fused.

I feel a sudden urge to reach out to him, ask him for help. It would be the perfect opportunity to make contact, but something stops me calling to him.

The doors open and everyone begins filing off. I sit there watching them, and one or two passengers look at me curiously, probably wondering why I'm not moving.

My man stands up fully, and when there's a gap, he steps into the aisle.

I can't stop staring at him. Pushing away thoughts of Jack.

I feel my muscles tightening further, gripping my flesh like hot fists at the bottom of my back.

Passengers shuffle by me, and he gets closer and closer until…
he's right in front of me. I glance down at the envelope and see a
name written in big black letters: JAMES WILSON. Poking out
under it is the corner of his brown leather satchel, which bears
the monogram *JW* printed in faded gold.

James. It suits him.

Finally, he turns and looks straight at me. Time stands still for
a few seconds as our eyes lock.

His are a warm hazel, his hair thick and shiny.

I search his features for a hint of that special smile he's given
me before, wait for his fingers to flutter in a small, discreet wave.

But his eyes flicker over me and move on to glance out of
the window beside me, and then he passes by me and the queue
shuffles on behind him.

The last people get off, and suddenly I'm all alone in the empty
carriage.

CHAPTER 14

Louise

Ten years earlier

After that first meeting with Martyn, Louise's nights at home watching soaps and early bedtimes were suddenly a thing of the past.

During the first couple of weeks, she saw him three or four times, and they did so much together – a day trip to the coast, the cinema, dinner in various upmarket restaurants.

The third week, they sat together in a tiny cocktail bar in Hockley. There were only a few other couples in there, and classic Duke Ellington tracks played subtly in the background. The dimly lit bar shimmered with candles and fairy lights, adding a romantic and intimate air.

The waitress came over and Martyn ordered a beer.

'I'll have a Bellini, please,' Louise said, possibly feeling the most sophisticated she'd ever done in her life.

'On a work night?' Martyn teased.

'It is Friday tomorrow.' She grinned. 'So I'm allowed.'

'I've never met anybody like you, Louise. Every day I find myself counting the hours until I can see you again.' He looked at her, searching her face for a reaction. 'I know some people would say it's far too early, but I… I need to know if you feel the same way.'

'I do,' she whispered without hesitation. Her face burned with embarrassment and she felt glad of the low lighting, but she made herself say it. 'I… I want to be with you all the time, Martyn.'

'You don't know what it means to me to hear you say that.' He pulled her in close and sealed her lips with his. She felt breathless with desire.

The waitress appeared with their drinks and gave Louise a knowing smile. She placed Martyn's beer and a tiny white coaster on the table for the Bellini before leaving them alone again.

They talked about everything that night. Martyn told her all about his gym business, explaining he was in the process of developing it into a franchise. Louise told him about her ambition to set up a corporate events company catering to small and medium-sized businesses.

Then they moved on to family.

'So there's just me, my younger sister Alice, and my mum,' Louise told him. 'Mum and Alice are close; I had more in common with my dad. I don't think they really get me, you know?'

'Story of my life,' Martyn said, and then softened his voice. 'You lost your dad?'

Louise nodded sadly, willing herself not to get upset. The last thing she wanted was to spoil this wonderful evening. 'He died two years ago. He left me and my sister a small amount of money I haven't touched yet. That's why I'd like to set up the business; do something meaningful with it. Something he'd be proud of.'

'I think that's a brilliant idea.' Martyn nodded. 'In fact, I might be your very first customer if this franchise deal gets signed off soon. I'll have plenty of wealthy investors and clients that I'll need to look after and impress.'

'Really? That sounds amazing.' Louise took a sip of her Bellini and enjoyed the squeeze of excitement in her stomach. Martyn's business experience was clearly going to be invaluable to her when she got her new business up and running.

*

The next evening, Martyn sent a cab to pick her up. He'd told her to dress up smartly and bring an overnight bag.

Her mother and Alice could be inquisitive, so Louise thought of an excuse that would satisfy them. She was twenty-three, she had nothing to hide, but she'd choose her own time to tell them about Martyn when she was good and ready.

'A group of us from my hotel are going out for the evening and the manager is giving us complimentary rooms for the night,' she mentioned casually as they watched TV together.

Her mother nodded in acceptance, but of course Alice had to be clever.

'The hotel must be quite full,' she remarked. 'That brochure you brought home said there were only ten rooms in the entire place.'

'Yeah, well we're doubling up.' Louise shot her a look that she hoped conveyed that her sister should mind her own business.

As per Martyn's instructions, the cab took her to a brightly lit building displaying ornate Victorian architecture on the outskirts of the city. Louise gasped as he opened the door of the cab himself, dressed in a smart black suit and crisp open-necked white shirt.

She was speechless as he took her overnight bag. The best hotel in Nottingham, which she'd previously only seen in pictures, with the man of her dreams… Maybe she should pinch herself to make sure it was actually happening.

They checked in to the suite Martyn had reserved and then enjoyed a wonderful meal in the hotel's top-class restaurant with wine and champagne. When they went back up to the room, Martyn unlocked the door of their room and gestured for Louise to walk in first.

She gasped and then squealed at the sight before her. Rose petals were strewn on the bed and lit candles dotted all around the room.

'Louise?'

She turned to see Martyn down on one knee.

'Louise, I love you, and I can't bear to be without you. Would you do me the honour of being my wife? Will you marry me?'

CHAPTER 15

Alice

Everyone else on the tram has got off, but I'm still sitting here.

I swallow hard and look up from my vacant stare to see an elderly man looming over me.

'Are you feeling all right, love?'

'Yes. Yes, thank you,' I say, shuffling to the edge of my seat. 'Sorry, it's just my back, I—'

'Oh, I know all about aches and pains, I put up with them all day.' He grins good-naturedly. 'You'll be OK once you've had a good stretch.'

I know he means well, but I wish he'd leave me alone to get up in my own time.

I grip the metal pole behind my seat and hoist myself to standing, trying not to grimace.

'There you go, see, nothing to it!' he beams, continuing his ambling down the carriage. 'Have a good day.'

I stand for a moment at the edge of the exit step. I can see above the heads of the people on the street. It's only been a couple of minutes since James got off the tram, but that's plenty long enough to disappear up one of the many streets snaking away from the main square.

I step down onto the pavement and am instantly swallowed up in the bustle of busy workers, all with somewhere to go. It's still on the early side for shoppers, and half the shops aren't open yet.

I look to the left. The big Debenhams windows are lit up, but its double doors are closed. Next door, the interior of a pizza restaurant is in darkness and I can just about make out the chairs still upside down on the tabletops.

My heart sinks as I look the other way, above the sea of heads, and I curse myself for not getting off at the same time as James.

I allowed myself to get lost in my thoughts of why he might have blanked me like that. He was probably embarrassed to see me there; it would have been most unexpected, after all.

I have an overwhelming urge to put things right, to try and explain to him why I was on the tram this morning and not sitting in my window as usual.

As I step forward, I catch sight of a man in a beige coat and stripy scarf emerging from Costa Coffee. I follow as quickly as I can, fighting against the flow of bodies until I have him in sight again.

He is cutting across the square, walking quite fast, clutching his takeaway coffee. His head is slightly down, against the cool wind, and he keeps his eyes on the pavement as he moves forward.

I'm going to lose him.

I speed up a little, pushing through the throng, but despite my efforts, he's moving further and further away.

As I step onto Old Market Square, he approaches the front of the Council House. Soon he'll disappear amongst the teeming crowd of people currently funnelling into the narrow confines of shop-lined Exchange Walk. He'll be at St Peter's Gate before I can even glimpse which direction he takes, never mind catch up with him.

I gulp in big breaths of air. A mad compulsion within me insists I must keep going. I don't know where this drive is coming from.

And then he stops walking.

Right there at the edge of the square, he leans against the enormous art deco stone lion that lounges regally on the right-hand side of the Council House.

As I hurry towards him, I wonder… is he waiting for me? Has he realised I'm following him? And then, as I draw closer, my heart slips just a little when I see he is holding his phone up to his ear.

I'm close now, so I slow down in an attempt to regulate my breathing. There are several small groups of young people dotted around in front of the Council House steps, and I manage to linger incongruously on the fringe of a quiet huddle of French students.

Craning my neck a little, I have a good view of James. He's wedged his satchel between his feet and is now talking animatedly. One hand holds his phone, the other is raking through his hair repeatedly in what looks like a nervous mannerism.

He frowns and opens his mouth to say something, and then clamps it closed again, as if he can't get a word in edgeways with whoever the caller is.

One or two of the French students have noticed me now. The girl nearest to me swaps her shoulder bag onto the other side, as if I might nab it any second, and another nudges her friend to indicate my ominous presence.

I don't care. I've come this far; I'm not passing up the chance to possibly see where James works, or at least where he goes next. That way something constructive will have come out of this crazy journey into town.

I watch as he abruptly pulls the phone away from his ear and stares at the screen. He looks a little shocked, and I wonder if the other person has hung up on him.

I get ready to start walking, but he doesn't move. He rakes his hair again and leaves his hand there, at the top of his head, staring down at the cold grey concrete in front of him as if he's waiting for an answer to some vital question to show itself.

He squeezes his eyes shut briefly and then his jawline sets. He looks as if he's steeling himself to deal with something unpleasant.

I wonder if it's a work matter, if he's in some kind of trouble with his boss. That's the sort of look he has on his face, as if something bad is on the horizon that must be faced.

One of the French students turns to me and says something. Her face is pale, thin and twisty. I haven't a clue what she's saying – sadly I studied German, not French, at school – but I get the gist of it.

Who are you, why are you standing here with us? Or something similarly challenging.

I glare back at her, reflecting her animosity, and take a step back from the group, but I make sure my eyes don't leave James for more than a second or two.

Slowly he reaches down and picks up his bag, slips his phone into it. I watch as he takes a big breath in, as if he's steeling himself for something, and then, as suddenly as he stopped, he's on the move again.

I scuttle around the group of students and head after him, down Exchange Walk. He steps out onto St Peter's Gate and turns left. I follow suit, and catch the back of him as he makes another quick left turn, disappearing from view.

I wait a second or two outside a silver jewellery shop and then head for the corner of the tiny street on the left where he turned. It's a dead end, but up at the top, there's a rather grand, glossy black door complete with a large brass knocker.

When I'm satisfied he must have entered this doorway and isn't going to unexpectedly emerge again, I sidle up and read the brass plaque that's attached to the wall on the right-hand side.

Emperor Knight.

I think this must be where he works.

CHAPTER 16

On the tram on the way back home, I feel encouraged that I've seen James's possible workplace.

I'd have thought a solicitor would have to look smarter than he did, although he probably wears a suit under his usual beige mac. I certainly spotted a tie.

It's a good career, though, if that's what he does for a living. I can't imagine anyone dreaming of being a lawyer unless it's one of those glamorous ones who deal very publicly with celebrity divorces. But it takes all sorts, I suppose.

A few years ago, when Mum was well and I had no problems to speak of, I landed my own dream job purely by accident.

Three years earlier

I found myself with time to kill in the middle of town, waiting for Mum to finish scouring every clothing shop in Nottingham for a new jacket to wear at a friend's wedding, so I wandered into Moderno, the big contemporary art gallery in the city centre.

I'd always liked coming here, loved its big, open creative spaces and the leafy terrace café. If you felt like being less visible, there were stairs at the back that led to the lower floors, where a warren of small, intimate rooms packed with art offered a quieter experience.

You could easily while away a few hours in Moderno, although it wasn't usually to my taste in its selection of exhibiting artists. I generally found the pieces too eclectic, and the exhibitions were often verging on the bizarre and unfathomable.

My own preference was for artwork that was original, of course, but with slightly more commercial appeal. I loved a stunning landscape or portrait pieces that ordinary people adored enough to save up for and hang on their walls to live with day after day.

Pieces that meant something to them, were evocative of their personal happiest times or distant places visited.

Not wanting to limit myself to one kind of art – just as avid readers enjoy a broad sweep of book genres – I'd always made the effort to seek out all kinds, and so it seemed a perfectly pleasant way to kill half an hour while I waited for Mum to appear with her elusive jacket.

The gallery wasn't busy that day, so there was plenty of time to linger and contemplate some of the unusual clay sculptures in the main gallery. I moved on to an exhibition on the far side that explored graphics, music and poetry from the Far East. I was reaching for the headphones to enable me to listen to a curator's opinion on it when I heard a familiar voice behind me.

Turning and peering through a suspended trio of giant monochrome prints depicting ruined cities, I saw my old university tutor, Montague Forster, chatting to the suited gallery manager I'd seen on my previous visits.

Using the prints as a useful cover, I walked down the middle of the gallery and lurked around closer to where they stood.

'When does your friend need someone in post by?' the gallery manager asked Monte.

'Well, The Art Box is scheduled to open at the end of the month, so ideally in the next week or so, if possible.'

My breath caught in my throat and I fought a splutter.

Lots of people in the online art appreciation groups I was a member of had been chatting about the opening of a hot new gallery called The Art Box. Owned by legendary Dutch sculptor Finn Visser, the exclusive boutique gallery would be the first offshoot of his award-winning sculpture gallery, The Steel Box, which was located in Sheffield. The fact that he had chosen Nottingham as the location for his next art venture was a massive coup for the city.

'I can ask around,' the manager told Monte doubtfully. 'But our temporary help comes mainly from students who can't work full-time, and I'll be straight with you, I don't want to let any of our permanent assistants go or that in turn gives me a problem.'

'Understand completely, Col.' Montague held out his hand. 'Well, if you hear of anyone looking, let me know. I'll be in next week to see the Aztec Lights exhibition.'

I watched as he strode out of the gallery with that distinctive long-legged gait I remembered from uni.

I rushed out after him.

'Monte!'

He stopped walking and turned sharply, his hooked nose hawk-like. The furrows lining his brow quickly dissolved into a wide toothy grin.

'Alice, dear girl!' I ran up to him and we embraced. 'How perfectly lovely to see you. How're things... you still painting?'

'A bit. Sometimes.'

'Remember what I told you in class. You've got to just keep at it.'

I felt my face flush a little as I realised my next question would probably reveal my earlier eavesdropping.

'Actually, Monte, I'm looking for work and I overheard you saying back there that you knew of someone who...'

'... needs a gallery assistant!' He beamed. 'Would you be interested?'

'Well, from what I overheard you saying, it sounds like just the sort of thing I'm looking for.'

'Sly little fox, listening in.' He narrowed his eyes and gave a hearty laugh as I felt a burst of heat in my face.

'I wasn't… I mean, I didn't mean to…'

'Only joking, dear girl.' He checked his watch. 'Time for a quick coffee and a chat?'

Mum and I had agreed to meet outside the Cross Keys pub in fifteen minutes' time. But she hadn't texted yet and I couldn't afford to pass up this opportunity. If I didn't do something to cut Mum's apron strings soon, I despaired of ever starting a life of my own, away from home.

'I'd love to,' I said.

Monte led the way across the road to a small Fairtrade coffee shop where the city's arty types hung out.

While he queued for drinks, I texted Mum to say it would be another thirty minutes before I could meet her.

I looked around me, enjoying the spread of warmth inside with a mixture of excitement and terror. I'd had this place pegged as an art student hangout, but in actual fact, there were people from all age groups in here.

When I was still at university, I didn't fall into the trap of making judgements about people and places, but since leaving, I'd become more cautious and, I suppose, afraid of putting myself out there. Although nobody could accuse me of not pushing myself forward today.

I saw that Monte was currently being served. In a few minutes, he'd be back at our table with the drinks and I'd find out if I really had a chance of working at The Art Box.

I couldn't help reflecting on the strange turns life could take. I'd left the house two hours ago for a shopping trip with my mother, and now here I was with a possible dream job opportunity on the horizon.

'Here we go.' Monte placed a white mug in front of me. 'One latte, as requested.'

'Thanks.' I picked up the mug and cradled it in my hands, willing the sting of the heat to sharpen my persuasive skills. 'It's so great to see you again, Monte. I can't believe it's been two years.'

'Tell me what you've been doing with yourself.' He took a sip of his cappuccino and licked the froth from his upper lip before raising his eyebrows.

'Nothing particularly exciting,' I said, wondering how I could make spending my days trailing around after my mother sound entertaining. 'After uni I made a concerted effort to get my portfolio together. I was painting abstract portraits for a while, and then I tried some mosaic pieces but found I hadn't really got the patience for it.'

'Good that you're trying new things, though.' Monte nodded approvingly. 'Keep giving yourself the time and space to experiment and sooner or later you'll find your niche.'

I smiled and took a sip of my latte, shifting in my seat. I didn't want to get bogged down in what my preferences were. I wanted a job in art.

Monte was a perceptive man. He coughed and put down his mug on the small, scratched table.

'Well. Let's not veer from the important matter in hand, which is the gallery assistant vacancy at The Art Box.' He smiled at me. 'When would you be available for interview?'

In that moment it felt like all my dreams had collided in a wonderful explosion of possibility. How could I have known it was just the opposite?

CHAPTER 17

Three years earlier

Mum's expression was thunderous as we crossed the road to the taxi rank.

'I didn't get your text until I'd been waiting here for a full five minutes, and now it's nearly fifteen minutes after the time we agreed to meet. Where on earth did you get to?'

Undeterred, I linked my arm through hers and squeezed.

'Remember Monte, my old university tutor?' Her face remained blank as we clambered into the back of a green Hackney cab. 'Well anyway, I bumped into him in Moderno, and guess what? I've got a job interview tomorrow morning!'

I knew the deal wasn't done yet, but my heart felt like bursting. I just had to tell someone.

'A job interview, where?' Mum remained unimpressed.

'There's a new gallery opening in town soon. It's going to be really important to our art scene here, and—'

'I thought you meant a proper job. A career.' She rolled her eyes as if I'd misled her, and looked out of the cab window.

I felt a flare of annoyance, but stepped on it before it gathered strength.

'You know that's what I'd like, though, Mum, a career involving art in some way.' The taxi swung around a corner and I grasped the overhead handle. 'Monte knows the gallery owner well. His name is Finn Visser. He's quite a famous artist.'

'Never heard of him.'

'He's Dutch, and unless you're into your art, you wouldn't know of his work.'

'If you're ignorant,' she remarked drily. 'Like you obviously think I am.'

'That's not true, please don't…'

'Please don't what?'

Ruin everything like you always manage to, I wanted to say.

'I didn't mean it like that,' I said instead. 'I know it probably doesn't seem like much to you, Mum, but for me it's a very big deal.'

'You haven't any gallery experience, though.'

'That's what makes this chance so amazing. Mr Visser is a good friend of Monte's and wants to employ someone he can trust from the off, someone who comes with a personal recommendation. He asked Monte to try and find a suitable local candidate.'

Despite Mum's jibe, I had got lots of experience viewing art in galleries, as well as my degree, and Monte said I should use that as a selling point in the interview.

'Well, I wouldn't get your hopes up until this Visser man actually offers you the job,' Mum said briskly. 'That way, you won't be disappointed.'

I stared at her smug, closed-off face. There was a sort of know-ingness in her expression, an appreciation of my limitations. I'd seen it before, though it was usually aimed at Louise.

Mum was wrong, though. I'd be more than just disappointed if I didn't get the job.

I'd be totally and utterly crushed.

The next morning, I arrived at the private members' club in Hockley ten minutes before my interview time of ten o'clock.

I'd been awake since five a.m. I hadn't slept all that well, but in a good way, because I was fizzing with anticipation of what might be.

I'd googled Mr Visser the evening before, and knew what he looked like. So a couple of minutes before ten, when a short, bald man wearing a loud printed shirt appeared in reception, waved to the concierge and breezed past without so much as a glance in my direction, I knew he had arrived.

At five past ten, the concierge showed me through into a carpeted corridor. He tapped on a door and pushed it open, then disappeared again.

'Come in, please.' Visser appeared unsmiling at the door. He extended a small, clammy hand. 'Finn Visser, pleased to meet you.'

His English was perfect, and the very slight accent was charming, but he didn't look enthralled to be here.

'Alice,' I said feebly.

So much for having a recommendation from Monte. He didn't seem overly friendly. Then again, what had I expected? 'Hello, Alice, you've got the job'? Very doubtful.

I followed him into the small but tastefully decorated room and took a seat opposite what looked like an antique oak desk, complete with a blotter and an old-fashioned telephone.

'So, Montague informs me you are interested in the gallery assistant position at the soon-to-be-opened Art Box?'

'I am,' I said. 'Working in a gallery is something I've been wanting to do for a long time now.'

'So why haven't you?'

I paused before answering, watching his stubby fingers drum on the desktop. I found myself wondering how those hands could create such delicate sculptures.

'There haven't been any openings here in Nottingham.'

'You won't travel?'

'I would, if the right job came up,' I said, hoping that was what he wanted to hear.

He asked me about my experience, and I told him about my degree, studying under Montague Forster, and also spoke briefly about my preferences in terms of the art I liked to look at.

'And tell me, Alice, why do you want to work in a gallery?'

He interlaced his fingers and placed them in front of him on the desk.

There were a thousand stock answers I could give that would sound intelligent, cultured and impressive, but I suspected Finn Visser had heard them all before.

So I told him the truth.

'I want to bring art to real people.'

He raised an eyebrow. 'And how would you propose to do this?'

'By talking to people, interacting with them in a real way. Not alienating them with jargon.'

'Jargon?'

'Yes, like talking about the metaphorical significance of the artist's colour choice when someone has come in to look at a coastal landscape because they have memories of childhood holidays there.'

Was it my imagination, or had Visser's face softened just a touch?

'I see,' he said, and then waited, as if he wanted more.

'I'd like to take the time to show people how the artist has managed to infuse a piece with light, or how the angle of a sculpture changes the way you view it.'

'To educate them.'

I shook my head.

'To discuss art with them in a way that's meaningful and that might help them to see why they should buy a piece with their hard-earned money.' I think for a moment. 'Equally, because of my own knowledge and interest in art, I would like to think I could talk metaphors all day long with a customer who initiated this approach.'

Visser smiled. He actually smiled.

'This, I find, is a refreshing view. One I like and I think would fit very well in my new shop.'

My stomach bubbled in anticipation. It was a very positive reaction, but he hadn't offered me the job yet.

'I have already appointed a manager to run the shop; his name is Jim Saxby. He is at the premises now. Would you like to take a look?'

'I would love to!' I beamed, unable to rein in my enthusiasm.

Present day

The past dissolves like candyfloss as the tram approaches my stop.

It's much quieter on board now that the rush hour has passed, and as I disembark and look up at the apartment block and my own empty window, my energy suddenly deserts me as though someone has pulled the plug.

I can't wait to get inside and lock my memories and the whole world out.

CHAPTER 18

'It's like a flaming oven in here.' Louise wafts her face when I open the door to her and a glum-looking Archie the next morning. 'No wonder you never buy any new clothes; you must spend all your money on heating bills. You should treat yourself.'

I've never complained about lack of money to Louise, but she's right, I haven't bought anything new for ages. Mainly because there's little reason to when I hardly go out.

I pull my T-shirt down over my sweatpants as if that might make them look a bit less ragged.

I did feel a bit of a state yesterday on the tram. A new pair of jeans, a warm but fashionable coat and some trendy ankle boots would be a big improvement. I could start with that anyway; even a few updated garments would help make a big difference.

'You look really nice today,' I tell her wistfully.

She's wearing a three-quarter-length black mac over a navy shift dress. She's paired it with black knee-length boots and some simple pearl dress jewellery. As usual, her make-up is flawless, and her dark auburn hair falls to her shoulders in soft, full waves.

'I don't know how, I had to rush like mad this morning to get ready.' She sighs. 'It's such a pain having to drop Archie off here before I can go to work.'

I immediately feel as if it's somehow my fault. It's a talent she has that capitalises on a flaw that's all mine.

'I don't suppose you've got time for a quick coffee before you go?' I say spontaneously.

I know I'll probably regret it later, but I'm desperate to speak to someone about getting on the tram and seeing James yesterday.

Maybe I could even use this opportunity to chat as a step towards getting a little closer to my sister. She has lots more experience when it comes to men after all.

'If only. I'll try and drop in to see you one night after work later in the week.' She calls through to Archie, who I'm pleased to see has already taken it upon himself to remove his shoes in the hallway. 'See you later, pumpkin!'

When Louise has left, I take a glass of juice through to Archie.

'We get juice at the breakfast club,' he says, reaching for the TV remote. 'I'm not allowed any at home. Mum always says I have to wait until I get to school.'

'Oh well, I've poured it now.' I hold out the glass. 'How was school yesterday?'

'OK, I suppose.' He takes the drink and turns his attention back to the TV.

Sometimes, engaging Archie in conversation is difficult. I've read somewhere that technology is systematically robbing the young of decent communication skills, like talking face to face, for instance.

I pick up the remote control and turn off the television.

'Hey!' He lunges for it and I move it smartly aside, holding it mischievously behind my back.

'Let's make a deal. When you're here and one of us wants to chat, we'll turn off the television or your game. Deal?'

'OK,' he says slowly, looking at me as if I've gone mad.

'We've got a lot of catching-up to do. We're stuck with each other for a while, so we might as well be friends, right? Talk about interesting things occasionally.'

'I suppose.' He shrugs and thinks for a moment. 'But I haven't really got anything interesting to say.'

'Oh, I doubt that. I'd love to learn more about science and stuff and I know you study all that at school.'

'Really?' His eyes widen. 'Did you know there's enough DNA in your body to stretch from the sun to Pluto and back?'

'No way.'

'It's true, honestly, Auntie Alice. And there are EIGHT TIMES as many atoms in a teaspoon of water as there are teaspoonfuls of water in the Atlantic Ocean.'

'That's an awful lot of atoms,' I gasp.

His face is alive now, his hands flying around in the air as he expresses himself. The lethargic, reluctant boy who arrived ten minutes ago is nowhere to be seen.

'OK, my turn.' He sits upright to listen. 'Did you know that… in space, the skin on your feet peels off?'

'That's gross!'

'Gross, but true. In the microgravity environment, astronauts don't need to walk, so the skin on their feet starts to soften and flakes off. When they eventually take off their socks, the dead skin cells float around in the weightless environment.'

'Cool,' Archie gasps, frowning slightly as he thinks it through. I feel a bit of a fraud having googled a couple of facts before he arrived. I'm certainly no expert on space.

'See, having a chat can be far better than having the gogglebox on 24/7. We both just learned something. We might as well make the most of our time together.'

'Mum says I won't be coming here for long.' He looks towards the window as if he's deciding whether to say something. 'Auntie Alice, Mum says you don't do anything ALL DAY LONG. Is that true?'

'I think it's time I had a word with your mum,' I say crossly as I hand him back the remote.

Archie turns his head sharply.

'Why?' His face looks a little paler.

'Well, it sounds like she's saying some pretty mean things about me that aren't really true.' Even as I speak, a little voice in my head asks what exactly I *do* do all day, but that's hardly the point. 'And it's… it's just not very nice.' I wiggle the remote control at him. 'I'm going to get ready now, so you can put the television on again for a little while if you like.'

Archie doesn't snatch it back like I expect. 'What will you say to her?'

'Don't look so worried.' I smile. 'I'll just ask her to stop saying snide things.'

I place the control on the seat cushion and turn to leave the room. Archie jumps up and grabs hold of my arm.

'Auntie Alice, please don't… don't say anything to Mum.'

His cheeks are flushed now and he's biting the inside of his cheek.

'Hey, it's OK, it's not your fault.'

'No, but…'

He is still staring at me, his eyes wide and shining. I realise he's close to becoming really upset.

'Tell you what, just forget it,' I tell him. 'I won't say anything, OK?'

'Thanks, Auntie Alice.' His shoulders relax again as he slumps back in the seat.

I leave the room but hover at the door, peering through the small opening. He doesn't put the television back on, but sits quietly, nibbling at his fingernails.

If I didn't know better, I'd say the kid looks really worried.

CHAPTER 19

Louise

When her mother was still alive, Louise visited the old family home once a week. To her shame, she spent all week dreading Friday evening, which seemed to come around tremendously fast.

She was locked in a battle with her own demons, a deep depression that nobody knew she was being treated for. Since meeting Darren, she'd discovered that the hair and make-up and smart clothing disguise worked an absolute treat. People – even those closest to you – saw an individual who looked as though they were fully functioning, and that was enough for them.

That was the thing with poor mental health, she pondered. With no bandages or crutches or wheelchairs on show, you could keep it all tucked away inside, for short spells at least. What people couldn't see didn't seem to exist in their eyes.

And nobody ever looked beyond the glamour, close enough to see the haunted look in her eyes. Nobody knew about the insomnia. She was able to keep that easily hidden from Darren, who slept like a log.

Two years earlier

Visiting her mother had become a challenge that went beyond Louise's coping capabilities. Her visits grew less and less frequent and shamefully shorter as time went on.

Alice, openly damaged by Jack's death, which she blamed herself for entirely, had developed a care routine for Lily that bordered on obsessive. Tasks must be undertaken on the dot; their lives were ruled by the clock. They found a sort of warped sanctuary in it.

Louise would often turn up out of her scheduled time slot, delayed at work or by traffic or simply life, and get short shrift from her mother.

Sadly, her illness had seemed to loosen Lily's tongue when it came to her opinions, and her default opinion of Louise had always been low.

'Hi, Mum.' Louise breezed in with her smiley mask firmly in place. 'Sorry I'm a bit late.'

Lily looked up from her jigsaw tray in disgust.

'Your sister dedicates herself to caring for me, but *you*… you can't even get yourself here on time.'

During her visits, Alice either ran around like a loon, organising Lily's medication or meals, or sat staring into space without comment while Lily told Louise exactly what she thought of her.

'Falling for that con man,' she'd sometimes cackle. 'Alice and I saw him for what he was the day you met him. We tried to tell you – didn't we, Alice? – but you wouldn't listen. You'd never listen.'

'I never would. I'm such a terrible person, aren't I, Mum?'

'Why can't you just take it?' Alice had once whispered to her at the door. 'Why can't you just say you're sorry and take it? It would be so much easier for us all. It takes me ages to calm her down after you've gone.'

'I've taken it my whole life,' Louise snapped back. 'All through our childhood, not that you ever noticed. So I'm well in credit. It's your turn now.'

She felt bad when she'd left that day, but Alice had asked for it. She was such a bloody martyr. She couldn't wait to tell Louise she'd been diagnosed with that ambiguous 'disease' ME, and how she felt so dreadful and life was so hard. Blah, blah, blah.

Louise couldn't deny that looking after Lily must be no walk in the park, but Alice had as good as stopped living after Jack's death anyway.

This way, at least she had a roof over her head, a carer's allowance, and no reason to leave the house if she didn't want to. And mostly, she didn't want to.

But the day Louise called and Alice told her to sit down because they had something important to tell her, she felt her forearms prickling with dread.

'I'm selling this place,' Lily said simply.

Louise looked around the sitting room where she'd spent her childhood. Their father had sat in the very chair she herself sat in right now.

'But… where will you go?'

'I've found a small apartment on the outskirts of the city,' Alice said. 'Mum's seen all the photographs and we think it'll be perfect, don't we, Mum?'

Lily grunted, but all Louise could think about was what was going to happen to the money. The family house must be worth a packet, even in the current economic climate.

'It will be easier to manage, easier to get into town, and it'll free up funds to pay for some home help,' Alice added.

'Your sister is killing herself looking after me.' Lily looked at Louise accusingly. 'I have two daughters but only one cares about me. I'll pay for some extra care, and also for the tablets we can't get indefinitely on the NHS.'

Louise thought about how she was currently living hand to mouth, raising Archie as a single mother, working and paying ridiculous childcare fees, not to mention the constant juggling of paying overdue bills. Generally running herself into the ground. Even a couple of thousand would make life so much easier.

But there was something else that cut her like a blade.

It was painfully obvious that the two of them had discussed and debated the whole moving house thing without once mentioning it to Louise. It was as if she didn't matter, didn't warrant consultation… it was as if she barely existed at all.

That day, it felt like they had finally excluded her from their lives once and for all.

CHAPTER 20

Alice

I stock up on bits I need at the small Tesco up the street, including some healthy treats and snacks to keep in for Archie.

It's a really convenient store but I've hardly ever been in there, preferring to do a big monthly food order online up until now.

Since I've been out more, popping up the road to the shop seems far more doable, and it gives me a satisfying sense that I'm pushing myself out of my comfort zone.

I walk slowly up and down the aisles, perusing the fruit, the mixed nuts and the small snack-size yogurts. As I amble around, I think about Archie and the shadow that passed over his face when I said I'd have words with his mum. His twisting fingers and wide, imploring eyes. The big sigh of relief when I promised not to say anything.

Such a visceral reaction doesn't really make sense over something so minor. It makes me feel uncomfortable. Perhaps Archie is just nervier than I thought, has too good an imagination.

I load some things into the basket and make my way to the checkout.

Although I've been careful not to buy anything really heavy, it's still a struggle to get the stuff back home. Every joint in my body seems to be throbbing today.

It's with relief that I zap my fob on the security keypad and struggle into the foyer of the apartment building with my bags. I see the large white handwritten notice immediately and groan out loud.

I don't need to read it to know exactly why it's there.

'Bloody great.'

The lift is out of order at least twice a month, and especially, it seems, if I have a load to carry upstairs. I knew I should have come straight home, but unexpectedly I've found I quite like getting out again.

It had crossed my mind once or twice that I might be getting agoraphobic, but it turns out I just needed a reason to take the plunge to walk out of the door again.

I redistribute my load a little and am steeling myself to begin the climb when I hear feet shuffling behind me.

A girl is leaning into the corner next to the entrance door. I've walked past without noticing her.

She's very slim, with blonde hair and one of those dark regrowth-style partings that's been done on purpose to follow the latest fashion trend. She has small, delicate features with big, soft brown eyes. I'm guessing she's in her early twenties.

'Oh! I didn't know there was anyone else here.' I jerk my head back at the lift and roll my eyes. 'It's broken down *again*.'

She attempts and just about manages a weak smile, but now I see her eyes are swimming and red-rimmed.

'Are you… OK?'

'I'm fine.' She wipes her nose with the back of her small, pale hand. 'Thanks for asking, though.'

She's staring wide-eyed into space, tapping the toe of her boot on the floor nervously, and I wonder fleetingly if she's taken something.

I'm desperate to get back to my apartment, but it seems rude to just leave her like this.

'Are you waiting for someone? Or looking for a particular apartment number?'

Her skinny black jeans, heeled ankle boots and trendy parka with fur-trimmed hood look brand new. She certainly doesn't look as if she's sheltering here because she's got nowhere else to go.

She ferrets in one of the deep pockets of her coat and pulls out a tissue, giving me a weak smile.

'No, I live here. On the fourth floor. I just… I'm trying to get myself together before I go back up there.'

'I see.'

This is a cryptic conversation I'd rather not continue. I'm tired and aching all over, with what feels like a mountain up ahead of me.

'Well, I'd better start the mammoth climb,' I tell her. 'So long as you're all right.'

'You haven't got to trek right up to the top floor, have you?' She holds the tissue up to her face and blows her nose noisily.

'What?' I turn, one foot on the bottom step. 'Oh no, thank goodness. I'm third floor. Flat 332.'

I bite down on my tongue. I don't know why I volunteered that information.

The girl looks surprised. 'That's the one directly below me. I'm in 432.'

'Small world,' I say, thinking about the phone vibrating on the hard floor, the thumping noises that startled Archie, and the footsteps pacing back and forth night after night. Not to mention the shouting.

She coughs.

'I hope… I'm not too noisy up there.'

'It's difficult, isn't it, living in an apartment block? You can't help but hear stuff all the time.'

She tilts her head to one side. 'Does that mean I *have* disturbed you?'

I just want to get back to my own apartment. My body feels like it's been through the wringer, and I've got three flights of stairs to climb yet.

'No. Not really. Like I said, it's difficult, isn't it.' It's not a question and I don't phrase it as one.

She pushes herself off the wall and takes a step forward.

'Anyway, I'm Jenny.' She holds out her hand. 'Pleased to meet you.'

'Alice,' I say, looking regretfully at the bags that mean I'm unable to shake her hand.

'Give us a couple of those, I'll walk up with you.'

'No, it's fine.' I tighten my hold on the thin plastic handles, which are already cutting into my fingers. 'Honestly.'

'I'm not being funny, but you look as if you're about to flake out,' she says, and pulls at one of the bags until I let go. 'Give us that one as well, it looks heavy.'

She sets off upstairs with the bags, leaving me trailing behind feeling like an old woman. There's probably only about seven or eight years between us, but right now it feels more like thirty.

I stop at the top of each flight of stairs and take a few breaths before plodding on. When finally I reach the third floor, exhausted and almost bent double, Jenny is there, smiling and looking as if she could have easily carried on to the eighth floor.

'There you are.' She grins. 'I was about to send a search party to airlift you up.'

I lean against the wall and drag in a deep breath.

'Sorry.' Her smile fades as she sees my face. 'I was only joking.'

'It's fine, honestly.' I smile, panting but willing myself to just chill out a bit. 'I'm really grateful for your help. Thanks.'

She bends down to pick the bags up again. 'I'll take them into your apartment for you. I can put the stuff away as well, if you like.'

'No, there's no need for that,' I say quickly. 'But I really appreciate the offer.'

This morning, I left the apartment in a bit of a mess: dirty dishes on the worktop and stuff scattered around the living room. When we were younger, Mum used to have a rule about always leaving the house tidy.

'That way you're never caught out,' she'd say, although now I realise it was probably another one of Dad's ridiculous demands.

Jenny nods and starts to walk towards the next flight of stairs before hesitating.

'If you're ever at a loose end, feel free to pop up for a cuppa. I've been here over six months now and don't know a soul.'

'I will, thanks, Jenny.'

I pick up the bags and we say our goodbyes.

It's only when I get inside that I realise I never asked her why she was so upset, or why she was so keen to avoid going back up to her own flat.

CHAPTER 21

I finish a late sandwich lunch and think about having a nice relaxing bath and an early night with a good book later. I flick on the television and settle on Sky Arts as a background buzz while I close my eyes. Not to sleep, as daytime napping makes me groggy, but just to rest a little.

After actively trying not to leave the flat for so long, the last couple of days have been taxing in terms of both physical and nervous energy.

I listen to the presenter's pleasant smooth voice as she tours the Van Gogh Museum in Amsterdam, a place I've always wanted to visit.

As I relax, the voices fade out and my mind moves back again to the day I got the job at The Art Box.

Three years earlier

After agreeing to accompany Mr Visser to meet Jim, the Art Box manager, he suggested the quickest option was to walk there. It was a fine, dry day and the gallery wasn't far from the private club where we'd started my interview.

It felt strange, a little uncomfortable, walking with him through the streets of my home city. Nobody gave us a second glance despite his eminence in artistic circles.

Like my mum, most people, unless they were ardent modern art fans, would have likely never heard of Finn Visser, creator of the world renowned *Ordinary Man* series of exquisite wall sculptures.

The Art Box was tucked away up a side street in the Lace Market area of the city known locally as the Creative Quarter.

It was just a two-minute walk from Moderno, where I'd bumped into Monte the previous day. I smiled as I thought about all the art fan speculation online about where the new gallery might be situated. It had been right under their noses all the time!

The street was in popular use as a short cut from the shops into the Lace Market car park. I recalled that the new premises used to be a vinyl record store called Spinners. Visser had made a clever location choice by staying in the bustling city centre yet also bagging his own piece of quiet space a little off the beaten track.

'Here we are.' He tried the front door, which was locked. As he fumbled in his pocket for a key, I noticed there was no signage in place out front yet. Plain cream Roman blinds were pulled down fully on the two big picture windows and also the glass door. No visible clues at all about what it would soon become.

I felt a little thrill shiver down my spine when I thought of the reaction I could cause online later if I wished to do so, teasing the members of my Facebook art group with clues about the top-secret location of Finn Visser's latest venture.

Finn turned the key in the lock and pushed open the door.

'Hello?' He called out. 'You there, Jim?'

I stepped inside the shop behind him.

'Wow!' My mouth dropped open. I didn't know what I'd expected, but it wasn't this.

'I like your reaction.' Finn grinned. 'We have done a lot of structural work here. It used to be a very cramped, gloomy old record shop, I am told.'

I nodded. The last time I'd come to Spinners, I'd still been at comprehensive school. One of the girls had wanted a specific Beatles LP for her dad's birthday, and a few of us had come here with her to look for it.

At that time, the shop had had a cast-iron 'two schoolchildren at a time' rule, so three of us had to wait outside in the cold while she browsed the never-ending discs. We'd pressed our noses up against the window, marvelling at how so many boxes of records could be crammed into such a tiny space.

Now, I looked up and around in sheer admiration at how it had changed.

Mr Visser had obviously knocked through to the back rooms and also the attic, which had previously not been part of the main retail area, to create a dazzling white space with high ceilings and a mezzanine level running across the back. The floor was bleached hardwood, and tiny LED spotlights were dotted generously across the walls.

It was still a shell. There wasn't a single piece of artwork, display plinth or furniture in there.

'We are scheduled to open in precisely one month's time,' Finn told me. 'The first job of the new gallery assistant will be, in conjunction with Jim, to organise the publicity and PR for our opening event.'

'Sounds fantastic,' I told him, tearing my eyes away from the interior at last. 'I've been to lots of gallery launch events. I'd like to think I've got a good idea of what works and what doesn't.'

Finn nodded and called out for Jim again. I hoped he was impressed. It was hard to tell with his poker face, but the thought did cross my mind that Monte would be proud of me, selling myself like that.

At last, footsteps sounded and a tall middle-aged man with salt-and-pepper hair, a long, thin nose and twinkling eyes appeared from a door at the back.

'Hello, boss.' He grinned. 'Found us a customer already?'

'This is Alice,' Finn said as Jim and I shook hands. 'She lives in Nottingham and is interested in the gallery assistant position.'

'Ay up, mi duck!' Jim laughed. 'That's what I'm told they say around these parts by way of a greeting.'

I nodded and laughed, warming to him immediately. It sounded as if this place would be welcoming to ordinary local people, not just educated arty types. That was the kind of inclusive atmosphere I wanted to be a part of; bringing art into the wider community.

Mr Visser cleared his throat. 'So, this would be your place of work, Alice. What are your thoughts on our proposed accommodation?'

'Astonishing,' I breathed, looking round again. 'There's so much light and space. It would be any artist's dream to exhibit here.'

They both nodded and exchanged a glance.

'I think Alice would make a fine gallery assistant, Jim… if she wants the job, of course?'

The two of them looked at me expectantly, and it was all I could do not to burst into tears.

'Yes please,' I managed to squeak.

Present day

My hands jump up from the armchair as my phone gives out a shrill tweet to both rouse me from my reminiscing and signify an incoming text. I reach for it, feeling a little raw as I'm ripped away from my happy early memories at the gallery.

OK if Archie stops at yours tonight? Sorry, wouldn't ask unless urgent. L x

I twist one hand up to rub at my sore shoulder. I can hardly say no, and it's not worth asking where she's going at such short notice because I learned long ago that Louise always has a smart answer at the ready.

That's fine, I text back.

I wonder if she's given Archie the bad news yet. I'm guessing that my flat is the last place he'd choose to come.

You're a star! I'll bring him over about 6.

I lean my head back on the sofa and close my eyes. It's going to be a long night unless I can formulate some kind of a plan to win my nephew over.

CHAPTER 22

Louise's cheeks look very pink and she's chewing her lip as Archie slips inside past us both.

'I'm sure that kid winds me up just for the fun of it,' she says between gritted teeth before blowing out a breath. 'He tests my patience every day. Thanks for having him, though, you're a lifesaver.'

'I think there are lots of kids with worse behaviour,' I say lightly. 'He's a good boy really, when he's got things to do.'

'Spend a lot of time with eight-year-olds, do you?' Louise grins but I sense the steel behind it.

She hands me Archie's stuff, bids us goodbye and swiftly disappears off down the communal landing.

'Nice to see you, Archie. Had a good day at school?'

He stands in the hallway looking a bit distracted, as if he's thinking about something else, but then he registers that I've asked a question and grunts by way of reply.

I've braced myself for a difficult evening, but before I know it, he's kicked off his shoes and hung up his school coat without any prompting at all from me.

'What's this?' he says as I follow him into the lounge.

He's looking at the Scrabble board and bag of tiles I've set out on the floor, flanked by two brightly coloured bean bags that I found in the spare bedroom.

'I've been sorting through some old board games, stuff me and your mum used to play years ago. Your gran brought them here from the old house. So many happy memories linked to them, I suppose she couldn't bear to throw them out.' I've already hidden the TV remote control, and although Louise has brought his Xbox in a bag again, I left it at the door and shuffled him quickly through to the other room. 'I thought, if you fancied it, we might have a game.'

He looks at me, confused. 'What, *you'll* play with me?'

'Of course. Board games need at least two players.'

'Oh wow, thanks, Auntie Alice! At home I have to pretend to be the other player, too.' He runs over to the game and I feel a pull on my heart. 'I'll sit this side, is that OK? Will you be able to get down here with your bad back?'

'I think I'll be fine getting down, it's getting up that'll be the challenge.' I'm only half joking, but it's sweet of him to ask. 'You might have to leave me in here for the night, Archie.'

'If you can't get to your bedroom, I'll bring my pillow and quilt in here.' His face remains serious. 'I wouldn't just leave you here on your own.'

I grin to mask the rising emotion that threatens to embarrass me and ruin our upbeat mood. 'Come on then, let's make a start. I'll get juice and sliced apple while you prepare for me to give you a Scrabble masterclass!'

He whoops in delight and punches the air.

The next hour flies by. Archie tells me he's never played Scrabble before, but once I've explained the basics, he is a delight and a more than worthy opponent. I'm in awe of his vocabulary and word skills.

'Z-E-N-I-T-H,' he spells aloud as he places his tiles on the board. 'Eighteen points and... I win!'

'You're a hustler! All this time and I never knew you were a Scrabble master.' I shake my head in disgust. 'How does an eight-year-old boy even *know* a word like that?'

'I'm nearly nine,' he corrects me politely. 'And zenith means the highest point of something. In science, we learned about planets colliding at the zenith because of the magnetic pull.'

'Like learning about the planets, do you?'

He nods. 'Mrs Booth, my teacher, says I'm really good at it too.'

'Very well done, Archie, I'm impressed.' I clap my hands. 'OK, you pack the game away and I'll make us more drinks and snacks, and then we'll watch a bit of TV together.'

I brace myself for a loud protest swiftly followed by a demand to set up his Xbox, but it doesn't come.

'OK, thanks for playing with me, Auntie Alice,' he says, pulling the Scrabble box towards him.

I place my palms on the floor and clamber with difficulty onto all fours. After a few seconds, I sit back and upright. Easy does it.

'Hold onto me if you like.' I look up to see Archie standing next to me with his hands out. 'It might help you to stand up.'

'Thanks, Archie.' I smile weakly, trying not to show how bad the needling pain is. 'That's kind of you.'

'That's OK, Auntie Alice,' he says simply. 'I used to think it was boring coming here, but now I like it.'

'That's good news. I like having you here.'

'Best of all, we can look after each other when we feel bad.' He smiles as I get to my feet. 'This is what it must be like to have a friend.'

Once I've lost the stiffness, I carry a tray through with our drinks and two small bowls containing crisps and cheese biscuits.

The game has been neatly packed away and the bean bags have been placed against the wall.

'Good job tidying up, Archie,' I say, taking the remote control that's been hidden in the kitchen drawer from the tray and aiming it at the television.

'I suppose you're going to watch soaps now,' he says morosely.

'Wrong!' I sing out. 'I thought *this* would be far more interesting.'

Archie looks at the TV expectantly as I press a couple of buttons and the screen flickers into life. Whilst in the kitchen, I had a bit of a brainwave and searched catch-up viewing for programmes about planets, finding one I felt Archie was sure to enjoy.

'Whoa… the 2017 eclipse!' he gasps when the intro comes on. 'So cool! Are we actually going to watch this *together*?'

When he's not scowling, he looks like a different boy.

'Yep, we actually are. I think you're definitely the expert on this stuff, though,' I tell him. 'So you might have to explain bits to me if it gets a bit technical, OK?'

'Deal!' He grins. 'I already know all about this, Auntie Alice. They called it the Great American Eclipse and it was a TOTAL solar eclipse if you happened to be viewing it from a certain part of the USA.'

'Wow.'

The programme is interesting. I learn a lot about the 2017 eclipse, but I learn even more about my nephew.

Louise has told me on a number of occasions that Archie struggles at school and that he's currently under assessment for ADHD. But the kid sitting next to me right now is totally focused. He's bright and hungry for knowledge.

We watch the programme together, and for forty-five minutes, Archie barely moves.

He doesn't fidget, manhandle the cat or throw anything at the wall.

He doesn't even touch the crisps or cheese biscuits.

The only time he takes his eyes from the screen is to fill me in on bits he's learned at school. It's a wonderful thing to watch him emerge from a combative, angry shell and come alive right in front of me.

Later, he changes into his pyjamas, and when I tuck him up, there are no scowls to be seen. I sit on the edge of his bed as we continue to chat about the programme for a few minutes.

We both feel a bounce at the bottom of his bed and Archie looks startled.

'You *are* honoured!' I say. 'Magnus has stopped by to say goodnight.'

The cat stalks up the bed and Archie pulls the quilt up under his chin. Even I'm unsure of Magnus's intentions.

'You know, I think he must be impressed by your knowledge of the planets.' I smile, scooping Magnus up as I stand. 'Cats are really intelligent too, so he'll appreciate what a boffin you are.'

Archie's face relaxes into a grin. We say goodnight and I turn off his lamp.

'I hope I dream nice things... like about the eclipse,' he says nervously. 'I hope I don't have a nightmare.'

'A nightmare? What about?'

'I don't know,' he says in a small voice. 'Just bad things... angry shadows.'

'I'm sure you'll be fine. There are no angry shadows here, poppet.' I smile, bending to kiss his forehead. 'And I'm only next door if you need me. Night, night, Archie.'

'Night, Auntie Alice. Thanks for doing stuff with me.'

And again I feel that pull on my heart.

CHAPTER 23

Three hours later, I wake with a start from a deep sleep. The glowing digits on my alarm clock inform me it's well past midnight.

Buzz, buzz, buzz… The phone is vibrating again on the floor upstairs.

I've only met Jenny once, but maybe I should take up her offer and call in for a cup of tea. Somehow, I might find a way to casually mention the phone problem. It must disturb her rest too, unless she's lucky enough to sleep so deeply it's not a problem.

But tonight, it's not just the phone that's woken me. There's something else too. A shuffling noise, near the door.

I half sit up in bed and squint into the semi-darkness, my heart hammering, trying to tell me something is wrong.

As my eyes adjust, I see that Archie is in my room, standing at the bottom of the bed. His eyes are wide and he's shivering.

'What is it, Archie?' I whisper, sitting up fully and swinging my legs too quickly over the side of the bed, starting a dull ache in my hips. 'Are you OK?'

'I'm really sorry, Auntie Alice,' he whimpers, hugging himself. 'I've wet the bed.'

The next morning, I sit quietly at the table, my cup of coffee rapidly turning cold in front of me.

Archie is still sleeping; it's only 6.30, too early to get him up for school yet.

After sorting him out in the night, I feel like I didn't sleep at all. In reality, I probably grabbed a couple of hours, but no more than that. I just couldn't fully relax again, not with the stuff that's going round and round in my head.

Wetting himself like that, he was bound to be distressed, so there was no surprise there, but the way he *acted*… distressed was not the word; it was way more than that. He seemed terrified, not because he'd had a night terror but because he was really scared about what my reaction might be.

I realised my first job was to calm him down a little, which I managed to do. I told him it wasn't a problem and that it was easily sorted.

The thing I remember most clearly about last night was that he kept giving me this distrustful look as I repeatedly assured him I wasn't annoyed, like he was trying to decide, *does she really mean it?*

It was very upsetting to see him so afraid of me.

I ran him a shallow bath while he stood and watched silently. He insisted on keeping on his wet pyjamas until the bath was ready, and declined my efforts to help him undress, so I left him to it and went to strip the bed and sponge down the mattress.

It didn't take long. I gritted my teeth against the banging pain in my legs and shoved the soiled bedding into the washing machine, then moved some ironing from the spare room bed so it was ready for Archie to use.

Then I walked across the hallway to the bathroom and tapped lightly on the door.

'Archie, you done in there?'

No answer. I heard water splashing as if he was standing up, ready to get out of the bath.

'I have your towel here.'

I pushed the door gently, just so it would open enough to stick my arm through and hand him a soft towel, warm from the airing cupboard. But the door was locked.

'Archie? Are you OK in there, love?'

I heard the click of the lock and the door opened a crack. I stepped back, startled as he grabbed the towel.

'Thanks.' In his haste, he stumbled and gasped, quickly shutting the door again – but not quickly enough to stop me seeing.

The lock turned on the other side but I couldn't move. The breath caught in my throat and I steadied myself by leaning on the door frame.

I stood there for a few more seconds, trying to process what I'd just seen.

Five minutes later, dressed in clean underpants and one of my plain T-shirts, Archie climbed into bed in the smallest bedroom. I checked him after fifteen minutes and he was already fast asleep.

As I sit at the table now, stuff is starting to piece together in my head. Things that didn't mean much to me before take on a far greater significance when placed alongside other pieces of information.

I feel trapped, terrified of doing nothing but afraid that my imagination has gone into illogical overdrive.

Regardless of possibilities, there are some worrying facts and I know deep down that these are what I need to focus on right now.

Archie always seems to be on the edge of his nerves. He's either kicking off for next to nothing or he's withdrawn, as if he's expecting something bad to happen.

I've suffered from anxiety long enough myself to know what that looks like from the outside.

I used to think his sudden bursts of anger were just signs of spoiled bad behaviour, but now, after spending more time with him, I can see that the smallest obstacle to an observer is just one thing too much to cope with in Archie's world.

I run my fingers through my hair and realise it's been three days since I washed it. I'm a mess, inside and out. It's fairly easy to sort out my appearance, but there's a far bigger problem looming now.

Who is hurting Archie and why is he so afraid of me speaking to Louise?

My sister may be many things, but above all she is Archie's mother and I know she loves him. I think she loves him very much and so none of this makes sense.

Musing over the facts is not going to be enough to clear my conscience. The very least I can do is to ask some considered questions of my sister.

I don't even know what I'm hoping to achieve, I just know it has to be done. I have no choice, and yet…

The difficulty is going to be not making things worse for Archie.

He's already terrified of me telling his mother anything at all that happens while he's here.

And I've got a good track record of making entirely the wrong decision and ruining the lives of the people I care about the most.

CHAPTER 24

The knowledge that you are responsible for ending someone's life is a terrible, terrible cross to bear.

It's a weight that remains untouched by the placatory efforts of others who seek to ease your pain.

You weren't to know what would happen, or *You have to learn to forgive yourself.*

These are all phrases that sound so logical, so sensible. They're phrases that are easy to say but that I have found impossible to absorb and believe.

I know this because I've tried. I've tried so hard.

Words don't really matter, because the end result must always remain the same. The person is gone. Their life cut short because of *you*.

I sometimes let myself think about what might have been. That probably hurts the most, like a hot blade slicing through my guts, my organs.

The past will never shift or change, so that just leaves the future.

All I can do from here on in is make sure I don't harm anyone else again, and the best way to do that is not to make any rash decisions. I must watch myself, keep my mind sharp and balanced.

I didn't mean to hurt Jack, yet I did.

'Please, God,' I whisper. 'Don't let me cause harm to anyone else.'

But even as I say the words, I know I can't shut myself off from other people any longer. I have a duty to make sure Archie is safe.

I just wonder why bad things always seem to happen to other people when I'm around.

CHAPTER 25

Louise texts to say she's stuck in traffic and will be late picking Archie up from mine. She usually picks him up directly from school, but today she asked if I could do the school run and bring him back to the flat.

I fret and debate what I'm going to say to her about my concerns about my nephew.

Not that *she's* ever had a problem saying exactly what she thinks to me.

All my life I've had the dubious benefit of Louise making sure I know in no uncertain terms what her opinion is on the way I'm living my life, or decisions I have made.

There are hundreds of examples of her getting on her soapbox and taking the moral high ground, but the one that comes to mind right now is the disapproval she displayed so openly when I landed my dream job.

Three years earlier

'Mum said you've got yourself a job,' Louise said as she walked past me in the kitchen, popping a piece of toast in her mouth and munching.

I looked up in surprise from my drawings. It was rare that my sister showed any interest in my life these days. I could understand it. Louise was ambitious herself, trying to combine a challenging career in PR with motherhood and keeping a home.

She'd declared she wasn't interested in men any more after her experience with Martyn Hardy... and who could blame her?

I'd carefully rehearsed all the good points of my new job before telling Mum, painfully aware that however I dressed it up, it wasn't the position of art lecturer that had always been her ambition for me.

I told her about the new gallery, where it was and how I hoped she'd be able to come to the opening event as an important guest.

'Mr Visser wants to be inclusive, show all different types of art, especially from local artists,' I said, the enthusiasm bubbling inside me. 'I'll have to work the odd late night and weekend when we launch a new exhibition, but I don't mind that at all, and Jim's said it works both ways, that he'll be flexible if I need the odd hour off.'

For the first time in my life, I felt so vital, so alive.

'I know it seems to be your ideal job, and that art is important to you.' Mum sighed, and I braced herself for the 'but' that I knew was about to follow. 'But was it worth doing an art degree for? Essentially, you've got a job in a shop, love.'

And there it was: the sentence that would stick in my head every time Finn or Jim praised me, every time someone appeared to be impressed by my position at the gallery...

Essentially, you've got a job in a shop.

I knew right then that those eight words would stick with me for a long, long time.

'So,' Louise brushed crumbs from her hands onto Mum's cleanly swept floor, 'what is this exciting new career then?'

I felt myself reverting to type and playing down the position. 'It's just assistant at a little gallery that's opening soon in town.'

'Oh well, I suppose it's a start,' Louise said tartly. 'It's what you want to do, though, isn't it, arty-farty stuff?'

'It is.' I laid down my pencil, feeling ridiculously grateful that even if she was making fun of me, my sister had registered what my career preferences were. Louise had always been far more interested in her own life and aspirations than those of others. 'I know it doesn't sound much... a gallery assistant, but it is my dream.'

'And were there many people interviewed for this position?'

Louise's lips sealed together in a small, mean line and I realised I'd fallen straight into one of her traps. Mum must have told her how I'd heard about the job. My mood slumped. I might have known her interest was misplaced.

'I'm not sure how many people Mr Visser interviewed. I was lucky, bumped into my old tutor at the Moderno and overheard him telling the manager about the vacancy. I was a bit cheeky really, just boldly asked him about it.' I chuckled conspiratorially, hoping to get Louise on side. Sadly, it didn't work.

'Oh, I get it now. Nepotism at its best.' She frowned.

'Don't be silly... it wasn't like that at all, nobody just *gave* me the job.' I tried to cajole her.

Louise shook her head. 'To be honest, it infuriates me when this sort of thing happens.'

'Come on, Louise, don't be like that.'

'Like what? Annoyed, you mean? I think I've every right to be. Opportunities falling into your lap while the rest of us have to claw our way into a job and then work damned hard to stay there once we get there.' She inspected her fingernails. 'Yet it seems if you know the right people, you can just waltz right in, no effort at all.'

I sighed openly. I couldn't win this conversation if I tried, so I might as well give up right now.

'I've obviously hit a nerve,' Louise remarked. 'Nothing you can say to that, is there?'

'It's a shame you've made your mind up exactly what happened when you weren't even there,' I snapped back, surprising myself.

'I've told you it wasn't like you describe at all. I had to have an interview with Mr Visser like anyone else would've done.'

'But your tutor had already put a word in for you.'

'Not really. He told Mr Visser I loved art, that I had a first-class degree and—'

'You always have to get that in, don't you?' Louise's nostrils flared. 'Having a go because I didn't go to university.'

'Oh for God's sake!' I slammed my hand on the tabletop, rattling my pencils. 'Just stop it with the pity party, can't you? This isn't about you, Louise. Can't you just be pleased for me... for once?'

Her jaw dropped, and I stalked from the room, my hands shaking.

CHAPTER 26

The doorbell shrieks and I jump up and rush through to the hallway.

I can hear the television on in the lounge where Archie is watching cartoons back to back.

When I open the door, my palms are sticky and a trickle of sweat wriggles down my back. 'Hi,' I croak, my mouth dry.

'Hello, how are you?' Louise breezes past me without waiting for an answer or offering an apology for her late arrival.

'The traffic just gets worse around here. I reckon if you sold this place, with your share you could get a neat little terrace with a garden in a nice quiet suburb. You can't actually enjoy being in the middle of this crazy melee.'

She's talking too fast. There's a nervous energy about her, as though she's high on something. I suspect it's probably a leftover from running on adrenalin at work all day.

'I like living here,' I mutter. I've got to try and keep the upper hand in this conversation. 'Do you have time for a quick cuppa?'

Her phone pings and she stops in the hallway to read the text, chewing the inside of her cheek as she types out a reply.

She's wearing a navy trouser suit with a faint cream pinstripe. The wide-legged trousers are well cut and hover above beige strappy sandals that show off French-polished toenails. Her shoulder bag is in a matching shade of beige leather with a gilt trim.

If I didn't know her so well, I'd think she was completely together as a person, but as her sister, I'm very aware there's something about her today that's just slightly spoiling the pristine image she usually conveys.

Her hair is loose and curled but looks a little mussed at the back, and as she taps at her phone, I see she has a broken nail.

'Louise… drink?'

She bites her lip and looks up from her phone. 'What? Oh… no, sorry. Darren was away last night and I have to get back and tidy the house before he gets home later.'

'I really need to have a quick word with you about something. It's important.' I speak calmly whilst dying inside when I imagine her reaction to what I have to say. 'It won't take long.'

She clicks off her phone and drops it into her bag. It seems that at last, for the moment at least, I have her attention.

'Go on, then. I suppose another ten minutes won't hurt.' She slips her handbag from her shoulder and places it on the worktop. 'Let's have that cup of tea and you can tell me about your fancy man on the tram.'

If she thinks that's the subject of our chat, she's got a big shock coming. I fill the kettle and flick it on, and then lean back against the sink.

She's looking critically around the kitchen. Over the past year or so, she has commented on the poor-quality units, the dated flooring and voiced how distasteful I must find the view, having to overlook the residents' parking bays.

Around eighteen months ago, Louise and Darren bought a new five-bedroomed house on an exclusive estate in Ruddington. It's a palatial affair, the sort that has fancy white pillars either side of the outsize door, as though mimicking a Georgian mansion in the middle of suburbia.

There are several primary schools close to the new house, but even though Archie was at the perfect age to make the move without his education being disrupted, they decided to keep him where he was.

'Less of an upheaval, and he won't have to leave his friends,' Louise said breezily at the time. 'Anyway, I hear the schools around here stick their noses into your business too much.'

According to Archie, he doesn't have any friends at school, and isn't school nosiness simply a case of taking an interest in the pupils' well-being? Still, it wasn't for me to question their decision.

We were closer then. Louise used to bring over brochures and samples of fabrics and wallpapers for the interior of the new place, and we'd sit and discuss her favourites. On the surface, everything seemed wonderful, but I detected a reticence, a sort of hesitation that she brushed over every time the subject of the new house surfaced.

One day I decided to run the gauntlet.

'Is everything OK at home, Louise?' I asked casually. 'I mean, of course your new place is going to be totally amazing, but is it what you want? I just get the feeling something is bothering you.'

Her expression dropped as if I'd slapped her around the face.

'What on earth do you mean? I couldn't be happier. Who wouldn't be if they had my life?'

'Of course. It's just that I wonder if moving house is really what you want. Sometimes, you still seem a bit unsure.'

'Oh, you'd love that, wouldn't you?' Her eyes sparked with fire. 'You'd love to think we're unhappy. Well, things are perfect. Life's amazing, remarkable... is that enough superlatives for you?'

'Louise! I'm sorry, I didn't mean—'

'It just unnerves me when you think you know me better than I know myself. I understand you're only trying to help, but I don't know where it comes from.'

'I just want you to be happy, that's all. And to say that if you want to talk about anything, anything at all, them I'm here.'

'I appreciate your concern, Alice. But you must never voice this stuff to anyone, least of all to Darren. Just worry about your own life and keep out of mine. Otherwise, you'll be very sorry. That I can promise you.'

I was used to my sister's temper, used to her changing like Dr Jekyll and Mr Hyde in front of my very eyes. But that day she actually scared me.

What should have been just a put-down felt distinctly like a serious threat.

I don't want to tread the same path today, but I have no choice but to risk her wrath.

I owe that much to my nephew.

CHAPTER 27

Louise taps at her phone yet again and I wait for the next disagreeable feature of my flat to be pointed out to me. But if she's seen anything new here that she objects to, she's thankfully keeping it to herself today.

The silence feels dense and impenetrable around us. I scratch at an old burn mark on the worktop, thinking how best to broach my worries about Archie.

'So.' She sits on a tall stool and spreads her manicured fingers on the counter. 'You said you wanted to talk.'

I turn and look at her, and she smiles distractedly and nods, encouraging me to speak. I open my mouth and close it again.

'*Is* it about your man on the tram?' She winks.

'No, it isn't that.' I tap my fingers on the worktop. 'It's hard to know how to start really.'

'Oh, just say it.' She flips her palms upwards. 'You don't have to worry. I'm your sister, for heaven's sake.' She hesitates and gives me a coy look. 'I think I know what you're going to say, actually.'

'You do?'

'Yup. Something that's probably been on your mind for some time. All I'll say is, don't feel embarrassed. We've all made decisions and then changed our minds… it's allowed, you know.'

'Decisions?' I echo.

'I'm assuming you're finally thinking of moving.' She sighs. I start to speak, but she holds up a hand to silence me. 'There's absolutely no need to justify anything to me, Alice. I'm just pleased you've finally come to your senses. With house prices as they are, it's a great time to—'

'It's nothing to do with that!' I shake my head in frustration. Can't she just *listen* for once? 'I've no intention of moving from here. Can we get that straight?'

'Oh!' The polite smile slides from her mouth. 'Well, what is it, then?'

'I'm worried about Archie.'

She wraps a foot around the leg of the stool. 'And why's that?'

A trace of indignation has entered her tone, but I can't be dissuaded by it. I need to gather my few remaining scraps of courage and say what needs to be said.

'I think he might be being bullied at school, Louise.'

'I don't think he is.'

'Have you asked him about it?'

She sniffs. 'I've talked to him about this before, asked him time and time again if there's a problem, but he just clams up.'

'Maybe he's scared to say.'

'I've spoken to his class teacher, Mrs Booth, but she hasn't seen any evidence of him being bullied either. He's a good storyteller, I know *that*.' She inspects her broken nail nonchalantly, but I see her jaw clench. 'May I ask how you've come to this conclusion?'

'He gets so angry over small things, but I think he's using his temper as a ruse to cover up anxiety.'

Louise laughs. 'I think you spent too many hours in that therapist's office, Alice. We're talking about an eight-year-old kid here. Fortunately he hasn't learned yet how convenient it is to blame everything on *anxiety*.' She uses air apostrophes when she says the word.

I choose to ignore the barb.

'I don't think he's aware he does it, it's just a reaction.' I keep my voice calm, but it needs saying. 'I think, for a young boy, he is very anxious indeed. It's as though something is really worrying him.'

I stop. I reassured Archie again before Louise got here that I wouldn't mention the bed-wetting incident. I feel like I can't break that promise, but unfortunately it makes it difficult for me to mention the marks I saw on his body, because then I'd have to explain his bath in the middle of the night. But it's too important to keep to myself, so I need to find another way to talk about it.

'Do you check him for bruises and stuff?'

Her face pales. 'What a strange thing to ask.'

'I thought I saw a bruise on his arm, but he seems guarded about taking off his fleece.'

She laughs and indicates her jacket. 'I'd be guarded about taking my clothes off in here; you might turn the heating up even higher.'

I feel like I'm playing a one-sided game of tennis. She's batting away every concern I attempt to raise.

She sighs. 'Look, I admit he does seem to have a problem controlling his anger at times, but as I've said, he's being assessed for ADHD. If they find that's what's wrong with him, they can prescribe some medication that'll calm him down a bit.'

Archie doesn't need calming down and shutting up; he needs to be encouraged to open up to the people he trusts. I try and work around this idea rather than risk alienating my sister by speaking too bluntly.

'I wondered… if there might be a school counsellor Mrs Booth could arrange for him to talk to?'

Louise stands up. Her fingers glance against the teacup in front of her, and brown liquid slops over the lip of it, puddling on the worktop.

'If I need any advice on how to handle my son's problems at school, then I'll ask for it.' She snatches her bag up. 'Although I can't imagine what help *you'll* be able to give, never having had any kids.'

I follow her into the hall. No wonder Archie is nervous; Louise's mood swings are out of control. But I'm annoyed too.

'You might be surprised to know it's perfectly possible to tell if another person is unhappy and worried about something despite never having gone through the act of childbirth.'

She doesn't answer, doesn't give any sign she's even heard me. She wants to swat me away like a bothersome house fly but I'm not going to let that happen.

She pushes the living room door open with force and I see Archie jump up from the sofa, his face pale.

'Archie! Get your stuff, we're going. NOW.'

The television goes quiet and Archie appears at the lounge door holding his school rucksack and overnight bag. His eyes are wide and I can see his feet are fidgety.

'Louise, you're scaring him,' I say gently.

Archie glances at me and then back at his mother. 'Mum, can I stay here with—'

'Now is definitely not the time to be asking me for stuff, Archie,' Louise says firmly. 'Say goodbye.'

'Bye, Auntie Alice,' he says without looking at me, forcing his socked feet into his shoes without undoing the laces.

'Bye, Archie,' I kiss the top of his head as he passes me. 'See you soon.'

Louise marches past me at the door and turns when she's on the communal landing. Her tone is acidic.

'You know, the best advice I can honestly offer you is to get over what happened back then and find yourself another job.' She juts her chin forward. 'Maybe then you'll stop interfering in other people's lives and take a look at your own sad existence.'

CHAPTER 28

Louise

Louise stormed out of the apartment, vaguely aware of Archie scuttling behind her trying to keep up.

How dare Alice presume to tell *her*, Archie's mother, how to parent her son? Not only had she no children of her own, she'd barely been in the company of kids at all, so far as Louise knew.

It was fairly easy to see why her sister had turned out this way, though. Favoured and spoiled by their mother from an early age, she'd grown up thinking she could conquer the world.

Louise found herself wishing her mother had lived to see the utter mess Alice had made of her life, and in contrast how well Louise was doing. She was a fighter.

But then Lily probably would have made an excuse for her favourite child as she always did when they were younger.

'Come on, hurry up,' she snapped at her son, opening the car door. 'Get in, we're already late and your dad will be home soon.'

'Can't I stay with Auntie Alice, Mum? I'll be—'

'Get in!' she snapped, rushing around to the driver's side.

A few minutes later, they were stuck in traffic. Archie was immersed in the handheld game console she kept in the glove compartment, and Louise, still fuming from Alice's interference, drifted into remembering how it felt to be their mother's firstborn and least-favoured daughter.

Twenty years earlier

'Now that's what I like to see. My two girls playing nicely together for a change.' Their mother stopped by the kitchen table and began folding the smalls she'd just brought in from the washing line. 'What nice bright colours!'

Louise held her painting aloft. 'Mine is a picture of you, Mum, in the garden. Look, you've got your pretty pink flowered dress on.'

Lily tipped her head to one side and pursed her glossy red lips as she considered the artwork. 'So I have.'

Mum had thrown that dress out now because Dad didn't like it, but she didn't point that out.

Louise held the picture out. 'It's yours to keep, Mum. I made it for you.'

'How nice, thank you, darling.' Lily didn't take the painting but glanced over at Alice, who hadn't said a word, her fair head still down and focused. 'Let's see your painting then, Alice!' she said brightly.

Alice paused in her brushstrokes and frowned down at her work. Lily laid down the clean washing and walked over to the table, standing behind her.

Lily tapped the corner of her painting with a pearly pink nail. 'Well now, that *is* something special. A real work of art!'

'She hasn't even finished it yet,' Louise said. 'And Morris's ears are the wrong shape.'

'Nonsense.' Lily leaned forward and picked up the painting by its top corners, turning it around so it faced both the girls. 'See how Alice has filled the space, Louise? See the detail, the careful application of paint rather than those fast, clumsy splodges? And don't worry, darling.' She kissed the top of Alice's head. 'Morris is a gnarled old thing now, he's been in his share of cat fights. His ears look *exactly* like that in real life.'

Alice smiled and tipped back her head to look gratefully up at her mother.

Both Lily and Alice visibly jumped as an almighty crash sounded on the other side of the table. Palettes containing a rainbow assortment of paints exploded onto the terracotta tiles of the kitchen floor.

'Oh!' Alice said in a small voice.

'You little…' Lily bounded over to Louise and grabbed her by the arm.

'Owww!'

'Get up to your bedroom this minute, you spoilt little—'

'YOU ALWAYS LIKE HERS THE BEST!' Louise screamed, glaring over at her sister. Alice looked down at the table and covered her ears with her hands. 'I'm the eldest and my pictures are tons better than hers. She's *always* your favourite.'

'Don't be ridiculous.' Lily pressed her lips together and pinched Louise's arm harder. 'That's a terrible thing to say. Take it back this minute!'

'I won't! I won't take it back!'

Louise twisted out of her grip and ran from the room.

Through the crack in the door, she watched as her mother turned to face Alice, her slender back straining against her silk blouse. Lily smoothed down her immaculate blonde curls and addressed Alice.

'You'll come across this all your life, Alice. *Jealousy.*' Lily's light brown eyebrows knotted together. 'You must learn to bear the burden of it.' She moved closer and laid her hand on Alice's arm. 'You're gentle, creative and special. Remember that. Promise me you'll never let your sister's poisonous tongue dim your shine, my darling.'

'I promise,' Alice whispered.

Louise wanted to walk away, but she could not. She watched as Lily carefully lifted Alice's painting from the newspaper spread over the table and fixed it to the refrigerator door.

'There. All ready to show when Dad gets home,' Lily said, and Louise felt something inside herself harden forever like stone.

Present day

The traffic started to crawl and then progress at a reasonable pace as the council roadworks lorry blocking their lane finally moved.

Alice might have grown up as their mother's favourite daughter, being taught she was the cleverest girl who was never in the wrong, but in Louise's opinion, that scenario had changed a good few years ago.

Judging by the conversation they'd just had in Alice's kitchen, her sister thought she was onto something. She thought she'd got things sussed when it came to Archie, but she was way wide of the truth.

Even Louise herself didn't want to think about what was really happening to the boy.

CHAPTER 29

Alice

Speaking to Louise about Archie didn't go well. In fact, that's probably an understatement, but I'm satisfied with how I dealt with it. I couldn't think of any other way of saying those unpleasant things. She was always going to blow.

But I know from past experience that although she is fast to lose her temper, she also doesn't stay mad for long. In the past, she has often said unpleasant things in the heat of the moment and then approached me afterwards with an olive branch of sorts.

Her accusations about using underhand means to get my job at the gallery was one of those times.

Three years earlier

Later the same day that she'd accused me of nepotism, Louise came into the kitchen again.

I was still drawing at the table as Mum prepared soup for our tea at the hob and we worked in companionable silence.

Louise walked over and leaned on the table.

'I'm sorry if I upset you earlier,' she said.

I looked up. Had my sister just apologised?

'You always get oversensitive with these things,' she remarked. 'I was just saying that although I'm pleased you got the job, you have to admit, it's not that easy for most people.'

'Fine.' I sighed, keen to avoid rekindling the argument. 'It didn't feel easy at the time, but thank you for apologising.'

Louise didn't go away. Instead, she pulled out a chair and sat opposite me.

Mum looked round at us, still stirring the pea and ham soup, but she didn't say anything.

Louise leaned forward.

'Actually, I've been doing some thinking, and it's occurred to me that I can help you in your new job.'

I frowned.

'What's that look for?' Louise sounded offended. 'I thought you'd be pleased.'

'When you say help,' I said cautiously, 'what exactly do you mean?'

Louise spelled it out slowly, as if it should be obvious. 'You work for a new art gallery with an upcoming high-profile launch event, yes?'

I had an uncomfortable feeling about where this conversation might be leading, but I didn't interrupt her. Nonetheless, the realisation that Louise had actually done a bit of research about The Art Box surprised me.

'I work for one of the best public relations companies in the East Midlands.' She clapped her hands. 'See the connection? We can help each other!'

'You mean with the launch event…' I said slowly.

'Yes, with the launch event. The planning, the ideas… everything really. Surely your boss, Vasser, will be using a PR agency.'

'It's Visser,' I corrected. 'Yes, he's looking at local companies, but he's already mentioned one or two that he already had his eye on.'

'Well you'll have to take his eye off them again, won't you?' Louise winked at me. 'It would really do me a massive favour if I could show our CEO that I've brought a high-profile event like the Art Box launch on board.'

'Would it help your promotion prospects, Louise?' Mum asked.

'Help them? It would probably secure the promotion,' Louise replied in a sniping sort of way. 'And God knows Archie and I could do with the money.'

Clever: she'd always known how to get Mum onside.

An uncomfortable feeling started in my solar plexus, but I ignored it. Louise had a boss too; perhaps I could appeal to her experience of managers pulling rank.

'Mr Visser is quite single-minded in his ideas. I can mention your company but I wouldn't hold out much hope.' Louise's face dropped. 'How come you know so much about the gallery anyway?'

'I've heard one or two people in the office mention it. Art fans.' Louise said it like that was an affliction. 'They were talking about how great it would be if our company could spearhead the launch campaign. It would seriously mean the world to me if I could bring this one to the table, Alice.'

'It would be wonderful if you girls could help each other out,' Mum added.

I felt like a bug under a microscope. Mum turned from her cooking to gauge my reaction and Louise's eyes were still glued to me.

Didn't they realise it wasn't that easy to bring a company on board? I was the gallery assistant, not the manager, and a brand-new employee at that.

'I can't promise anything,' I said again. 'I can try—'

'If you don't want to help me, then just say so,' Louise snapped. 'I'd much rather you were honest than treating me like an idiot. Don't forget, I've worked in the business of promotion and PR far longer than you have. I can tell when someone is fobbing me off.'

'Louise, please!' I ran my hand through my hair, exasperated. 'Will you just stop being so defensive? I'm not trying to fob you off at all; quite the opposite, in fact. I'm being honest when I say Mr Visser may already have made arrangements. If he hasn't, I can mention your company. I can't do more than that, can I?'

'Actually, you can,' Louise said thoughtfully. 'You can do a lot more than that without putting yourself out at all.'

I looked at her, dreading what was coming.

'The launch event is on the second of May, right?'

I nodded.

'Well, if you can give me some insider info about your boss and the kinds of colours and styles he prefers, I can get some invitations mocked up for you to take in to show him. What do you think?'

'I… I don't know, it might seem…'

'It might seem what?'

With each added increment of frustration Louise added to her voice, I became more and more uncomfortable.

I'd literally just started this job, a position that was a dream come true for me. Mr Visser didn't know me well enough yet to be taking recommendations, and I hadn't worked with him long enough to gauge his tastes when it came to things like invitations. Plus, Jim was the gallery manager. I didn't want him to feel that I was stepping on his toes.

'There's a procedure to follow, Louise. I'm sure you have them at your place too.' I ignored the rolling of my sister's eyes and looked to Mum for support, but she turned back to her soup. 'I'm not saying I can't help, but I have to do it the right way.'

'Little Miss Goody Two-Shoes,' Louise mumbled under her breath.

I felt a hard lump in my chest. That hated phrase was what Louise had called me all the years we were growing up. It was a put-down then and it still felt like one now. Still, I bit my tongue.

'Like I said, I'll see what I can do,' I said lightly, and with that, I stood up and left the room.

Present day

I feel more frustrated after thinking back than I did when Louise just left.

The best thing I can do, I decide, is to get out of the flat for a short time. A few basic things like milk and bread need replenishing.

Fresh air and a bit of exercise might bring a new perspective on things.

CHAPTER 30

'Darren!'

My brother-in-law stops dead in his tracks on the stairwell and looks up at me, his face almost as surprised as mine.

'What are you doing here?'

'I'm coming up to see you, of course.' He flashes me a healthy white grin and strides up the last few steps with no effort until he reaches where I stand on the second-floor landing. 'Didn't expect to bump into you on the stairs, though.'

'I was just off to get a few bits from the shop.'

He's wearing jeans and looks broad and fit in his close-fitting fine wool sweater. His hair is a bit messy and he has the faintest shadow of whiskers on his face. He's not a vain man, but I've always thought him attractive in a rugged kind of way.

'Useless lift is broken again.' I pull a face. 'Still, it's all much-needed exercise, I suppose.'

'I meant more that…' His face reddens and he fiddles with the strap of his small rucksack.

'Yes?'

'Louise mentioned you don't get out much these days.'

'That's true, but I'm probably nowhere near the mad recluse she enjoys making me out to be.'

'Course not.' He stuffs his hands in his pockets, glances up the stairs behind me.

I realise it'd be rude not to ask him back to the apartment. 'Come up and have a drink. The shop will wait.'

'I don't want to disturb you, Alice. I'll call again some other time.'

'It's no trouble, honestly. And you must've come to see me for a reason.'

'Oh… yes. It'll wait, though…'

But I insist on going back upstairs and he follows me inside the flat.

'I'll stick the kettle on,' I say, slipping off my coat and shoes. 'Make yourself comfy in there.'

'Don't bother with a hot drink for me; a glass of water is fine, thanks.'

I take two glasses of water through and sit down in the lounge and he walks over to the window, peers down at the street and then sits down himself.

'I just came to see how you are, really. I never get to see anyone any more, with my work schedule.'

'As you can see, I'm fine.' I take a sip of my water, fully aware that despite his politeness, I haven't got to the reason for his visit yet. 'More to the point, Darren, how are you?'

He sighs and hangs his head, but he's smiling. 'You were always the astute one, Alice. Can't fool you, can I?'

'Is something wrong?'

'No. Well… maybe.' He pinches the top of his nose. 'It might be. I wondered if you'd had any thoughts at all… just lately, I mean. That's why I came here.'

'Thoughts on…?'

This is not such a satisfying guessing game.

'Look, I'm just going to say it,' he sighs. 'Have you noticed anything different about Louise these past few weeks?'

I think for a moment. 'In what way?'

'The way she's been acting and… the way she looks.'

'I can't say I have, not really.' But even as the words leave my mouth, I know I have noticed one or two things.

'I appreciate that I'm putting you on the spot here, and I'm sorry. I thought long and hard about it before calling in, but I'm just desperate to talk to someone really. Maybe I'm getting paranoid and imagining stuff. I don't know.'

His features look drawn and I think he's lost weight since I last saw him about a month ago, when he picked Archie up.

'I've noticed Louise is working much longer hours than before and she's dressing smarter, but—'

'Yes!' He looks vindicated. 'Those are the sorts of things I've noticed, too.'

'She's had a promotion, Darren,' I say gently. 'It's not unusual for people to smarten their image to better fit the expectations of a new role.'

'You're right, but you know these after-work meetings she's been going to? Well, I bumped into one of her colleagues the other day who I knew from years back. I just happened to mention that Archie and I aren't seeing much of her at night lately and he looked really taken aback. He didn't say anything, but I think he just didn't want to speak out of turn.'

'Hmm. There are the breakfast meetings too,' I say thought-fully. 'She says she'll have to drop Archie here for a few days at least.'

In an instant, I realise from the way he looks at me that he didn't know.

'She's dropping him off every morning?'

'Not *every* morning.' It's so obvious I'm backtracking. 'It hasn't been happening for long, only just lately she's needed me to take him to school.'

Darren's foot starts to jiggle.

'I didn't know this was happening, Alice. I'm really sorry she's been putting on you.'

'Not at all, I don't mind.' Louise's furious face looms large in my mind. This could easily be relayed quite innocently by Darren and end up sounding as if I'm trying to drop her in it. 'I'm very fond of Archie, you know that, and I was under the impression you're working longer and longer hours.'

'I do work long hours, but no more than I've always done. I've come home early two nights this week but Louise has been out.' Darren's face seems to crumple, and for a moment I think he's going to get really upset, but he takes a deep breath. 'Just between you and me, Alice, I worry about Archie.'

I sit up a bit straighter.

'In what way?'

'I don't know.' He shakes his head, fighting with himself.

This might be the only chance I get to speak to him about Archie.

'Darren, you know you can tell me anything, and this is important. If Louise is overly distracted with work, then it's up to us to make sure Archie isn't suffering in any way.'

'Has he said anything to you… about being unhappy?' He looks wretched, as if he's blaming himself.

'No, but I can tell something's not right. I tried to raise it with Louise, but she got annoyed, thought I was criticising her parenting skills.'

'She's so defensive, snaps my head off every time I try to get her to sit down and talk to me. Especially if it's anything to do with Archie.'

I know how *that* feels only too well.

'I know I'm just his stepfather, but I love that boy. I'd do anything for him, and it breaks my heart…' his voice cracks, 'when I think Louise is taking her frustrations out on him.'

'Archie thinks of you as his father, Darren,' I say firmly. 'He always has and that's what's important. But what do you mean about her taking it out on him?'

He looks at the floor.

'Sometimes I think he's scared of her.' He drops his voice lower, as if he's worried someone might hear. 'These past few weeks she's been acting so weirdly at home, not like herself at all. She's short-tempered and we've both felt the sting of her vicious tongue. I'm out of the house so much and I worry that Archie is taking the brunt of it.'

I consider this. I've witnessed her snapping at Archie and brushing away my concerns about him at school.

'I told her I suspect he's being bullied, but she seems to think the school have it all in hand.'

I wonder whether to confide in Darren about Archie's bed-wetting. He didn't want anyone to know, but it's often the sign of a troubled child. Archie, at eight years old, is hardly the best judge of what the important adults in his life need to know.

'You look as if you were going to say something,' Darren prompts me.

I decide I can't do it. Not this time.

'Not really, just thinking about what you've said. Maybe you should speak to Archie, reassure him he can speak to you in confidence.'

Darren nods thoughtfully.

'There's something else.' He shuffles to the edge of his seat and looks right at me. 'I'm pretty sure Louise is having an affair.'

CHAPTER 31

I don't know whether to expect Archie the morning after my set-to with Louise, but he arrives at seven as usual.

'Thanks,' Louise mutters, leaving him at the door.

Not overly friendly, but civil at least.

Archie seems a bit cagey as he skirts around me, takes off his shoes and then sits quietly in the lounge without turning the television on.

'How's things?' I ask him brightly, wondering if Louise gave him a hard time last night when they left.

'OK.'

'Put the TV on if you like. I'll just get dressed.'

I wait in the hall a few moments, listening, before heading for my bedroom, but the television remains silent.

I get dressed quickly, wincing but tolerating the twinges in my lower back. I'm distracted by trying to think of a way to get Archie to open up to me, to ascertain if there's anything he's worried about in a way that doesn't put him under any pressure and doesn't violate Louise's probable instruction not to talk to me about personal matters.

When we step outside the apartment building, I pause to look up at the sky. I'm relieved to see the fine drizzle has stopped and the cloud is beginning to break up, allowing weak rays of sunlight to arrow through. The good weather is late coming this year.

I've left a few minutes early to give us time to take a more leisurely walk this morning.

'Soon be the Easter hols.' I smile down at Archie as we set off walking, but he keeps his eyes on the pavement. 'Has your mum got anything planned… trips out, perhaps, or a holiday?'

'I don't know,' Archie says.

'I used to love school holidays because I got to do lots of artwork. Do you like art? Have you got paints at home?'

'Mum doesn't like the mess.'

'What about your dad, does he like doing stuff with you when you're at home?'

'He's busy.'

OK, clearly time to change tack. After a short pause, I try again.

'Hey, I heard about this great game the other day. Want to play?

'What sort of game?' he says suspiciously.

'It's called the word association game.'

'It doesn't sound like much fun.'

'It is, though. Wanna try it?'

'OK.' He shrugs.

'Here's how it works. I say a word, and you say the first word that comes into your head. So if I say *salt*, you might say *pepper*. Get it?'

'Sounds easy.' Archie is unimpressed.

'Ah, but there's a catch, see. You're not allowed to think about your answer at all, you just have to say the first thing that comes into your head. That's the golden rule.'

He kicks at pebbles but doesn't say anything.

'Let's have a go. The first word is… flower.'

He hesitates. 'Rose.'

'Legs.'

He waits a second too long. 'Errm… trousers.'

'That's good, but if you want to beat the best time, you have to answer like *that*!' I snap my fingers.

'OK.' He grins.

'Here we go then… Face.'

'Ache.' He comes back like a flash.

We both laugh.

'Nose.'

'Snot.' Archie doubles over laughing.

'Apple.'

'Pie.'

'Dog.'

'Breath.'

'Ha, ha, nice one.' I grin. 'You're good at this, Archie.'

'I like this game. Do I get to ask you some words?'

'Sure,' I say. 'Few more from me first, though.'

'School.'

'Boring.'

'Teacher.'

'Strict.'

'Friends.'

'Football.'

'Mum.'

'Angry.'

'Carrot.'

'Cake.'

'Home.'

'Work.'

'Dad.'

A slight hesitation again. 'Cry.'

'Brilliant, Archie. Your turn to ask me, now, though I don't think I can beat that.'

In between the silliest replies I can give to make him laugh, I review Archie's own answers. They weren't what I expected. His response for the word *mum* was *angry*, which makes sense. Louise seems to be snappy with everyone right now, myself included.

His response to *dad* was *cry*, which I found sad and made me feel like I was intruding in private family matters, but it fits with the stuff Darren told me himself yesterday.

There was no mention of bullying or hurting around the words related to school, but I'm still going to carry through with a plan I was thinking about all night, on and off.

'Last word for me this time,' I say to Archie as we approach the school gates.

'OK… The last word is: Alice.' He grins, pointing at me.

'Weak,' I say without thinking.

'Weak?' Archie stops walking. 'You're not *weak*, Auntie Alice. You're strong and kind and you're very intelligent, too.'

I turn to look at him, wondering if he's being smart, but his face is open and honest.

'Well, that's… nice of you to say so, Archie. Thank you.' I almost feel uncomfortable, which is silly because it's only a game.

'You're welcome.' He steps forward and squeezes my hand. 'I like spending time at your flat. I feel safe there.'

'Do you feel safe at home, Archie?' A look of alarm crosses his face. 'You know you can tell me anything you—'

'I forgot! It's my turn to help make the toast at breakfast club. Bye, Auntie Alice!' And in a flash he's gone, trotting through the gates and into reception.

I've made some mistakes in my life I'd dearly like to reverse. Who hasn't? I can never forget the past, but looking out for Archie is something I can do right now.

I can make a difference, if I find the courage.

I've tried talking to Louise about my concerns, which didn't work, and I know Darren is worried about him but isn't around enough to monitor the situation.

I'm certain someone is hurting and upsetting Archie and I feel completely justified in following that up, however awful the outcome might turn out to be.

A shiver of discomfort trickles down my spine into the pool of darkness at my coccyx.

I don't know what I really think might be happening to my nephew.

I don't want to second-guess, and I don't want to try and identify the twisty, faceless shadows that play at the edge of my consciousness.

Instead, I'm going to do something I probably shouldn't.

I'm going to do it right now.

CHAPTER 32

I wait until the school receptionist has buzzed Archie through into the main building and then I go back inside.

I know he'll be going straight into breakfast club and they're not allowed inside the classroom until the bell rings, signalling the start of the day.

'Can I help you?' The young receptionist slides open the glass hatch and offers me a faint smile.

'I'm Alice Fisher, Archie Thorne's auntie, and I wondered if it would be possible to speak to Mrs Booth, his class teacher, please?' The faint smile disappears. 'I literally just need a couple of minutes, that's all.'

'Can I ask what it's about?'

An older woman sitting at an adjacent desk looks up from her paperwork.

'It's a health issue the school really needs to know about. The doctor said his teacher should be informed for health and safety reasons.'

She reaches for the phone. 'Of course, I'll try the staffroom now. Please, take a seat.'

The double whammy of mentioning the doctor *and* health and safety has clearly done the trick. In society's new culture of blame, schools have to be careful to follow procedure to the letter.

I push away the twinge of guilt, telling myself I'm doing this for Archie.

While I'm waiting, my mind drifts back to my conversation with Darren yesterday. On the one hand, I feel vindicated in talking to him and hearing we have similar concerns about Louise. She's always had a knack for making me feel as if I'm overreacting or imagining stuff. But on the other hand, hearing what he had to say has increased my worries about my nephew exponentially.

Obviously Darren seemed distracted by his suspicion that Louise might be having an affair. He didn't elaborate much on why he believed it and I certainly didn't tell him that I'd seen several clues that pointed to the very same conclusion.

Her increased focus on how she looks, her preoccupation with her phone, and the 'meetings' at unusual times… it doesn't bode well.

Soon as Darren left the flat yesterday, I felt an absolute conviction that I have a responsibility to make sure Archie is safe, and if Louise isn't taking that seriously, then as his aunt I feel entitled to make my own enquiries.

And consequently, here I am, waiting for his class teacher, feeling a little queasy at the thought of what I'm about to do behind my sister's back.

A few minutes later, the secure doors open and a smiling woman in her thirties appears. Her hair is styled in a neat brown bob and she's wearing minimal make-up and a knee-length floral cotton dress with sensible sandals.

'Ms Fisher? Lovely to meet you.'

I stand up and we shake hands and find I warm to her immediately.

'Thanks so much for seeing me,' I say. 'It won't take long.'

'No problem at all. We can talk in my classroom before the children come in for registration.' She holds the door open and ushers me through with her arm, and I follow her down the corridor.

From outside, the school building looks very old. I think I recall being told at some point that it was built in the late 1800s and was a fine example of typical Victorian architecture. But inside, the rooms and corridors are very much up to date. The decor is bright and welcoming and it's obvious that money has been spent on keeping the interior modern and an inspiring place for young people to learn.

Mrs Booth opens the glass-paned classroom door and again invites me to walk inside before her.

I look around Archie's classroom with wonder. It's a lovely bright space with a large picture window that overlooks the playground. The walls are crammed with vibrant artwork and I find myself walking towards a display taking over one entire corner, entitled 'Our Solar System'.

Mrs Booth sees me smiling.

'Ah, you've spotted our new whole-class display!'

'It's wonderful.' I look up at the papier-mâché planets suspended on wires from the ceiling and twirling slightly in the draught from the door.

'Thank you, we're very proud of it. The children all contributed to it; in fact Archie played a big role in making our moon.'

She points to an impressive grey globe, its surface pitted with craters. I imagine Archie working on it, keen for the detail to be realistic.

'We watched a programme on the eclipse together and he knew so many facts about the moon…' For some inexplicable reason, I feel emotion welling behind my eyes.

'Are you OK, Ms Fisher?' She touches my arm gently. 'Come on, let's sit down a moment to talk. Would you like a glass of water?'

'No, no,' I say, sniffing like an idiot. 'I'm fine. Just a little worried about Archie, that's all. That's why I came to see you.'

'The office said there's a medical concern?'

I hang my head, unable to continue my cover story. 'There isn't really… it's not exactly medical.'

'Oh!' She looks a bit put out.

'But I *am* worried about Archie, Mrs Booth. My sister has left him in my care for the past week, and spending more time with him has highlighted to me that there might be a problem at school.'

The teacher nods but stays quiet.

'Louise is very busy with her job at the moment and she suggested I have a quick chat with you about how Archie is doing at school because I think there's a distinct possibility he's being bullied.'

'I see.' Mrs Booth sounds guarded. 'Can you tell me a bit more about your concerns?'

I can't betray Louise by telling her I think my sister isn't taking enough interest in what's happening to Archie. I also know that if I admit I've spoken to Louise and she's told me in no uncertain terms to back off, it might spook Mrs Booth. She could just shut the conversation down and go straight to Louise instead.

'As I say, spending a lot of time with him recently has led me to believe he's quite anxious behind his facade of being angry and uninterested in everything.' I remind myself to take it slowly. I won't mention the stuff that's *really* worrying me just yet. 'It's hard to get him to engage in talking about school at all, but he has mentioned he doesn't really have any friends. I wonder whether someone is upsetting him in class. Louise told me he's being assessed for ADHD, but to be honest, during the time he's been with me, he's been focused and articulate, and I question the wisdom behind this decision.'

I worry that I've gone too far, attacking the school's decision, but Mrs Booth laces her fingers together and smiles at me.

'I have to say I find your views on Archie refreshing, Ms Fisher.'

'Alice, please.' I brace myself for a put-down. By *refreshing*, she probably means naïve.

'I've said much the same thing to Archie's mum myself. He can be quiet and withdrawn in class when he first gets here, but once he's involved in something like our planet display' – she glances at Archie's splendid suspended moon – 'he is focused and brimming with ideas. I think if he were being bullied, he wouldn't blossom like that. Our class teaching assistant, Miss Bramley, has a good relationship with him and she has spoken to Archie. He's denied anyone is upsetting or hurting him in school. And as a recent report home showed, he did very well in his last set of practice papers in all subjects.'

I stare at her. 'Then may I ask why you are adamant about assessing him for ADHD?'

'The school isn't involved in that decision, Alice,' she sighs. 'I'm afraid, despite advice to the contrary from me, Archie's parents are undertaking the assessment privately.'

CHAPTER 33

Louise

Ten years earlier

After the night that Martyn proposed, things moved fast.

'We need to get our own place,' he told Louise, causing her heart to blip with pleasure. 'Somewhere nice to call home.'

'Your apartment is plenty big enough for us, though, and I love it there.'

'It's a bachelor pad,' he said. 'I want a new place that's completely and only ours.'

It was so sweet of him to think of it like that, she'd almost been moved to tears.

She'd only been to Martyn's place once in the three weeks she'd known him. It was an amazing duplex flat overlooking a park on the outskirts of the city.

They'd just stayed one night there, but when Martyn took a shower the next morning, she'd walked around touching the glossy surfaces and staring out of the floor-to-ceiling windows in the impressive lounge. She could imagine herself living here, the envy of everyone who knew her.

There wasn't a single thing out of place. She'd peeked inside the dishwasher and it was empty. The two wine glasses they'd used last night had already been washed by hand and upended to drain on the side.

Martyn was obviously a clean-freak and it crossed Louise's mind she'd have to really buck her ideas up to come anywhere near his slightly obsessive standards.

Back in the bedroom, the shower was still going so she had a quick look in the wardrobe.

She'd never seen so many suits hanging together. Expensive fabrics and designer labels – it was a revelation. Martyn rarely wore anything but jeans and a white T-shirt when they were out.

But he had explained to her about his exciting business expansion. He was dealing with some very wealthy and influential investors right now who could make or break his franchise bid. She didn't see him during the day, but he'd told her about lavish business lunches in the best restaurants in town with clients and investors.

Louise knew how important it was to look the part, even in her own insignificant job.

'We could be millionaires this time next year,' he'd told her on more than one occasion.

We could be millionaires. She'd loved how it sounded when he said things like that.

Martyn was everything she wanted in a man and she was determined to make their relationship work. Whatever it took.

In reality, that meant tolerating his strange ways. She gathered pretty quickly that he was a proud man. He'd asked her not to come to his gym until the massive refurbishment programme had been completed.

'I want to see your face light up when you see what I've achieved,' he told her bashfully. 'People don't seem to understand that success doesn't happen overnight. It's a slow process.'

He would also sometimes pay for a very modest bed and breakfast when they wanted to stay the night together. It seemed ridiculous when he'd got such an amazing pad sitting empty, but it was just one of his little quirks.

Needless to say, however, her curiosity was piqued. She tried to push away the warning whispers in her mind, but they wouldn't be silenced.

One day, on a slow afternoon at work, against her better judgement, she googled Martyn's name. After a few seconds, the page loaded with search results and it became clear from the summary of each article that most of them referred to a Martyn Hardy who had been involved in a litany of financial disasters.

Her hand shaking, she clicked on a couple and read about a Martyn Hardy, the same age as *her* Martyn, living in Nottingham, who had appeared in court to face fraudulent charges and been discharged due to insufficient evidence.

She read about a Martyn Hardy who had been attacked and beaten by unknown masked men after running a house-building business into the ground and claiming not to have realised that investor funds had been spent on inappropriate items.

She scanned down the page to see dozens of reports, all covering the same awful stories. She pressed a button and the printer next to her began to clank and gurgle as it spat out a hard copy of the devastating results.

She took a breath then, and instead of reading through each item, she clicked on the tiny cross at the top right to close the page of search results down.

Feeling sick, she cleared it with her manager to leave work early, and soon as she reached her car, she texted Martyn.

Need to see you right now. I can come to the gym or meet somewhere but have to talk. L x

Twenty minutes later, they were staring at each other across a table in Starbucks. Her heart hammered inside her chest and the sick feeling had increased threefold.

'For God's sake, Louise, what is it?' Martyn's face looked creased with worry. 'You've dragged me away from work, so it must be important, but you're just… sitting there, saying nothing.'

Wordlessly, she took the printed sheet from her handbag, unfolded it and slid it across the table.

He picked it up and barely glanced at the printed words before his face drained of colour.

'This is… it's not what you think,' he said. 'If you don't trust me, I'd rather you came and asked me than dig around in the dirt like this. I'm disappointed, Louise.'

'*You're* disappointed?' She felt a stab of annoyance. 'How do you think I felt when I saw all this?' She prodded at the paper with a finger.

'Will you let me explain?' He stroked her hand, and despite everything, she felt a flood of affection towards him. His voice cracked slightly as he went on. 'Am I at least worth a listen?'

'Of course!' She sighed. 'Martyn, I love you, but when I saw this, I thought—'

'I know what you must have *thought*, I just wish you'd asked me.'

'I can't ask you about something I don't know! Why didn't *you* tell me?'

She saw his jaw clench, but his voice remained calm.

'It was all a conspiracy against me, Lou. All of it.' He pushed the paper away. 'People jealous of my business success and trying to squeeze me out of the industry.'

'One of the reports said you were involved in house-building, not fitness.'

'It was just a spin-off from my main business.' He wafted her comment away. 'You know what the newspapers can be like, taking something small and magnifying it for effect.'

'But the investors' money… the fraud allegations. What did—'

He shook his head and she stopped speaking.

'I'm going to ask you something, Lou, and when I hear your answer, I'll know whether we have a future together.'

She swallowed hard. Was he threatening her that he'd finish things? In her mind, the bright future sparkling on the horizon started to slip away like the last vestiges of a sunset.

'Do you love me enough to believe in me? To take me as you find me now, not on the basis of these… these lies?' He grabbed the paper and screwed it up.

'Of course I do. But you understand I had to ask? We shouldn't have any secrets from each other, Martyn, we're going to be married.'

'I do understand, darling, of course I do. But I'm not your average guy. I'm not your nine-to-five regular sheep who'll give you a mediocre life. I want more than that and I will work my socks off to give you the best I can.' He sighed and squeezed her hand. 'I've been betrayed by a lot of people, Louise, including women. I could go through each of those stories you found and give you a perfectly watertight explanation, but what would be the good in that?'

She blinked at him.

'Our time is *now*, not what's happened in the past. I love that you understand me and believe in me, and you are going to be the most amazing wife and mother to my children. Please don't let the jealousy and lies of others ruin what we have.'

She squeezed his hand back, emotional at his words.

'You mentioned women. Was there someone special who—'

'There have been girls before you, but there'll be nobody else for me now, ever. You're my queen, can't you see that? I want everything shiny and new for you. Even that flat feels tainted to me now. I respect you too much to take you back there.'

The part of her that had wanted to scrutinise his past, the part that wanted answers… she could feel it growing weaker by the second. He wasn't trying to hide that he had a chequered history, but he was asking her to put her faith firmly in the man he was today. Was that so bad? She loved and believed in him and that hadn't changed. Did she really want to let the faceless enemies in his past ruin their wonderful future together?

'I'm going to make a big ask of you, Louise.'

She looked up from her hands, gazed into the deep, genuine eyes of the man she loved and believed in.

'Please don't look back any more. Don't do any more Internet searches, don't listen to anything you might hear about me. *You* are my future. You are the only thing that matters to me and I will make you proud. Can you promise me you'll leave all those old lies buried?'

'I promise,' she whispered. And she meant it.

A few days later, when Martyn mentioned they might start looking for their own place, she couldn't control her excitement.

'Take a look on Rightmove, see what's on the market and find a few places you like the look of, and we can take it from there,' Martyn said.

She fought a twinge of disappointment.

'I thought that would be something we could do together,' she said gently.

'And we will. It's just that I've got so many meetings over the next couple of weeks, it's going to be virtually impossible for me to find time.' He tucked a stray lock of hair back behind her ear. 'I don't want to wait. You're too important to me.'

Louise glanced at the sparkling diamond on her finger and smiled.

She wanted Martyn to see that she was someone he could rely upon. She regretted her probing into his past, giving credence to people who just wanted to see him fail. All she wanted to focus on now was their future together.

'Don't worry,' she said. 'I'll sort it.'

*

'It's lovely,' Alice said, looking around Louise and Martyn's new flat, which sat just a stone's throw from the River Trent. 'You found this place yourself?'

'Not exactly.' Louise sniffed, adjusting a window blind. 'I saw it online and made the first viewing, and then Martyn came with me. We both loved it.

'The rent must be a pretty penny, being so near to the river.'

'Ooh, let me show you the boiling water tap. It's a marvel,' Louise said suddenly, moving away. 'We don't need a kettle any more.'

She turned the tap on and showed Alice how easy it was to make a cup of tea without filling and boiling a kettle. She was keen to get off the subject of money as soon as possible, suspecting that her sister was likely to ask awkward questions such as who had paid the deposit on the flat, and were they going halves on the rent.

Alice could never begin to understand Martyn the way Louise did, and Louise wouldn't even try to begin explaining.

He had told her how his money was tied up in knots at the moment. He said he'd had sleepless nights worrying how he could get his hands on a deposit for the new flat.

'It's only a few weeks' leeway I need, and then I'll be awash with cash,' he'd said glumly. 'But we've no choice, I'm afraid. We'll have to wait.'

Louise understood that he was the kind of man who liked to be independent. He wanted to be the one to provide a good life for them. She didn't want to undermine that, but it seemed silly to wait when she had the cash from her dad's modest inheritance.

When she'd suggested using it, his face had lit up initially and then become serious again.

'I can't let you use that money.' He'd shaken his head. 'It's not right.'

But she'd insisted. 'It's for our future. We're in this together, Martyn. I want to support you until the gym franchise project is sorted. Then our problems will be over.'

He'd held her face in both hands and kissed her gently on the lips.

'You are so special, do you know that?' She'd smiled, basking in the glow of his compliment. 'I love you so much.'

She'd paid the deposit and the first month's rent on the flat, just to tide them over.

'I'll be paying your dad's money back with interest soon,' Martyn had assured her. 'I give you my word on that.'

CHAPTER 34

Alice

I leave the school and walk quickly back to the main road, where I realise I've just missed a tram.

I notice there are people waiting at the stop, and see that the next one is due in just two minutes' time.

I'm distracted during the journey into town; I don't really notice anything outside the window at all. I'm too busy going over the conversation with Mrs Booth.

Before I left, she made me promise I'd tell her if I had any more concerns about Archie, and in the meantime, she said she would be watching him a bit more closely in class, just to ensure nobody was upsetting him in any way.

She seemed so certain that there was no problem with bullying at school; just that Archie was a solitary sort of boy and consequently hadn't got many friends.

This seemed a logical conclusion but left me with a dilemma. If kids at school weren't thumping Archie and leaving bruises, then who was?

Louise's scowling face flashes in front of my eyes and I turn to look out of the window to escape it.

Archie's nightmares, the *angry shadows* he spoke of the night he wet the bed… was it just normal childish fears, or was somebody really scaring him?

When the tram reaches the centre of town, I shuffle down the aisle with everyone else, silently questioning why I've come here. As I step down onto the kerb and look across the square, I see what I'm sure is James's back entering a coffee shop on the other side.

I usually avoid coffee shops like the plague. They tend to be a hive of noise, overpriced coffee and a lack of seats. It sounds stupid, but I always think people are looking at me in these sorts of places. Judging me.

I look down at my new jeans and coat I bought online. I've no reason to believe that anyone is thinking badly of me. These sorts of fears are like a program in my head that took over when all the bad stuff happened and has been running ever since.

I don't need it any more. I don't want it to be part of my fresh start.

After the accident, I talked it over with my therapist and she pointed out that actually, people were usually far too interested in their own lives to notice or indeed care about what my outfit choice for the day might be.

There's no need for me to feel I'm an imposter amongst normal folk.

Sadly, acknowledging it on an intelligent level, knowing you're just imagining what people are saying about you, doesn't make the feelings of inadequacy go away. That takes much longer, but at least I've made a start.

I push open the shop door and rise up onto my tiptoes in an attempt to see above the crowd. I scan the room, but no luck.

He came in here, I know it.

At least I felt sure it was him, and yet now, I can't see anyone who looks similar. Perhaps he was meeting a friend or a work colleague and they slipped out when I looked the other way.

Then the queue shifts and I spot him in the corner, hunched over his phone. Squeezed on one side of a table for four, opposite an amorous young couple so knotted together behind a stack of empty coffee cups and wrappers that they probably haven't even noticed the room has filled up around them since they first sat down.

The queue to be served snakes along the counter and almost all the way to the door. In the time it takes me to get a drink, he'll probably have already finished his and left.

I pick up a tray with a used cardboard cup on it and move slowly across the room as if I'm looking for a seat. An older lady gathers her coat and bag nearby and vacates her shared table, but I ignore that space and carry on walking towards the corner.

When I get close to James's table, I hover a bit, looking vacantly over people's heads.

He must sense someone is standing fairly close and looks up from texting.

'Hi!' I wait for a reaction, but there is none. 'Do you mind if I…'

'Course.' He indicates the chair next to him. 'Help yourself.'

'Thanks.' I set down my tray. The couple opposite don't even glance my way.

He's back to his texting now, but his face looks a little flushed and I wonder if he's recognised me but is too embarrassed to say anything.

We've only seen each other from a distance until the tram ride earlier in the week, and now here. Maybe he thought I looked different, more attractive, when I sat in the window of my apartment.

Maybe he's trying to let me down gently by pretending he doesn't know who I am.

I feel sick. I should never have come in here.

He glances sideways at me and I sit up a little straighter when I feel my own face glowing. I'm staring and he's noticed. I can't just sit here like an idiot.

I pick up the empty coffee cup and raise it to my mouth, pretending to sip through the plastic lid. I don't actually allow it to touch my lips; the thought of someone else's saliva on it makes me feel sick.

I sit like that for a few moments, and then put the cup down and look around. James is absorbed in his phone, the couple opposite in each other, and the surrounding tables are filled with people talking and laughing.

This is what it must feel like to be invisible.

I chew the inside of my cheek and watch my foot dancing at the end of my leg. Jiggling around in time with the thoughts that are coming thick and fast now.

I never asked for James to look up at my window. I wasn't the one who smiled and waved first. I asked for none of it.

So now, sitting right next to him, why should I be too afraid to make contact? He can't do all that and then expect me to accept the fact that he is blanking me.

'It's quite cold out there,' I hear myself say, but he doesn't reply.

The girl opposite unsticks herself from her boyfriend's lips and stares over at me.

I turn in my chair, away from her and towards James. He looks up.

'Sorry! I didn't realise you were speaking to me.'

'I said it's cold outside.' I give him a little smile.

'Yes, it is. Freezing for the time of year, in fact.'

There! His gaze settles on me just a second too long. I think he's made the connection.

Part of me squirms with embarrassment, but another part, a part that's been ignored for a very long time, is taking over.

'I wasn't going to say hello, but… well, it sort of feels as if we know each other.'

'Do we… know each other?' he says.

I press my lips together and he seems to catch himself.

'I mean, you look familiar, but…'

I feel my face dropping. Why is he playing this stupid game?

'I live in Carlton Court, the apartment block next to the tram stop. I see you every morning.'

I feel like the girl opposite is listening in to our conversation. I glance over, but she is resting her head on her boyfriend's shoulder and she has her eyes closed. I'm being paranoid again.

I turn back to James and his face has paled. 'I'm sorry, you must have the wrong person.'

And there it is… Now that he's seen me close up, he's not interested.

CHAPTER 35

I wonder if it is possible to die of embarrassment. If so, I'm probably going to die right here, in the middle of a city-centre coffee shop.

I feel hot under my coat and sweater, and illogically, I want to run outside. But I've come this far, and if I back off now, I know it will be the end of it… the end of *everything*. I'll probably never speak to a man again in my life.

So I clear my throat, ignore my burning face and say what needs to be said.

'I see you from my window every morning.' Did his eye just twitch, or did I imagine it? 'Sometimes you look up and smile and wave.'

His gaze searches my face. He's a very good actor, but I'm feeling quite vulnerable now. Why did I even start this conversation in the middle of such a busy place?

Just because he looks up at my window and waves doesn't mean he wants to take things any further… doesn't mean he has any wish to speak to me in real life.

And then I have an awful thought that sets my heart pounding.

I glance at his left hand. There's no wedding band there, but not all men wear them. Especially ones who like to flirt openly with other women on their journey into work.

The girl opposite has gone back to canoodling with her boyfriend. I lean forward.

'Are you married?' I whisper.

'What?' His eyes widen. 'God, no! Look, can we start again. I'm James Wilson, pleased to meet you.'

I shake his extended hand. 'Alice Fisher,' I say.

'Hello, Alice. I do recognise you, you know.'

'Then why did you act as though you didn't?'

He glances around and shrugs. 'Believe it or not, I'm a really shy person.'

'You seem much bolder when you're on the tram.' I feel a trickle of sweat inch down my lower back. 'The way you stare up at my window like that…'

'Well, it's easy looking confident when distance is involved, isn't it? So, what's it like, living in Carlton Court?'

'Not for everyone, I suppose.' I shrug. 'My flat is quite small, but I like it.'

'Let's see, you must live on the…' He mimes counting the floors.

'Third floor,' I say.

'Yes, I thought it must be. I hope you don't mind me looking up at your window.'

I glance at my hands. 'It's fine. I don't mind at all.'

He starts slightly as his phone begins to ring. He glances at the screen and ends the call without answering.

'Don't mind me,' I say. 'Take the call if you need to.'

He seems a bit edgy. 'No, it's fine, honestly. They can wait.'

He slips the phone into his pocket.

I wonder what happens now. How do two people get from waving from a tram to chatting and then possibly arranging to meet up for drinks or maybe go to the cinema?

I can't ask him out, I just can't. It feels too forward. The first time we've met in real life, at least.

The shrill ring starts up again and he snatches the phone back out of his pocket, presses a button to end the call once more.

'Somebody's persistent.' I grin.

'Yes. Annoyingly so. It's just work. Think they own you, don't they?'

I nod, and am about to ask him where he works when the phone rings for a third time. He glances at the screen and then springs up out of his seat.

A woman with two small children standing directly behind him cries out as his elbow knocks her tray sideways. Coffee and cake fingers fly out at all angles. The little boy screams as hot milk splatters over his face.

'Sorry! Oh gosh, I'm so sorry,' James exclaims, his hands flying up to his hair.

'What the hell are you doing?' The woman picks up the distressed child.

'Sorry… I have to go.' James looks at me, his eyes dark and haunted. 'I'm so sorry… Alice, but…'

And with that, he grabs his bag, scarf and mac and scurries away without looking back at me or the woman and her son.

'What an idiot! Do you know his name and address?' she snaps at me. 'I could sue him for this, you know.'

She dabs the child's face, which fortunately isn't marked but is rather flushed, with a wedge of napkins provided by a concerned member of staff.

'Sorry, we don't know each other,' I tell her.

I bend down to pick up my own bag, eager to get out of the place, and that's when I see it. A slim silver phone, lying under James's chair.

It must have slipped from his pocket as he jumped up.

I grab my bag and scoop up the phone in one smooth movement.

My throat is dry and my face feels very hot.

I ignore the woman's accusing stare and make my way out of the packed shop with James's phone nestled cold and comforting in my sticky hand.

CHAPTER 36

Outside the coffee shop, the road is now choked with cars.

I rushed out to get to the cool fresh air, but instead I find myself among revving engines and frustrated motorists glaring into the middle distance as they wait for the gridlock to ease.

My fingers tighten around the phone in my pocket and I look up and down the street, just in case James has realised it's missing and returns for it.

Not that I'd have to give it back right away if I didn't want to. Nobody saw me pick it up.

As soon as the thought of keeping it appears, I have to smile at myself. Who am I kidding? I'd return it to him without hesitation, but still, the delicious feeling of having something almost forbidden… it feels so good, so *exciting*.

It occurs to me then that perhaps the right thing to do is take it back inside and leave it with the staff behind the counter in case he calls back in for it at some point. But I imagine the staff are annoyed at James causing an incident with the woman and her son. They might not be too obliging after that.

A woman huffs as she brushes by me, and I realise I'm standing in the middle of the pavement. I step back towards the coffee shop window and slip James's phone into my pocket. It will be safe there until I can return it to him myself.

I inch through the stationary cars that snort like disgruntled metal dragons and head back down towards Old Market Square. I can see the tram stop from here.

Impulsively, I stop at the small Italian deli on the way and buy a square slab of freshly made vegetable lasagne and a bag of salad for tea.

I feel so extravagant when I emerge from the shop clutching one of those stylish brown paper bags that signify artisan food. People buzz around me and the streets are busy. I'm in the city alone, and most importantly, I'm OK. I'm really OK!

It's a normal thing for most people, but today, to me, it feels like I'm actually living again for the first time in a very long time.

There's a loose gathering of passengers waiting at the tram hub.

I huddle inside the shelter, pressing myself back against the Perspex screen, the phone seeming to throb like a living thing in my pocket.

But I can't take it out here. I don't feel comfortable being in close proximity to crowds of people, haven't done for some time.

I think back to only a few years ago, to when I worked at the gallery, meeting and greeting important customers, organising art exhibitions and VIP pre-viewings… I took it all in my stride, confident of my own abilities.

Now, it feels like I'm thinking of a different person altogether. A stranger.

An old lady with a wheeled shopping cart hobbles inside the shelter and I inch a little further up. I feel a twinge in my back and I know what's coming. When I push the pain aside, it always wreaks its revenge on me.

I'll have to find time for a rest when I get back home.

The tram arrives after a few minutes. Once I take my seat, the tension in my neck and shoulders starts to dissipate a little.

I take a breath and congratulate myself that I did it. I escaped the solitary confinement of the apartment and got myself out here again.

The high-pitched whine starts up and the tram begins to scoot forward. I stare out of the window as we glide past the people, the cars. Odds are, somewhere not too far away from here, James will still be thinking about the incident at the coffee shop.

He's probably questioning himself: should he have stayed to make sure the young boy was OK? Of course, he most definitely should have done.

He seemed so distracted by the phone calls he claimed were nothing important. Yet his face told a different story.

Now I come to think about it properly, he acted rather oddly from the moment I sat down to share his table.

I accept he probably felt embarrassed when I pointed out I'd noticed him passing the apartment building each morning, but pretending he didn't recognise me at all was taking it a bit far.

He admitted it in the end, though, and I suppose that's all that matters.

We were getting on so well until those annoying phone calls set him on edge. He might've asked me to go for a drink or a meal… who knows? That final call was the one that did it. Up he jumped, sending coffee flying everywhere.

Still. All is not lost, and it's obvious what I need to do next.

I've now got a great excuse to board tomorrow's early tram. Sitting next to him would seem a little forward at this stage, but it's a completely natural thing to do when I have a good reason like returning his lost phone.

It's the perfect opportunity to get to know him a little better.

CHAPTER 37

The tram glides past a road that I know leads up into the Lace Market, specifically to Moderno, which is still the biggest art gallery in the city.

Not that I've been able to face visiting recently, but those times are still fresh in my mind.

Three years earlier

The first few weeks at the gallery were a whirlwind of activity, and I loved it.

Setting up social media accounts, working with a local company on building The Art Box's website, and organising the printing of flyers, banners and other promotional material.

Jim had also set up several meetings with PR firms, so that we could decide which would be most suitable.

'Are you happy for me to leave the decision to you?' he asked me. 'I think you'll have the freshest, most adventurous approach to this.'

Was he kidding? I felt honoured to be given such responsibility so early.

'I'd love to,' I beamed. 'Thanks, Jim.'

'We can have a ten-minute meeting daily just to keep me in the loop. I'm going to be in and out a lot of the time, but you know you can get hold of me any time at all.' He held up his phone.

I both welcomed and embraced the challenge. I met with several agencies and finally settled on East PR, who I felt really understood the image we wanted to build. They also happened to be Louise's company.

I arranged for Finn and Jim to meet representatives from the company, including Louise, over coffee in the meeting space up on the mezzanine level, overlooking the city's rooftops from a big picture window.

Afterwards, both men articulated their approval. I mentioned that one of the key personnel was my sister, but Mr Visser just shrugged as if it was irrelevant.

'You really understand what we're trying to do here, Alice,' he said approvingly. 'You're going to go far.'

Jim nodded his agreement, smiling at me.

I tried to bask in their compliments, to enjoy the moment, but the ceaseless voice in my head reminded me that I'd have to do far better to be anything more than a shop girl in my mother's eyes.

As Jim had said, he was often out, driving up and down the country sourcing artwork and meeting other gallery owners. This left me alone for much of the day.

All the signage had been designed and was stored in the back room ready for securing out front just two days before opening, so that nobody would know the location of The Art Box until the last minute.

This suited me, left me the time and space to enjoy the serene atmosphere of the light, airy gallery. I enjoyed visualising how it might look when the stands and artwork were in place.

Jim showed me pictures of all the work he'd agreed to exhibit so far, and I was delighted at the rare mix of pieces that would initially be on show. Some were already coming in, and I personally took delivery of several enormous packages a day.

When Jim came back to the shop periodically, we would carefully unwrap the packages together and discuss the art within.

I often felt like pinching myself to see if this job I'd landed was real.

There had been other unexpected benefits, too.

When I awoke each morning, I stared at my image in the mirror, astounded at the transformation that was taking place.

My skin glowed, my hair seemed glossier, and best of all, food had already become a bit of an inconvenience, taking up valuable time when I could be working, rather than being the mainstay of my day.

One day, the weather turned cooler. Skeins of cloud knitted across the blue sky and a chilly breeze saw off any rays of warmth from the sunlight still managing to break through.

I'd carved out some time during the morning to look more closely at local artists. In the bidding to become a UNESCO City of Literature, Nottingham had a vibrant writing community, and likewise some excellent artists. I'd always felt proud that the city I lived in valued the arts and such a diverse culture.

Both Finn and Jim were delighted when I suggested they ring-fence a corner and perhaps a small section of the main wall for up-and-coming local artists to exhibit.

'I'm loving your ideas, Alice,' Finn remarked, and I smiled and vehemently pushed aside the negative voice still trying to pipe up in my head.

That day, I sat in the back office with the blinds down in the main showroom. I wasn't expecting any new deliveries, and if Jim was returning to the shop, his habit was to text me when he was on his way.

I turned to the outsize iMac and began working through the list of artist websites Jim had left me to take a look at. The first couple were promising. A young woman from the Meadows area of the city, whose art merged her African heritage with her English working-class roots. The paintings were vibrant and alive with colour and movement.

The second artist was a seventy-year-old man who took an avid interest in the old industrial structures of the city: the Raleigh factory, the Player's building… He had an eye for representing the wastelands where they had once existed.

I became so absorbed in his work that I only vaguely registered a noise, but then jumped at the sound of a louder knock. I glanced at the wall clock. Ten thirty. Jim had said he wouldn't be back until after one.

I stood up and listened. The knock had been here, at the back of the shop. Delivery drivers always came to the front; only staff used the back entrance.

I jumped again as someone rapped on the door, louder this time.

I moved closer, latched the chain and then opened the door a few inches.

A tall man, about my own age, stood there smiling. He had good teeth and shiny hair and was dressed in black jeans and a Morrissey T-shirt. My heart blipped and I swallowed to try and relieve the dryness in my mouth.

'Can I help you?'

'I hope so,' he grinned, sending my heart rate racing again. He held up an art portfolio case. 'I'm Jack Hampton. I don't suppose you've got a minute?'

CHAPTER 38

Three years earlier

That day at the gallery, I ignored everything I'd ever been told about opening the door to a stranger. I released the security chain without a thought and invited Jack Hampton inside.

'I'm Alice. My boss is due back any time now,' I said. 'If you'd like to leave your contact details, I can ask him if he'll see you.'

'That would be brilliant,' Jack said, stepping into the office. 'Thanks ever so much.'

I pushed a piece of paper and a pen across the desk. Jack placed his large black case against the wall and leaned over to write.

His glossy black hair caught the light and reminded me of a crow's feathers. I idly wondered if it shone different colours in full sun. I noticed his skin was olive, rather than pale. It stopped him looking like a goth with his black clothing and made him appear more exotic.

He looked up questioningly and I realised he'd said something but I'd been too absorbed in watching him write.

'Sorry?' I willed my cheeks not to flush, but I could already feel the heat.

'I said, shall I stick my email down here too?'

'Oh yes. That would be good, thanks.'

'No, thank *you*.' He smiled, laying down the pen and standing up straight. I gauged he was just about six feet tall, which was perfect alongside my five-foot-six-inch frame.

'How did you know we were here?' I asked him.

'Honest answer?' He looked bashful. 'My uncle is a delivery man. He mentioned in conversation that he'd dropped something off at a new place called The Art Box. Knowing I'm an artist, he asked me if I'd heard of it. You can imagine my reaction. I prised all the details from him. I accused him of telling stories at first, because everyone is talking about this place, but nobody has a clue where it's going to be.' I felt hypnotised by the intensity burning in his dark blue eyes. 'I woke up this morning and thought, today's the day I grow a pair and give it one more push to get my work out there. I'd sort of accepted it probably wasn't going to happen for me and that I was going to have to get a full-time job.'

I decided not to ask his uncle's name and which company he worked for. Mr Visser would probably want his head on a plate. He'd gone to great lengths to keep the location of the shop private until he was ready to reveal it.

'And I confess… I've been watching this place.'

'Watching it?' The back of my neck prickled. Contrary to what I'd told Jack, it would be a few hours before Jim returned to the office, and here I was, alone with a strange man who, despite being very attractive, could very possibly be someone who wanted to do me harm.

'Sorry, let me rephrase that.' He closed his eyes briefly and shook his head. 'I didn't mean it to sound like I'm a stalker or anything. When my uncle told me about this place, I walked past a couple of times. I saw you, and the man I assume is your boss, arrive yesterday morning. You both walked round the back and then the lights came on in the shop.'

'I see.' He was resourceful, if nothing else. 'So that's why you came to the back door.'

'Sorry.' He hung his head. 'It's just that I had to give myself this chance. You never know, right?'

'I guess.' I shrugged my shoulders and looked down at his portfolio. 'Your work is in there, I'm guessing.'

'I came prepared.' He grinned and then bit his bottom lip. 'I don't suppose you'd have time to have a quick look yourself?'

'Sure.' I nodded. 'I'd love to see your work, but the final decision—'

'I know, I know. The final decision doesn't belong to you.'

'Right.' I could have kicked myself for using the phrase. I'd had it said to me enough times when I'd tried to get work exhibited. 'Bring it through to the gallery, where the light's better.'

'I really appreciate this, Alice. More than you know,' he said, picking up the case and following me through.

He stood in the middle of the gallery space and looked up at the ceiling, letting out a low whistle.

'Fabulous, isn't it?' I grinned. 'It's going to look stunning once we get it fitted out properly next week.'

'I love it. The light, the space… And it's got such a great vibe, too.'

I knew what he meant. The place just had a nice energy about it.

'Anyway, let's have a look at your work and then I'll have to get on. Sorry.'

'Please don't apologise,' he said, crouching down to unzip the portfolio. 'I'm more grateful than you could possibly know just to have someone like you take an interest.'

I felt a frisson of pleasure to think that someone as cool and attractive as Jack obviously viewed me as a person of influence.

He slid out a couple of paintings and laid them out on the pristine white tiles, side by side.

'Wow,' I breathed.

I hadn't been sure what to expect, but this… this I most definitely did *not* expect. I stared at the unframed canvases, mesmerised by the swirls of pastel colours fading and deepening in various places, pulling the eye in and then distracting it all at once.

Jack walked to the front windows and sat on the low sill to give me some time to appraise his work.

As I stared, my mind started to make sense of the picture before me. I caught the movement of water, the rustling of soft green leaves and—

'It's the River Trent. At the Victoria Embankment in the spring,' Jack called out in a soft voice. 'Just in case you don't see it.'

'I see it.' I smiled at him. 'It's beautiful. And this one…'

I took a sideways step to view the second painting. This time I saw sky, birds and something fluttering in the sky. 'A kite!' I said, delighted.

'You got it!' He bounded back over. 'My grandad used to take me to the arboretum to fly my kite. It's one of my fondest childhood memories. Thanks for taking the time to look. I'm so chuffed you saw through the swirling mess… That's what the guy at the Brushstrokes gallery in Derby called it.'

I knew this particular brand of low self-esteem well. I'd felt exactly the same about my own work in the past, felt the fear that another person wouldn't get it, the meaning I'd wanted to convey through colour and texture.

'I did a history of art degree at Nottingham Trent,' Jack told me. 'Graduated eight years ago. It sounds naïve, but I honestly thought I'd be a full-time artist by now.'

'Believe me, I know how tough it is,' I sympathised.

'My dream is still alive.' Jack shrugged. 'Just. I've spent the last eight years in dead-end part-time jobs, working as a waiter, a shop assistant… Stuff just to keep the wolf from the door and to give me time for my painting. So I've no career to speak of. All I've got is this.'

He nodded to the artwork.

'I'm sure it would look even better displayed on the wall over there.' I smiled at him.

'Don't, I can't handle the thought of it!' He laughed and took a step closer to me.

I shivered involuntarily. He wasn't in my space and I certainly didn't feel threatened, but he was now close enough that I could smell his aftershave: a woody, subtle and very masculine scent. I was aware of his height, the breadth of his shoulders, his clean, even teeth showing through slightly open generous lips...

'Seriously, though, even if this doesn't come to anything, the fact that you've given me the time of day means the world.'

Our eyes met just for a second or two. I could imagine his hand lifting and touching my cheek, him moving closer and—

'Don't mention it!' I heard myself say brightly as I took a step back. 'Can you leave your work with me for a day or so? Give me time to show it to Jim.'

He clamped his hand to his forehead. 'Alice, I can't thank you enough, I—'

'It's fine, honestly.' I fought to get back in control and my tone was a little curt. These feelings had come out of nowhere and were ridiculous. I didn't know the guy and I was supposed to be representing The Art Box... I had to be professional. 'I'm happy to show him your work.'

He looked taken aback and I knew exactly why. In five seconds flat I'd gone from looking at him starry-eyed to taking all the warmth out of my words. It couldn't be helped. I had to cool off, get some distance between us.

'I just want to say thanks, that's all. Just let me know when you need me to come and pick it up. It doesn't matter about the outcome, I'm forever grateful you've tried to help me.'

After Jack left, I discovered that my good mood had somehow evaporated. I sat down at the desk and revisited the list of potential local exhibitors.

My earlier enthusiasm seemed to have faded away. Jack had been so amicable, so grateful. But there had been something else there… something dangerous that had both excited and repelled me.

It almost felt like he was making a great effort to appear a star-struck debutant artist when in actual fact he was confident and entitled. Looking at Jack was like looking at the surface of a calm and beautiful stream and unexpectedly catching a shadowy movement undulating beneath the surface.

I shook my head and tried to renew my focus on the local artists' shortlist.

My imagination was both a blessing and a curse. Why couldn't I just allow myself to be happy for once?

CHAPTER 39

Louise

Ten years earlier

Three months later, Martyn still hadn't paid her back his share of the deposit and the rent.

In fact, her inheritance was fast depleting, as he also hadn't been able to contribute anything to ongoing expenses due to sinking all funds into his new business venture.

Louise had grown tired of sitting on a deckchair in front of the television.

'What happened to the furniture at the duplex apartment?' she asked him. 'I know you said it came furnished, but you must've owned some bits… And where are all your suits?'

'I told you.' He scowled. 'I wanted a completely fresh start. You should be pleased I want to forget the past. I wish you'd stop banging on about it.'

She'd worked very hard at forgetting the stuff she'd seen online, and she'd kept her promise and done no further digging.

She had tried a couple of times to get him talking about some of the people in his past, but it always put him in a bad mood if she alluded to it in any way.

He told her all his close family were dead and had made it crystal clear that was as much as he wanted to say.

Eventually she'd managed to get the lounge looking nice enough on a shoestring. Her mum had given her some bits they didn't use in the house: a coffee table, a few cushions, and curtains that didn't look too dated for a modern apartment.

Admittedly, none of the stuff was really to Louise's taste, but she was grateful for it all the same.

She threw caution to the wind and splashed out on a bed, a black faux-leather three-piece suite and a small dining table and four chairs on a finance deal: buy now, pay later.

'Looks great in here now,' Martyn told her when he got home one day at eight p.m. She'd noticed, without comment, that gradually his working days were getting longer.

'I'd like to get the rest of the flat furnished properly,' she said, keeping her voice level. 'We've been in here a while now.'

'You don't need to tell me that,' he said irritably. 'I've got some good news, anyway.'

'Oh?' She felt immediately brighter.

'Yeah, the franchise deal is really close now. We're talking a week or two, maybe less.' He produced a bottle of fizz from behind his back.

'That's amazing!' She hugged him, the weight on her shoulders lifting by the second. 'At last. I'm so pleased for you… and for us.'

Martyn walked over to their open-plan kitchen and got the only two wine glasses they owned from the cupboard.

'There's just one final stage to get through, but my lawyer says that's just a formality, that there's no risk now that the deal won't go through.' He popped the cork and Louise let out an excited little squeal. 'On that basis, I thought we were safe to celebrate our success right now.'

'Sounds perfect.'

He handed her a drink and they clinked glasses.

'To *your* success and our future,' Louise said, inexplicably feeling a little teary. 'You've worked really hard on this deal, Martyn. I'm so proud of you.'

'Aww.' He looked bashful for once. 'I couldn't have done it without you, gorgeous. In fact…' He took a sip of fizz and placed his glass on the coffee table. 'I wanted to ask you something. You've not got through *all* your dad's inheritance yet, have you?'

'No, but I don't want you to feel bad about that. It's helped us through the lean time, and now the good times are here.' She held her glass up again but he seemed distracted.

'How much have you got left… of the money, I mean?'

Louise thought for a moment. 'About seven thousand.'

Martyn nodded and reached for her hand. 'It kills me to do this, but there's just one final payment to make so all the legal stuff can be completed. Is there any way you can lend me that seven thou just until the end of next week?'

A dull thudding started in her temples.

'We've already got five people ready to take on the first franchises around the country, Lou. The money is going to be pouring in in a matter of days and the first thing I'll be doing is replenishing your account.'

She cleared her throat. 'No problem. I'll transfer it right now.'

She picked up her phone and logged in to her online banking while Martyn watched. Afterwards, they made love and she felt like everything was coming right in her world at last.

With the business deal tied up, they could begin planning their wedding, and life as she'd imagined it would finally begin.

But her heart was growing steadily heavier and her chest felt tight. Why would she feel like this when she was about to get everything she'd ever wanted?

She swallowed hard and pushed the unwelcome feelings away as Martyn pulled her closer.

She couldn't quite believe that better times were finally around the corner. That was all it was.

CHAPTER 40

Alice

Three years earlier

Jim loved Jack's artwork.

'It's fresh, different... has an almost kinetic quality,' he said thoughtfully.

It was true, Jack's work did seem to have a kind of movement to it, a trick he'd played on the eye.

Still, I smiled to myself. Jim's typically convoluted language when describing paintings was the exact thing I wanted to step away from when speaking to people visiting the shop.

'I'll have to run it past Finn before we make a decision,' he continued. 'But I think he'll love it.'

For some reason, I felt pleased at Jim's reaction, as if his approval of Jack's work was somehow a reflection on me. Having only just met him, I wasn't sure I should overly care if Jack got a display spot or not.

But I did care. I wanted to help him. I genuinely loved his work, and if I was honest, I wanted to see him again.

He'd said he would call back to collect his art in a couple of days, and I would dearly love to be able to give him good news.

*

Jack was allocated a small space in the local artists' corner of the gallery.

'I can't thank you enough,' he told me when he emerged from Jim's office with his official offer and the terms and conditions of any sales made. 'I'd like to take you for a drink, if you'll come. I haven't really got anyone else to celebrate with.'

'So you've had to settle for me,' I said with a straight face.

'No! Sorry, I didn't mean it like that, I…' He shook his head as my stern expression dissolved into a wide grin. 'You had me there. I thought I'd offended you.'

'Course not. And thank you, I'd love to come for a drink.'

We went to a bar in the Lace Market that had been converted from a church to a drinking establishment. It was located very close to the gallery.

'Seemed appropriate.' Jack indicated the majesty of the interior and the original stained-glass windows. 'I reckon the big man upstairs was looking down on me that day I came into the gallery…'

'Please don't use that line on me… "and He sent one of his angels down to earth".'

We both laughed.

'You obviously know all my best lines,' he said, pouting.

We had a great night, felt as if we'd known each other for years. When it was time to leave, Jack asked me out the next evening and I accepted.

And so it went on, until two weeks later, when we were sitting in an intimate Thai restaurant in the centre of the city and Jack reached for my hand across the table.

'Can we make this dating thing official? Can we, like, say we're in a proper relationship?'

'What, you mean changing our Facebook status from "single" to "in a relationship"… as serious as that?' I quipped.

'As serious as that.' Jack nodded. 'We could even opt for "it's complicated".'

I burst out laughing as he squeezed my hand, and my heart, too. I felt light and warm and alive.

I fleetingly thought about my sister's pledge to keep away from men. It wasn't something I wanted to join her in.

I no longer felt alone. Jack and I were officially a pair.

CHAPTER 41

Louise informs me she won't be dropping Archie off in the morning.

It feels like my heartbeat is pounding in my throat instead of my chest. I immediately wonder if she's heard that I called in to school to speak to Mrs Booth.

'Any reason why?' I ask, trying to affect a casual tone.

'Just that I haven't got an early meeting scheduled for once,' Louise explains, her voice flat and uninterested. 'So I might as well take him in.'

Her eyeliner looks a little smudged, and for once, her lipstick hasn't been freshly applied. The pink has faded to a mere outline around her mouth.

'Hard day at work?' I ask her.

'You could say that, but then again, every day sucks right now.' She sighs. 'If I'm honest, I'm beginning to wish I'd never taken this new job.'

I wonder if Darren's suspicions are right and she *has* been seeing someone. Perhaps this new, subdued demeanour signals that things have started to fizzle out.

Despite my disapproval, I can't help but feel for her. I know what she's been through in the past and I do want her to be happy.

But I'm also disappointed that I won't see Archie. We've become so much closer in the last couple of weeks, both of us benefiting from each other's company, I'd like to think. Plus, until I get to the bottom of what's bothering him, I feel better checking he's OK.

'If you want to talk, you know where I am,' I say.

Louise doesn't appreciate the gesture. Instead, she laughs. 'Thanks for the offer, but I think your doctor would have to prescribe a stronger sedative if you knew the half of what was happening in my life.'

I hate the way she always manages to make me sound so flaky in a few well-chosen words. It's unfair for her to judge me on the medical advice I sought back then.

'Why not risk it?' I say quickly. 'You never know, I might not faint from shock.'

Her expression grows serious, and for a moment or two she actually seems to be considering my offer.

'If I'm honest, you seem a bit troubled.' I reach out to touch her, to try and reassure her, but she frowns and steps back. Within seconds, an indignant look settles over her features again like a veil. Her body stiffens and I prepare to receive her wrath with both barrels.

'Yes, well I suppose it would look like that to you, wouldn't it? You've no idea how it feels to try and keep all the balls in the air all of the time, the pressure of having to—'

'I'm trying to help you!' I startle myself as much as her and instantly drop my voice, mindful of Archie watching TV in the other room. 'I'm just trying to help, Louise. Why is your first thought always to assume everyone is trying to get one over on you?'

I expect one of her stock vitriolic replies to come back, but instead, her rigid stance deflates like a burst balloon right in front of me. I can't do or say anything, because the shock of seeing her bluster disintegrate so unexpectedly has plunged me into a frozen silence of my own.

'Because that's exactly how it feels…' she whispers, her eyes full. 'Like everyone is out to get me. Right now, Alice, I feel so utterly and completely alone.'

Later, when Louise and Archie have left, I decide to send a text to my sister.

Hope you're OK. Just call me day or night if you need to talk. A x

It feels as if the barrier between us has shrunk a little. Even though she left soon after my little outburst, the fact that she let me see her vulnerability at all is a big step forward. Maybe soon she'll be ready to talk and we can stop dancing around each other regarding my concerns about Archie.

When I explained that I'd grown closer to Archie and would like to continue to see him more regularly, even if she didn't need me to child-mind him, Louise didn't shoot me down in flames.

'We'll see.' She nodded. 'I know you care about him.'

I open the kitchen drawer and take out James's phone.

He'll definitely realise he's lost it by now. He'll have already scoured his pockets, and been back to the coffee shop, no doubt. He'll wake this morning knowing I'm probably his last chance, that maybe I picked it up when he left.

My chance to return it has arrived. I can take it to him directly by getting on the tram this morning.

I shower and wash my hair. Then I make coffee and slowly, ignoring the twinges in my back and hips, get myself ready.

I dress again in the new jeans and boots I bought online, and just before eight a.m., I shrug on my new dark pink duster coat.

Standing in front of the mirror, I consider my image as someone else might. My hair looks clean and brushed but is a bit shapeless. I catch a tiny glimmer of grey at my temples that I haven't noticed before.

But my skin is smooth and blemish-free and my eyes, enhanced with a little mascara, look bright enough. I turn off the light above the mirror and leave the room.

I think I look presentable, but with a good haircut and colour and maybe a make-up lesson at one of the department stores in town, I could make great strides in improving my image.

As I leave the flat, I decide I'll call in at the department store this morning and make a start on the new me.

I look around me, recognising some of the other passengers I usually view from my window above.

The tram stop is busy this morning, perhaps busier than usual, although it could just be that it feels that way, being one of the crowd instead of a detached spectator.

The digital display above me informs passengers that the tram will arrive in four minutes' time. I push through the bodies to the ticket machine and buy a return to the Old Market Square.

In my pocket, my hand closes around the cool casing of James's phone. I turned it off on the journey home from the coffee shop. It seemed like the right thing to do under the circumstances. Plus, I didn't really trust myself not to answer it if it rang.

It's only now that I realise I've prevented James from contacting me – he was probably calling his own number all last night.

Inside, a small wisp of cynicism flutters through me before I squash it flat. It's not true that I wanted a valid reason to see him this morning. That's not why I turned it off; it just made me feel a bit jumpy, knowing it was 'live' in my pocket.

The crowd starts to close in around me and I crane my head to look down the road. It's getting busy with traffic now, the start of the rush hour. Cars, buses and bicycles whizz by, and here is the tram, just coming into view at the bend.

It is brightly lit and the shiny silver and dark green livery brightens the dull morning. My heart rate picks up seriously and I know that as I board, my hands will be damp.

The tram approaches and I'm struck by how much the front of it looks like a snake: its slightly pointed nose with an incline that resembles a smooth reptilian forehead.

My insides are liquid when I think about James's reaction. Will he be relieved to see me when he realises I have his phone? Will he be pleased because it's another chance for us to chat?

The crowd carries me forward to the door and I fall in line as a loose queue forms. The doors whoosh open, and as I wait, I look back at the few passengers alighting to ensure James hasn't decided to get off in search of his phone.

When I'm sure he hasn't, and it's my turn, I step up onto the platform and scan my ticket. I move down the aisle towards the second carriage, where I know he will be sitting.

I have the strangest sense of being outside of myself. The voices around me, the faces that glance up as I pass… they all seem slightly removed from reality.

I pass through the first carriage and into the second. James's carriage. It's busy in here and I feel irritated as a woman and two noisy young children take their time getting seated, holding everyone up.

Finally they sit down and those of us still in the aisle shuffle forward. I'm straining my neck trying to spot James when suddenly his seat comes into view.

I carry on walking to the last carriage, looking wildly at all the seats until the realisation hits me.

James isn't on the tram this morning.

CHAPTER 42

As the tram starts to move, I turn and walk back through to the second carriage and sit down in what I've come to think of as James's seat.

An ageing rocker wearing a pair of white Beats turns and watches me for a moment, but I look away and stare out of the window.

It's been weeks now and James has never missed a single morning. Same seat, same time, same tram. It doesn't make sense.

After a few minutes, common sense prevails and I realise how ludicrous my reaction is. There could be a number of highly plausible explanations for his absence.

He could be ill; maybe a cold or stomach bug has laid him low. He might have an appointment or a day's leave booked from work.

I take his phone out of my pocket and turn it on, keeping my finger on the on/off button for a few seconds. I should never have turned it off; he's probably been ringing it for ages and been worried. I don't know what I was thinking of.

There should have been movement on the screen by now, but it remains black and unresponsive. I try pressing the button again, but still no luck. It must be out of charge.

I inspect the phone. It's an old-fashioned Nokia. I used to have a similar model until I traded it in for something a bit less basic.

It looks like the kind of low-cost handset you'd get on a pay-as-you-go contract and just use for calls and texts.

I pop it in my bag, pleased I made the decision to carry on into town. I should be able to buy a charger for it there, though first there's something else I want to do.

When I look up again, I see we're nearly at the Old Market Square. Deep in thought about the phone, I haven't even noticed people getting off and on, and now the tram is quite full, although nobody has sat next to me, thankfully.

When we reach our destination, I head off across the square to the coffee shop I sat in with James yesterday. It's less busy, so I join the short queue, and when it's my turn, I order a regular latte.

'Staying in or taking out?' the spotty, bored young man asks in a monotone.

'Staying in. Do you happen to know if a man has been in here asking about a lost phone?' I reach for a napkin.

'A lost phone?' he repeats unhelpfully.

'Yes. My friend lost his phone in here yesterday and I wondered if he'd been in to ask about it yet.'

The corners of his mouth turn down to indicate he hasn't a clue and doesn't much care.

He turns to the stocky young woman with short dark hair who is using the milk steamer behind him. I remember seeing her when I left the shop yesterday.

'Know anything about a lost phone, Cath? Anybody been in asking about it?'

'Sorry,' she calls, keeping her eyes on the stream of piping-hot milk gushing from a thin stainless-steel pipe. 'Nobody's asked on my shift.'

He bends down before standing back up again, his face blank. 'Nothing behind the counter here.'

'Thanks for looking,' I say.

I take my latte over to the table James and I sat at yesterday. I remember the annoying couple opposite us, canoodling and embarrassing themselves. I sip my coffee and think about how distracted James was during the last few minutes I was with him. I still feel certain he was unnerved by the phone calls flashing up on the screen.

I sit there for another ten or fifteen minutes, staring at the door. I admit I'm thinking there's a chance James might pop in here looking for his phone.

But the time drags slower than I thought it would and I realise I could sit here all day in the vain hope of seeing him.

As I pass the counter on my way out, Cath and the lanky young man who served me watch me leave. When I walk past the main window, they're saying something to each other and laughing.

It probably was a stupid thing to ask – if my friend had been in to ask about his lost phone – but I'm still surprised at how rude people can be. They're supposed to be helpful to customers, after all.

I walk up Long Row a little way and pause to look in the window of Debenhams. There's still fifteen minutes to go to opening time. Perhaps I'll call back in a little while to book that makeover appointment.

The windows feature mannequins dressed in stylish floral dresses and brightly coloured culottes. I feel more comfortable in conservative shades now, but when I worked at the gallery, I loved dressing up in striking outfits. You could get away with it in a place like that.

It's only two years ago, but it might as well be a lifetime away.

I realise the electrical shop I'm heading for probably isn't open yet either, so I sit on the low wall, looking into the square itself.

To the left is the Council House, with its iconic dome and friendly stone lions. At nine a.m. its bell will sound and will be heard up to seven miles away. To the right are the new fountains, a feature that's been constant since the square itself was redesigned in 1927. There's a photo in Mum's boxes in the spare room of the flat featuring me and a young Louise splashing around with our trousers rolled up.

I'm starting to feel a little more logical now I've stopped rushing around. I like sitting here. I feel almost invisible watching everyone around me walking with purpose, talking on their phones or trying to manage their kids.

The council house bell dings nine times and I get up and head for Beastmarket Hill, which flanks the square. Mr Partridge is just opening up at the small electrical shop I've used for years.

I always think it's a miracle that this shop, surrounded by the big chain stores, has survived, but Mr Partridge once explained that his family owned the building and were therefore not at the mercy of greedy landlords taking all their profits by constantly hiking up rent.

Five minutes later, I emerge with a charger for the Nokia. That's the beauty of this place: Mr Partridge rarely throws anything away, so it's the place to come for accessories for older models of phones.

I'm near the tram stop now, but rather than head over there, I hesitate, thinking for a few moments.

It's entirely possible that James came into town early for an appointment or a meeting. I remember the day I followed him across the square, and that gives me an idea.

I stand up and begin walking. Past the lions and down Exchange Walk to St Peter's Gate, where I turn left and head for the small street where I saw him disappear before.

I stand at the corner before walking a few steps further to the large black door at the end.

Emperor Knight.

I look at the shiny brass plaque and the button beside it. I could buzz up now, ask if James is in.

And then I realise I don't even know whether he works here. The reality of the situation is that he's just a guy I've seen on the tram and spoken to for a few minutes. Yet I feel I know him.

'Can I help you?'

A short, thin man in his early twenties, dressed smartly in a shirt and tie but without a jacket, steps out from the corner of the building. He takes another drag of his cigarette.

'I'm just… Do you work here?'

'Yeah, you could say that.'

'Are you a solicitor?' I look at him dubiously.

'I wish,' he laughs, flicking his cigarette to the floor and extinguishing it with his shoe. 'I'm just temping here, doing a bit of admin.' He walks towards me. 'Have you got an appointment?'

'No. I was… looking for someone who works here. A friend.'

He taps a number into the security keypad and pushes open the door.

'Oh yeah? What's his name?'

'James Wilson,' I say.

'James Wilson. James Wilson… Sounds familiar.' He pinches the top of his nose. 'I know! He came in the other day. But he doesn't work here, he's a client of Mr Forts. I checked him in. That's one of my jobs, see.'

A client?

'I don't suppose you know what he needed to see a solicitor for?' I say.

He laughed. 'Have you heard of the data protection act? As it happens, I don't know, but if I did, I couldn't say anyway. If I wanted to keep my job.'

'Of course,' I mumble, turning away. And then I have a thought. 'Can I just ask, what sort of law does Mr Forts specialise in?'

'Criminal law,' he says as he steps inside the building. 'That's all I can tell you, I'm afraid.'

CHAPTER 43

Once I'm back on the tram, travelling home, I google *Mr Forts, Emperor Knight, Nottingham*.

A picture of a smiling bald man in his late forties loads in the 'About Us' section of the firm's website. I scan through Andrew Forts' experience and biography, to the list of services he specialises in, and discover that he conducts work in police stations, magistrates' court, crown courts and appeal courts.

It's all very general and doesn't really tell me anything, doesn't give me a clue what James might have been seeking advice on.

Is he in some kind of trouble? He said the phone calls he received in the coffee shop were from work. He seemed irritated by the first two, but then that last call came in and he was definitely spooked by whatever he saw on the screen.

It's a mystery and almost impossible to second-guess why he was seeking advice at Emperor Knight.

My mind drifts as the tram speeds out of the city, and I find myself thinking about Louise again. I wonder if she's been thinking about opening up to me a little. I could see she too felt we'd started to break down the barriers between us last night.

I'm convinced something is really troubling her, but trying to get her to speak honestly about what is happening in her personal life is going to be a challenge. As is having her admit that Archie might be struggling.

She's stubborn and defensive by default. I remember only too well how her automatic response has always been to defend herself to the hilt, even when it's obvious she is in the wrong. One incident in particular comes to mind.

Three years earlier

My preparations for the gallery's launch event were going splendidly, but I needed to clarify a couple of things with the big boss. I asked Jim when we might expect Finn at the shop.

'We'll be seeing him less and less,' Jim told me. 'He's a busy man, still a working artist himself, and once the gallery is up and running, he'll probably only come over here two or three times a year.'

But the next morning, Finn called in.

He and Jim had some business to deal with in the back office, so I left them to it. The launch event was only two weeks away now, and we'd just taken delivery of a very important order from Louise's company, East PR.

I opened the box and took out one of the glossy, stylish pamphlets to inspect. They looked good, minimalist and yet managing to include all the information.

Next, I opened the smaller box containing the exclusive invitations that Mr Visser had chosen himself and Louise had personally overseen.

I gingerly unwrapped the cellophane and extracted one of the beautiful, weighty ivory cards printed in silver and black. She'd done us proud. I felt certain Mr Visser would love them.

I turned it over and read through the elegant script… and froze.

The gallery founder, Mr Finn Vasser, warmly invites you…

Vasser! The most important name on the invitation had been spelled incorrectly.

I slipped the invitation quickly into my bag and then hid the box under the desk and piled a heap of bubble wrap on top of it.

My heart hammered in my chest as I stared at the office door. How was I going to explain this?

The launch event was happening in just two weeks' time, and as per Mr Visser's detailed instructions, we were all set to send out the invitations by first-class post the next day.

'It's imperative we give people a two-week window,' he'd told us only a few days ago. 'The art world is full of busy diaries and we need to ensure The Art Box appears in many of them.'

I crept to the office and listened outside the door. Jim and Mr Visser were still deep in conversation, so I decided I should be safe to make the call.

I walked into the main showroom and brought up the list of contacts on my phone.

'Can I call you back?' Louise answered without a greeting. 'I'm just about to go into—'

'No, Louise. You can't call me back. The invitations have arrived and there's a spelling mistake on there. A huge one.'

'Oh! But you checked the proof I sent through, didn't you?'

'Yes, but Mr Visser's name was spelled correctly on the proof, I'm certain of it. The invites say Vasser. There's no way they can go out with such a glaring error. How soon can you reprint?'

'I'll have to check, hang on.' She put me on hold and I pulled the phone away from my ear as a barrage of awful electronic music started up. A minute later, she was back. 'OK, so the earliest we could get that done would be next Wednesday. I could have them with you again by next Friday lunchtime. How does that sound?'

I closed my eyes.

'That sounds like my worst nightmare come true.' I kept my voice low in the echoey space. 'They're supposed to be going out tomorrow night.'

Louise seemed completely unfazed.

'Well then, you'll just have to explain to your boss that you made a mistake and—'

'I didn't make a mistake! There's no way I'm going to be the fall guy for this,' I hissed through bared teeth, leaning against the cool wall near the front windows. 'You need to get that proof invite out and check it. I changed a phone number on the back and that's been amended correctly. I would've definitely noticed if the gallery director's name had been spelled wrong too!'

'Calm down. I can put the mistake right, but it's going to take time. I can't be any fairer than that, can I?'

Her nonchalant tone set my nerves jangling.

'I trusted you, Louise. We were all set to use a local company whose work Jim knows well, but I persuaded him to go with you. How is that going to make me look?'

'Look, I've really got to go.' Louise adopted a suddenly formal tone, as if someone had just walked in the room. 'I'll call you later and we can discuss the project in more detail.'

She ended the call and I stamped my foot in temper. The bloody project didn't need discussing; she just needed to correct her glaring error.

I paced around the showroom in a big circle, biting my nails and racking my brains about how I could put things right without losing the confidence of Jim, and more importantly, Mr Visser himself.

CHAPTER 44

Back home, after taking my coat off, I immediately set the Nokia charging.

I'm fully expecting that James will be back on the tram tomorrow, but just in case he tries to call the phone himself today, I think it's imperative I get it fully charged. I calculate it'll be at least an hour before it's ready for me to look through it, and so I shrug my coat on again, pick up my keys and head out again.

I'm seized by a compulsion to change things, and, as they say, there's no time like the present.

I leave the apartment building and turn left, walking about two hundred yards before turning left again and entering the small hairdresser's about halfway up the street.

I've never been here before, and that reassures me. I've no wish to return to the one I used when Mum and I first moved here, because, true to form, Charlotte, the owner, would want to know everything that's happened over the past two years in great detail.

'Can I help you?' A girl of about eighteen with cropped pink and blue hair smiles as I enter the shop.

'Yes, I'd like to make an appointment for a restyle.' I pull at a rope of my hair. 'As you can tell, it's been a while since I last visited a hairdresser.'

'We've just had a cancellation, actually, three o'clock this afternoon with Jeanie?'

My heart blips. I didn't expect an appointment so soon.

'I'll take it,' I hear myself say.

Next, I call at the small Tesco back on the main road. I consult my hastily scribbled list and put the items in the pull-along basket. Salad, fruit, tofu… I can't remember the last time I actually planned what I'll have to eat. My method is usually governed by what meagre supplies are in the cupboard or freezer, and that's generally something ready-made.

Growing up, Mum was a stickler for making sure we got our five portions of fruit and veg a day, right up until we were adults. You'd think all those years of having something drilled into you, it would stick, but sadly, it's the last thing I consider these days.

Sometimes you know what's good for you but you go and do just the opposite anyway. Louise has always been good at doing that too.

Like when she met Martyn Hardy and fell pregnant within three months.

Ten years earlier

They'd already got their own place by that stage, but she spent more and more time back at home. She told us Martyn was always working at his gym – towards their future, their dream, he was fond of telling her.

He liked to portray himself as the big businessman, but Mum and I had our suspicions from the start. It didn't take long to realise he lived permanently on the cusp of the next elusive big deal or opportunity.

I'd met Martyn on several occasions. He was a man who liked talking about himself and his achievements. He owned a spit-and-sawdust-type gym on the outskirts of the city, in an old garage unit in a run-down area, but to hear him talk, people came from miles around to benefit from his unique style of training.

Yet Louise herself had let slip that he never seemed to have any money. There was always some excuse why she'd have to pay the bill at a restaurant or get the tickets for the cinema.

He told Mum he lived in a brand-new duplex apartment in an expensive part of town, but when I went to the trouble of seeking out his address, which I found on Companies House online, it was an old concrete tower block at least a twenty-minute walk from the embankment.

And so it went on… an unlikeable habit of boasting that was very rarely backed up with any solid evidence of achievements.

In a very short time I had the measure of Martyn Hardy, but my sister seemed smitten.

At this stage I didn't tell her I'd been making tentative enquiries into her fiancé. She had an involuntary blindness when it came to seeing the truth about Martyn.

She used words like *aspiring, driven* and *committed* to describe him, while to Mum and me he was clearly a fantasist.

The wedding arrangements that Louise had excitedly said she wanted Mum heavily involved in never materialised either. I watched my sister grow increasingly sad.

'I'd go so far as to call him a liar,' Mum told me once when, on one of his rare visits to our house, Martyn spent fifteen minutes telling us he might have one of the major fitness chains interested in buying his crappy little gym.

Incredibly, Louise had never been to see his premises; at Martyn's request, she was waiting for refurbishments to be finished. From what I saw the day I went to look, they hadn't even been started.

It was pretty obvious it was always going to end badly.

But Louise never lost faith in him, so desperate was she to believe his unsubstantiated promises.

I remember the day I found her crying upstairs, clutching her stomach in the bathroom while Mum watched television downstairs, oblivious.

'What's wrong?' I'd dashed to her side, convinced she'd collapsed in pain through some kind of illness.

'Leave me alone,' she'd snapped in true Louise style. Usually I'd have taken the hint and left her to it as she asked, but this particular day I could tell she seemed really distressed.

I sat quietly on the edge of the bath and it didn't take long for her to open up.

'I'm four weeks pregnant,' she whispered.

I caught the unhelpful gasp that jumped up into my throat and reached for her hand instead.

'Does Martyn know?' I asked.

She'd cried harder then and I started filling in the blanks. It looked to me like Martyn did indeed know about the pregnancy and was probably none too happy about it.

'He wants me to get rid of it,' she sobbed, confirming my suspicions.

My skin felt cold when I imagined that tiny scrap of life growing inside her. The baby was my flesh and blood too.

'And what do you think about it?' I gently asked her.

'I don't know,' she whimpered. 'I just don't know what to think. Martyn says it's not the right time, that in a couple of years we'll be ready. But he says it can't happen right now.'

I recalled thinking it was a really stupid thing for her to do, getting pregnant so soon and by such an obvious loser, too.

Still, that was the day I decided to do a bit more digging on Martyn Hardy… a little deeper this time.

Present day

I put the last item in my basket and head for the checkout. I split the load between two bags, but it's still a slog back to the apartment.

As I enter the foyer, I say a silent prayer of thanks when I see the engineer just packing up his tools and the notice gone. The lift is operational again.

Back in the apartment, I empty the bags and put the food away. It feels so satisfying to see the fridge shelves stocked again and the salad drawer pleasantly full of fresh green stuff.

I fill the wire fruit basket on the worktop with satsumas and apples and place the fresh bread in the cupboard.

Then I turn my attention to James's phone.

CHAPTER 45

Three years earlier

The afternoon I discovered the error on the gallery launch invitations, I knew it would do me no good to postpone the awful truth. When Jim and Visser's meeting broke up, I was waiting with a hangdog face, ready to confess.

Mr Visser turned the invitation in his hands and then looked at me over the bright red spectacles he wore perched at the end of his nose.

I glanced at Jim, who winked at me and nodded.

I'd gone cap in hand to him while Mr Visser visited the bathroom and told him what had happened. Including the bad news that the company couldn't reprint and redeliver until the end of next week. He'd gone back to his office and made a quick call.

'And this spelling mistake of my name, you missed it on the proof invite?' Mr Visser asked calmly.

'No!' I said vehemently. 'It wasn't wrong on there, I'm certain of it. But the PR company has destroyed the proof so we can't check.'

'What's done is done, I suppose,' Jim chipped in. 'The good news is, Finn, my contact at the company we were going to use can redo them by Monday afternoon.'

'Hmm. It is not ideal as we lose a weekend, but under the circumstances, let's go for that.'

I let out the breath I'd been holding for what seemed like ages.

'However, I'll be writing to your sister's company stating that we will not be paying for the invitations unless they can produce the original proof,' Mr Visser said firmly. 'In this business, nobody destroys a proof until the job is completed.'

I nodded, chastised. 'I'm sorry, Mr Visser. I feel… responsible.'

'No matter on this occasion,' he smiled. 'Although perhaps mixing business and family should be avoided, yes?'

I nodded again, giddy with relief. That was definitely a lesson I'd learned the hard way.

The invitations were printed and posted out as planned and our event got a ninety per cent RSVP acceptance, which Mr Visser seemed delighted with.

The launch event went swimmingly.

I was standing with the glass of fizz I was making last all night so I stayed fresh and on my toes when someone tapped me on my shoulder. I turned to see Mr Visser himself and someone I was not expecting. I sprang back in delight.

'Mum!'

She'd said earlier that she felt a bit under the weather and wouldn't be coming to the event now that Louise had had a major strop about being blamed for the faulty invitations and wouldn't come with her.

'I couldn't not come in the end, so I got a cab,' she said now, her face brighter than I'd seen it in a while. 'I'm so glad I did; it looks magnificent in here.'

I followed her eyes, looking up and around the walls of our pristine gallery.

'It does look really wonderful, and a good part of that is down to Alice's brilliant work, Mrs Fisher. She's a gem and I'm so glad we found her. You must be very proud.'

'I am, thank you, Mr Visser. It's all she's ever wanted to do, you know, art and… suchlike.'

Mr Visser smiled at me knowingly and made his excuses, leaving me with Mum. When he had gone, I beckoned someone else over.

'Mum, I'd like you to meet Jack. I told you about him: he's an artist, and his work is over there in the local artists' corner.'

'Hello, Mrs Fisher. It's so nice to meet you.' Jack held out his hand.

He looked amazing, so tall and dark and sort of brooding, although he had a really sunny personality when you got to know him.

'Pleased to meet you, Jack,' Mum said, taking his hand. 'Alice talks about you a lot.' I blushed and Jack grinned.

'I know Alice is busy tonight, so would you like me to show you some of the paintings?'

'How nice.' Mum beamed, and I knew Jack had won her over already.

Over the next few months, The Art Box became a tour de force in the city and further afield.

One quiet day in the office, Jim made us a coffee and we sat down together for a rare ten minutes' peace.

'Finn is looking at new premises, Alice,' he said, wasting no time in getting to the point. 'Three times the size of this place and this time based in north Nottinghamshire, where there's a shortage of galleries like ours.'

'Wow, that sounds amazing!' I exclaimed, feeling excited. And then something awful occurred to me. 'What about… will I still have a job here?'

'That's what I wanted to talk to you about,' Jim said, sipping his drink. 'There's an assistant manager opportunity coming up as it'll be difficult for me to coordinate the two galleries on my own. Visser is impressed with you, Alice. I think you should go for it.'

'What?' I swallowed down a lump in my throat. 'But I've only got a few months' experience and—'

'You're a natural,' Jim interrupted. 'Is that something you'd want, more responsibility?'

'Yes! I mean, I love working in the gallery and I'd like to progress. Most definitely.'

'Well then, it's yours for the taking. There'd be an interview at The Steel Box, Finn's big gallery in Sheffield.' Jim hesitated. 'It'll be a panel interview, but that's nothing to worry about. I can take you through the things you need to know.'

I felt a bit sick at the thought of a formal interview, but as Louise often said, you had to claw your way up to get to where you wanted to be. And I'd wanted to visit The Steel Box since I'd started working here.

'I'm going to go for it,' I said suddenly, full of excitement about what lay ahead.

'Cheers!' Jim grinned and we clinked coffee cups.

CHAPTER 46

Louise

Ten years earlier

Louise lay in bed. She felt as though she was dying.

She didn't feel angry at Martyn; she felt angry at herself. How could she have been so stupid as to fall pregnant this early in the relationship?

She'd only forgotten to take her pill once. She knew loads of girls who'd done the same and they hadn't fallen pregnant.

She was certain that one tablet was neither here nor there… she felt sure she'd been on the pill long enough for it to build up in her system.

So she'd put it out of her mind and hadn't even mentioned it to Martyn.

And she'd ruined everything. *Everything.*

CHAPTER 47

Alice

'Auntie Alice, do you ever wish you could be somebody else?'

All the time. That's my knee-jerk reaction, but instead I say, 'I think everyone does at some point or another, it's normal. Why… do you wish you were someone else, Archie?'

'Yes,' he says matter-of-factly.

'And who do you wish you could be?'

'Anybody but me. Someone who doesn't always say the wrong thing, someone who's strong and good at sport and…'

'Yes?'

'Someone my mum could be proud of.'

I blink at him.

'Archie, have you heard of a man called Oscar Wilde?'

He thinks for a moment. 'Was he… a poet?'

'He was. A poet and a writer, and he said some very astute things that people still use today to help them live a better life.'

'Did he want to be someone else too?'

'No, I don't think so. He accepted himself for who he was and he said this: "Be yourself; everyone else is already taken."'

Archie frowns as he turns the quote over in his mind.

'Because everyone else is already themselves, so you can't be them?'

'That's right.' I smile. 'And more importantly, nobody else can be *you*.'

'But nobody else would want to be me,' he says, looking down at his hands.

CHAPTER 48

It's cool in the apartment, but my chest and face feel warm.

The battery icon on the screen indicates the phone is still charging, but it's been plugged in long enough now to give me a chance to see if James has called.

I disconnect the charger and cradle the phone in my hand, as if it's something precious. I'm not sure what to expect, but I've decided that if it rings while I have it turned on, I will answer it.

If it's James, then that will be fantastic. But if it's someone calling him, I can explain I'm looking after his phone temporarily until I can safely return it to him.

I can also ask them if they have any other contact details for him.

I hold down the on/off button and wait for the screen to come to life. Almost immediately, a notification box pops up.

11 missed calls

Eleven! Anyone calling the number after the phone turned itself off would have gone straight to voicemail.

I'm relieved to see that there is no password lock. This phone has the facility to do that, but obviously James didn't bother. Maybe it's his work phone and there's nothing personal on it.

I press a couple of buttons to take me into the call menu. I select the option to view the missed calls log and stare at the list for a moment.

My heart jumps into my mouth when my doorbell rings.

My first thought is that it must be James. He obviously knows where I live, it's not that difficult to get into the building if you're prepared to wait and it's easy to narrow down my flat number based on where my window is.

I stuff the phone into a drawer. The last thing I want is for him to see I've been snooping. I run my fingers frantically through my now tousled hair in an attempt to improve it and rush to the door just as the bell sounds again.

I open it, a forced smile on my face.

'Hi, Alice, hope you don't mind me just calling by like this but I wondered if you fancied a coffee? I could do with a chat.'

It's Jenny. The girl from upstairs.

With great effort, I keep the plastic smile in place.

'Oh! How nice. I…'

'I thought you might come upstairs to mine. I've got a new coffee machine and I need a guinea pig to try it out on.'

I laugh with her. I need to get my hair done, eat better and find some new friends. Coffee with Jenny ticks one of those boxes.

'Sounds great, give me a second.'

I grab my handbag and keys and follow her out into the corridor. We don't bother with the lift as it's only one floor up. As she puts her key in the door, I wonder whether to mention the buzzing phone on her floor that keeps me awake.

I decide to say nothing for now.

I follow her inside and close the door quietly behind me. One of the annoying things about living below Jenny is that she seems to bang doors for no apparent reason.

'Come into the kitchen and you can help me fathom this machine. It's a bit technical, to say the least.'

Her kitchen is identical to mine but she has a red and black colour scheme with the white units, whereas I've got duck-egg-blue tea towels and canisters.

A state-of-the-art stainless-steel coffee machine sits in the middle of the longest stretch of worktop.

'I was going to put it in the cupboard, but my boyfriend said it's a piece of kitchen furniture and should be on display.' She rolls her eyes.

'It's very… impressive,' I say. 'I'm sure it makes a fab cup of coffee, but I think I might stick with my kettle.'

We both laugh. I read out the instructions and she follows them, and a few minutes later we have two rather professional-looking cappuccinos.

'Qualified baristas, eat your hearts out,' Jenny declares as she does a little victory dance right there in front of the machine.

I really like her. Her energy seems to be rubbing off on me a bit. She asks me to take the coffees through while she puts a few biscuits on a plate.

While she's still pottering around in the kitchen, I get a few seconds to look around. It's so weird being in a carbon copy of my own lounge, which is right beneath my feet.

This room definitely looks more modern than mine. It's mainly beige and neutral colours, with a chocolate-brown rug and a glass coffee table in the middle, and dark brown faux-fur blankets scattered on the biscuit-coloured suite.

She's also got one of those electric fires that look like real flames, which adds a nice focal point to the room. It looks cosy and I feel a twinge of inadequacy that I couldn't have done something similar with my own space.

One thing that's not so good is that this room seems quite dark. Then I realise she has a cream Roman blind that has been pulled two thirds down, cutting out a lot of daylight.

'Here we go.' Jenny walks in holding a plate loaded with chocolate biscuits and cookies.

'I've just started a healthy eating drive.' I reach for a cookie. 'Looks like I might be delaying it until tomorrow now.'

I bite into the biscuit, savouring its crumbly sweetness.

'Life's too short,' Jenny agrees, reaching for a chocolate one. 'And biscuits are one of life's pleasures.'

'Easy for you to say.' I smile. 'Being so nice and slim.'

'That's because I haven't got much of an appetite most of the time.' A shadow passes over her face, but she doesn't elaborate and I certainly don't know her well enough to ask about anything personal.

'You've got your room looking lovely,' I say, looking around as I munch on another biscuit. 'It's much nicer than mine. After seeing your flat, I think my own is definitely overdue for a bit of an update.'

'I wouldn't be able to afford to do all this on my own,' she says honestly. 'My boyfriend buys me a lot of stuff for the flat.'

There doesn't seem to be any evidence around that a man lives here. Everything is very feminine, and I notice for the first time that there are no photographs in the room.

'We don't live together,' she says, as if she knows what I'm thinking. 'He lives… on the other side of the city.' For some reason, I sense that although she gives the impression of being quite a light-hearted and laid-back person, she's carrying a bit of a burden on her shoulders.

'Is it complicated?' I ask diplomatically.

'You could say that,' she mutters. 'And on top of everything, now my ex won't leave us alone.'

'Oh dear.' I'm beginning to wish I'd never got into this conversation.

'Yeah. I left him six months ago, we were engaged and everything. He took it really bad… still is.'

'Sounds difficult.'

'That's why I keep the blinds down. It gives me the creeps knowing he could be out there watching.'

'Your ex isn't a window-cleaner, is he?' I quip. After all, she lives on the fourth floor; he can hardly walk by and peek in.

'Ha! No, I'd have been better off with a down-to-earth window cleaner, though,' she says wryly. 'But he passes on the tram every morning, sends me a text to say he's out there. The last few times he's taken it a step further, staring up and waving at my window. I haven't a clue how he found out where I was living, but I feel really vulnerable now he knows which flat I'm in and everything.'

She's fading away from me. Her face, her voice… everything seems far away.

'My boyfriend reckons he's "sorted" it. I'm not sure what that means… I don't really want to know, to be honest. If you knew him, you'd understand why I'm worried, but… Alice, are you OK?'

I hear Jenny saying my name again and again, but I can't respond. Thoughts drift freely in my head, moving towards each other like they're trying to somehow fit together. But none of them are making any sense, no matter how hard I try to link them. I feel like I'm in the middle of a game where the rules have all changed.

James.

The strange unfocused look in his eyes on the tram, the non-reaction when he walked past me, the way he didn't recognise me in the coffee shop…

It was never my window he was staring at, but the one directly above. All this time, it's Jenny's flat he's been watching.

I begin to shake, and coffee spills into the saucer. My hands seem to belong to someone else as they place it on the coffee table in front of me.

I stand up quickly and catch the edge of the plate. It upends and the biscuits scatter all over the carpet.

'Alice, whatever's wrong?' I hear Jenny cry out.

But of course, I can't possibly tell her.

Instead, I pick up my bag and keys and dash from her apartment.

CHAPTER 49

Back in my own flat, I lock and bolt the door behind me. Then I rush to the bathroom and vomit my guts up.

When there's nothing left to come up, I slump back against the cool tiled wall and consider how I could have been such an utter idiot, an embarrassment to myself.

Within minutes, there's a frantic banging at the front door. Jenny's muffled voice calls out my name again and again. I ignore her.

I kick the bathroom door shut with my foot to further screen off the noise. My head is banging; my spine feels as though it's crumbling. The tiled floor is too hard and cold for my hips, but I don't move. I sit there for another twenty minutes. By then, Jenny is long gone.

Inch by inch, I slide my knees up to find my joints have completely seized up. Slowly, slowly, I turn to one side and, using the side of the bath as a support, ease myself up onto all fours.

Tears roll from my eyes with the pain. I need my tablets, I need a drink to ease my dry, scorched throat. I have to do this. Three times I try and get to my feet, but I can't manage that final push.

So I crawl. I crawl from the bathroom, down the short hallway to the kitchen. After a few minutes' rest and tentative leg stretches, I finally manage to stand up.

I drink a glass of tap water at the sink and then take another one to the counter. I perch on a tall stool and reach for my tablet container.

I know it's completely inadvisable, but I take tonight's painkiller and sedative too. I need as much help as I can get right now.

The hairdressing appointment I made flits into my consciousness and back out again.

I make it to my bedroom and flop down on the bed fully clothed, waiting for merciful sleep to come. Except when it does, it brings with it the beginning of the worst period of my life.

The day that really changed the path of where I thought I was headed.

The day that was supposed to be one of the most exciting in my life so far.

Three years earlier

I checked my appearance in the mirror.

Neatly pinned-up hair. Check.

Natural make-up. Check.

No bits stuck in my teeth. Check.

I felt ready as I'd ever be.

I ran the cold tap and allowed the water to trickle deliciously through my hot, sticky fingers. I wished I could have eaten my sandwich at lunchtime, but my appetite felt like it had disappeared, never to return.

Could I really do this job? Jim had worked hard at convincing me that I was a natural assistant manager for The Art Box... but did I really believe it?

Yes, this promotion would bring a significant hike in status and responsibility, but it meant so much more than that. My salary would rise by around twenty per cent, and it would mean that Jack could finally ditch his evening job as a waiter and we could think about getting a small place together.

It had been a quick process, but the two of us were so close. We were in love, and we both wanted to take our relationship to the next level, but we just hadn't got the funds.

Now, though, I was nearly there. Just one last hurdle to get over, and by the weekend, Jack and I could be celebrating with the bottle of Prosecco I had waiting on the top shelf of the fridge at home. Mum loved Jack, so I know she'd be supportive.

I turned off the tap and stuck my hands under the dryer, wincing at the harsh drone that only served to exacerbate my nervous headache.

For what felt like the hundredth time, I brushed non-existent flecks from my navy gabardine suit and picked up my handbag. It was time.

As I emerged from the bathroom, I glanced at my phone and smiled at the text notification from Jack. I clicked on it.

You'll slay them, my clever girl. Love you lots xxx

That was what he called me, his clever girl. I'd roll my eyes when he said it, but really I loved it. It felt wonderful that we supported each other in whatever it was we wanted to do. I was going for this promotion for both of us.

Somewhere deep inside me, a tiny voice asked if everything had happened too soon between Jack and me, but I squashed it flat before it could prosper. I knew who that critical voice belonged to and I'd heard enough of it over the years. Thoughts like that weren't positive or helpful. Not today… or indeed any day.

As I neared the conference room, where I knew the panel were waiting, I switched the phone to silent mode, just as the screen lit up to announce an incoming call from my sister.

Her vicious words from this morning ricocheted around my head. *You're a selfish cow who cares about nobody but herself.* Maybe she was calling because she'd thought of more insults to throw my way, but I had no wish to revisit our argument – about something minor as usual. Especially not right now.

My finger was hovering above the end call button when it occurred to me that Louise always preferred to text and hardly ever rang me during the day, unless she desperately needed something.

I glanced at the time at the top of the screen. I'd got four minutes before my interview officially started. I'd feel better explaining why I couldn't speak rather than just cutting her off like an inconvenience.

My finger slid over the screen and I answered the call.

'Alice?' The word escaped her lips and broke an octave higher at the end, and I knew something bad had happened.

'What is it?' I whispered as two people passed me in the corridor. 'What's wrong?'

The door of the conference room opened and Jim appeared, frowning at the empty seating outside where he was obviously expecting to find me. He looked up and down the corridor, and his face relaxed when he spotted me.

He held his index finger up and nodded when he saw I was on the telephone, signalling that they'd want me in there in a minute's time.

I swallowed hard as he disappeared back inside, my heartbeat picking up pace.

'Alice?'

I brought my attention back to the call.

'Sorry, Louise. Could I call you back in about an hour? It's just that—'

'It's Mum, she's in hospital.'

'What? What happened?' I leaned heavily against the wall, my chest pounding.

'Darren called to take her shopping and found her on the kitchen floor. They think it's a heart attack.' She pulled in a breath. 'They've taken her to the Trent Cardiology Centre at the City Hospital.'

'Oh no! I'm in Sheffield, at Finn's head office,' I said faintly. 'I'm just about to go into my interview, but I'll leave as soon as I'm finished. I can probably be there in under three hours if you can cover.'

'Are you joking?' Her tone sharpened. 'You need to come right now. Mum needs someone with her.'

'What? Didn't Darren go with her in the ambulance?'

'He had Archie in the car and he didn't think hospital was the right place for a six-year-old, and I totally agree.'

'But… aren't you there now?'

'No. I'm just leaving for a major client meeting in Stoke. I can't get out of it.'

'Louise, I need you to hold the fort just a little while and then I'll be there… You're already in Nottingham and I'm at least forty-five miles away.'

'You need to stop worrying about your promotion and think about your family for a change. A new job will wait for another day. Mum might not.'

'That's not fair! Mr Visser's main investor has flown down from Scotland just to sit on the panel. And you're already—'

'Not my problem. Mum's in a bad way. She was unconscious when they took her in, and she hit her head when she fell.'

'Oh no.' I pressed the palm of my hand to my forehead. *Think.*

'Please just delay going to your meeting, Louise. Or couldn't Darren—'

'No. He couldn't. Please yourself, but if something happens to Mum, on your head be it.'

A sharp click indicated that she had ended the call.

'Alice?'

I looked up sharply, my eyes shining. It was Jim, looking slightly irked that I was still halfway down the corridor instead of waiting bright-eyed and bushy-tailed outside the conference room.

He cleared his throat and opened the door wide behind him.

'The panel is ready for you now.'

Present day

When I wake up, I know instinctively what it is I have to do.

I jump at the harsh buzz of the door entry system. Someone is outside, asking to come up to my apartment.

Thanks to the entrance canopy, no matter how close I press my face to the living room window, I can't see who is standing outside the main building, buzzing to be let in.

So I have no choice but to ignore it.

I'm suspicious that it could be Jenny, trying another ruse to check on me. Even worse, it could be James, come to ask if I have his phone.

And I can't face either of them at the moment.

My phone pings and I realise it's still in my handbag by the door, so I ease myself off the stool and walk over there.

A folded piece of paper has been slid under the door. I'm guessing that when Jenny couldn't get an answer earlier, she left me a note.

After checking all the bolts are in place, with difficulty I bend and pick up the paper and then my handbag, taking both back over to the worktop.

The buzzer sounds again; this time, whoever is out there leaves their finger on it for longer. I ignore it and unfold the paper, stare at the black handwriting.

Mind your own business, bitch, or you'll be sorry.

I let out a small cry as the paper falls from my fingers.

That sounds far too similar to a voice from my past I'd rather forget.

Buzz… buzz… buzz… short, staccato interruptions driving me crazy now. But I'm resolved, especially after reading the note. I'm not letting anyone into the apartment.

I take my phone out of my handbag and see a text notification message from my sister. I open it up.

Where ARE you? I'm stuck outside buzzing to come in!! L

With perfect timing, the buzzer sounds again. Another long one.

I snatch up the handset and release the entrance door. A few minutes later, I open the apartment door to a panting Louise and an equally tired-looking Archie.

'This place is killing me!' She leans back against the wall and closes her eyes. 'Can't you just move to a nice little house closer to us with no bloody stairs to climb? You might as well have no lift here, the number of times it's out of order.'

I don't answer her; I just close the door again and lock it. I don't think she told me I was looking after Archie tonight, though I can't remember. So I say nothing.

'I'm not staying,' she says. 'I've got to…' She stops and stares at me. 'You look awful.'

'I feel awful,' I say.

'What's wrong?'

I've no intention of telling her about James; how it was the girl upstairs he was interested in. I know she'd barely be able to hide her glee at my embarrassment.

'I'm just having a bad day. Probably coming down with something.'

Her eyes immediately glaze over.

'I hope it's OK to leave Archie. Darren's working late and I've got an appointment… a meeting.'

Which is it? I feel like asking, but I don't. The last thing I need is an argument with Louise; that would just about finish me off today.

Instead I turn my attention to Archie. He looks pale and slightly troubled.

'You OK, Archie?' I smile at him.

'Of course he's all right,' Louise snaps. 'Go in the living room, Archie, put the TV on or something.'

He glances at me, but shuffles slowly to the door.

I look at Louise, about to quiz her on Archie's demeanour, and realise that she too looks a bit distracted.

'I'm dying for the loo,' she says. 'I'll go before I leave if that's OK.'

I watch her walk by me and disappear into the bathroom. All the way there, she never takes her eyes from her phone.

I don't know why I do it. I certainly haven't planned it, but when I see her handbag sitting there on the worktop, gaping open, I peer inside.

There's a silk scarf folded on the top and I push it aside gently to reveal her purse, a small mesh pouch containing items of make-up, and a hairbrush. I'm about to pull the scarf back in place when I feel something hard underneath my fingers.

I lift the scarf and spot something made of glass at the bottom of the bag. When I move her purse slightly, I see exactly what it is.

A small bottle of vodka that looks to be half empty.

CHAPTER 50

I hear the loo flush and make sure the scarf is undisturbed and in place before moving to the other side of the kitchen.

'How's the new job going?' I ask.

Louise looks up from her phone, surprised, as if she'd forgotten about her promotion.

'It's good, thanks, most of the time anyway.' She puts the phone down and sighs. 'Look, I know I'm always in a crazy rush, but I just want to say that I'm very grateful, you know. For how you're helping out with Archie.'

'That's OK,' I say, sensing an opportunity. 'I know you're a big tough businesswoman now, but you're still my sister. I worry about you, trying to be everything to everyone.'

To my horror, her eyes immediately fill and then overspill.

'Sorry!' She sniffs. 'I'm sorry, I don't know what's wrong with me.'

'Come on, sit down. Just for two minutes.'

I'd like to ask her about the vodka in her bag and whether it's helping her cope. I'd like to tell her about my awful mistake in thinking James was ever interested in me, and about the horrible note someone pushed under the door just before she arrived. I'd like to tell her about seeing Archie's teacher and about Darren's concerns too, but I haven't got my own head around any of it yet. So I know it's best to say nothing.

She sits on the stool next to me and takes the tissue I hand her. 'Thanks,' she says, blowing her nose.

'This is not like you, Louise. What's wrong?'

Usually when I ask about how she's feeling, she jumps into defence or attack mode, but today, she just sighs hopelessly, shakes her head and pushes around a toast crumb on the worktop that my cloth must have missed this morning.

'I'm dealing with a lot of… stuff at the moment,' she says in a guarded tone. 'I can't talk about it. It's not that I don't trust you, but it's just relationship stuff, you know?'

I feel the hairs on my forearms prickle as I remember Darren's suspicions that there might be someone else on the scene.

'Relationships are hard,' I say. 'But I know Darren really loves you, so whatever the problem is, I'm sure you can overcome it together.'

'Oh, Alice. There you go, off in your ideal little world again.'

I don't feel like taking one of her put-down lines today.

'I know what you think about me, Louise, but you have no idea what my life is really like. I can assure you it's far from ideal at the moment, whatever it seems like to you.'

'Touché.' She shrugs. 'I suppose we all make assumptions about other people. I didn't mean anything by it.'

'I know, but I wish you'd try not to voice your incorrect assumptions in front of other people.'

'Like who?' She bristles.

'I'm just saying, kids hear more than you think. I don't want Archie thinking I'm weird or something.'

She frowns. 'Why, what's he been saying?'

'Nothing,' I mumble. I forgot that Archie asked me not to say anything. 'I just used that as an example.'

She folds her arms and bites her lip and I need to say something to get her off the subject.

'Are you and Darren… OK?'

'That's not an easy question to answer in one word.' She looks at me steadily. 'You like Darren, don't you? You think he's a good man?'

It feels like a trap, but I'm going to answer honestly.

'Yes, it's fair to say I like him a lot. He seems to really love you and he treats Archie like his own son.'

'That's what I thought. And that tells me I'm right not to talk to you about my problems.'

I know what she's getting at. She doesn't want to tell me that she's having an affair because I have a good opinion of Darren.

'Look, Louise. I'm not married to Darren, so I can't judge you, no matter what's happening in your life.'

I can't say fairer than that and I ought to try and remain impartial, although that's difficult when I saw how worried Darren is about both Louise and Archie. My sister, on the other hand, seems to only be interested in thinking through her own problems, one of which is very likely her involvement with another man.

'You wouldn't believe me if I told you.' She gives a bitter laugh. 'You just look at me and think I have it all.'

She's way off target. I can see she's unhappy, and if she's seriously so deluded that she thinks I haven't noticed the recent changes in her – as Darren obviously has too, enough to ask what I think – then this is my chance to tell her.

'It's none of my business what's happening in your life,' I say carefully. 'But I can't deny I'm concerned about some of the signs I'm seeing.'

'What signs?' She sees me hesitate. 'Tell me, Alice.'

'You seem to be on a far shorter fuse than you used to be. You're often tight as a drum when you call here, and woe betide anyone – usually me or Archie – who says the wrong thing, because we'll get our heads bitten off.'

She looks down and doesn't say anything.

'I know I've never been as worldly-wise as you, Louise, but even I think it's unusual that you have early *and* late meetings most days.'

'What are you trying to say?'

'Just that.' I'm not going to let her set me up to accuse her of having an affair so she can tear a hole in me.

'It's really important you don't mention my meetings schedule to Darren, Louise,' she says firmly. 'He wouldn't understand.'

I bet he wouldn't, but I'm afraid it's a bit late for that.

'Surely Darren notices you're out of the house an awful lot. Does he have anything to say about it?'

'Are you serious? He's out more than I am. That's part of the problem.'

'Someone's got to pay for that fancy house and two cars, Louise,' I say, and before I even finish speaking, I see her shut down. Her *temper muscle*, as I used to call it when we were kids, flexes in her jaw.

'I'll say goodbye to Archie and get off then,' she says shortly.

With sadness, I watch her stomp out of the kitchen, unable or unwilling to take any responsibility for her own unhappiness.

Early in their marriage, it was always Louise who pushed for a better house in a better area. Darren was happy in their perfectly reasonable semi in Wilford until she started lusting after an address in an expensive suburb.

He left his job as a Nottingham-based salesman and went for more responsibility with a national company. And with that came the travelling, so to complain about his absence now seems a bit unfair.

I love my sister and my nephew and care about my brother-in-law too. I want them all to be happy, but that looks increasingly unlikely.

From where I'm standing, there's only one person who can't see the damage she's causing by refusing to acknowledge what's so obvious to everyone else.

CHAPTER 51

Louise

Three years earlier

The day Mum had her heart attack, Louise had had a big row with Darren about money. That was when his threats had started: to leave her, take Archie with him.

Since her split with Martyn and before meeting Darren, Louise had struggled to bring Archie up on one wage. Yes, her mum and Alice occasionally helped out buying him an outfit or a toy he wanted, but neither of them really understood how tough she was finding it on both a financial and an emotional level.

She knew this was due mainly to the fact that she clamped her coping mask firmly to her face before she left the house each day. Nobody would guess she spent her evenings crying and drowning her sorrows in cheap wine as many nights as her budget would allow.

Lily and Alice were close. There was just something about letting them know she was struggling that made Louise recoil inside. She simply didn't want them to find out.

Alice thought she was the one who had a tough life. It would be laughable if it wasn't so annoying.

She'd done some lame and largely useless art degree and then spent a few months pretending she was a real artist, producing what looked like bad Monet copies from the convenience of the spare bedroom.

She earned nothing, of course, relying on Lily's generosity to feed her and provide a roof over her head.

Despite what their probable opinion of her was, Louise wasn't stupid. She knew Lily must be giving Alice cash to buy clothes and art materials. You didn't have to be Hercule Poirot to see what must be happening behind the scenes.

Yet Alice still found plenty to complain about. The lack of gallery space for local artists, the bus being late two days in a row when she went into town, and how difficult it was to get a decent job.

Louise's heart bled for her. *Not*.

If Alice had only half of Louise's problems – feeding and cloth-ing her growing son, realising another year would pass without a break of any kind and passed over for promotion yet again at work – then she'd really have something to complain about.

Currently, Louise felt as though she was clawing her way out of a very deep hole from scratch each and every day.

So when Alice had landed her dream job, it felt like the last straw to Louise. She'd made an attempt to try and get her sister to understand how easy it had all been. She'd be working on the doorstep at some fancy gallery – no two-hour round trip for her – doing a job she loved. Predictably, Alice wouldn't entertain the idea that she'd been offered the job on a plate.

When her mum boasted to Louise that Alice was being promoted, despite a mere few months of experience on the job, Louise hadn't been the least bit surprised.

'You could ask her for a few tips in your own career,' her mother had suggested. 'You've been there years now with hardly any pay rise.'

And now she and Darren had big money problems that he was looking to her to solve.

Her head was full of it, full of worry and stress, and when Darren called to tell her that he'd found her mother on the floor, barely breathing, she couldn't take it a moment longer.

She called Alice and demanded she come home to deal with the situation.

Her mother had always made wisecracks about Louise's career; well, now she had an important meeting to go to and she was going to put it first. See how Lily liked *that*.

Darren had encouraged her.

'Tell Alice she has to come,' he insisted. 'Your mother has never cared about you, Lou. If she kicks the bucket, maybe this is finally our chance to get some money and solve our problems.'

CHAPTER 52

Alice

I'm just closing the door behind Louise when a foot appears, preventing me from shutting it.

I shriek and try to slam it.

'Oww! Alice, please… I just want to make sure you're OK!'

I peer through the gap to see Jenny hopping around on one leg.

'Sorry,' I say quickly, opening the door. 'I didn't mean to… I thought it was…'

'Look, can I just come in for a minute?' She looks nervously up and down the corridor. 'You know how nosy people are around here.'

I don't want her to come in, but I have no choice unless I want to be rude.

'I haven't got long,' I sigh, standing aside. 'I'm looking after my young nephew.'

I can hear the television blaring in the other room, louder than I usually allow it. But today, it suits my purpose that Archie is distracted.

Jenny steps inside, looking around her with interest as I did in her flat earlier.

'Come into the kitchen,' I say.

'It's so weird being in a mirror image of your own place,' she says.

'I'm sorry about earlier,' I say. 'I must have had some kind of stomach bug. I knew I was going to throw up and I just had to get out.'

'You could've used my bathroom,' she says. 'You didn't have to dash all the way back down here.'

Being sick sucks at any time, but it's even worse if it's not your own loo. And part of my excuse is the truth: I did feel very sick indeed.

'It was just instinct.'

'I came down straight away to see if you were all right. I banged on your door for ages.'

'I know, but I couldn't face anyone. I couldn't get up off the floor for ages.'

She looks at me and I meet her eyes. 'So long as it was nothing I did... or said,' she says slowly.

I can feel my heartbeat getting faster. There are some questions I really need to ask her, and I might not get a better chance than this.

I open my mouth to speak just as Jenny jumps off her chair and gasps. The kitchen door flies wide open and Archie stands there, blood streaming down his face.

'I'm sorry, Auntie Alice,' he whimpers as drops of blood spatter the kitchen floor. Then he sees Jenny and starts backing out of the room.

'Archie, it's fine, come here.' I grab a couple of sheets of paper towel and rush over to him. 'What on earth has happened?'

'It looks like a nosebleed,' Jenny says from behind me. 'I used to have them regularly as a kid.'

I'm dabbing Archie's face, but Jenny takes the tissue from me and holds it to his nose. Archie recoils, but Jenny isn't fazed.

'Like this,' she says, pinching the flesh of Archie's nostrils together. 'That's not too tight, is it, pet?'

Archie frowns and looks at me imploringly. 'I can do it myself,' he says curtly.

'You need to stem the flow of blood,' Jenny explains. 'It won't take long.'

We help Archie onto a stool. Jenny carries on administering her pinching method and I get some fresh paper towels.

'As far as I know, he's never had a nosebleed before,' I tell her. 'I'm going to have to call my sister.'

Archie starts blinking fast and I wonder if he's already worrying he'll be in trouble.

'It can't be helped, Archie,' I tell him. 'Your mum will be annoyed if I don't let her know.'

'She said it would be all right,' he says in a small voice.

'She said *what* would be all right?'

'When I hurt my head and got a nosebleed last night. She said I'm not to tell my teacher.'

I look at Jenny's shocked face and I feel both embarrassed and outraged at the idiocy of my sister. What on earth was she thinking?

I'm desperate to ask Archie what happened, but I'm concerned that Jenny, whom I barely know, has seen and heard enough.

'I can take over now, Jenny.' My hand hovers above her fingers, which are still pincered firmly onto Archie's nose. 'No need for you to hang around; we can catch up another time.'

'It's fine,' she says, leaving her fingers in place. 'I'll stay at least until the blood flow has stopped. Does your head hurt now, petal? How did it happen?'

Archie looks at her and back at me. He opens his mouth as if he's going to say something, but decides against it.

Jenny told me she used to work in a nursery, and she sounds like a concerned teacher right now, questioning Archie.

My head and face heat up as panic flutters in my chest. I'm torn between protecting my sister against an unfair assumption, and growing concern for Archie's well-being.

I need to know what happened last night, but it's fairly obvious Archie is not comfortable talking in front of a stranger, and neither am I, come to that.

If Louise has a drinking problem and has been neglecting Archie in some way, then I don't want it revealed in front of Jenny.

'Best not to question him while he's upset,' I say curtly.

'But he looks so scared,' she says, pressing her face closer. 'Is something worrying you, Archie?'

Archie glances away. He's obviously feeling vulnerable.

'He'll be all right, won't you, Archie?' I look at Jenny. 'He'll have slipped playing footie after school or something.'

Jenny doesn't look convinced and I realise I have to think of some way to change the conversation.

'Anyway, there was something I wanted to ask you. What's the name of that ex-boyfriend, the one who's been watching you on the tram?'

I'm talking too fast and my question sounds random, out of context.

'What a strange thing to ask!' Her brow furrows. 'Why do you want to know that?'

'I just wondered, after you said yesterday that your current boyfriend had "sorted" it. I wondered what that meant exactly.'

My blunt intervention has worked. Jenny's expression changes and now she looks like she's definitely on the back foot.

'Oh, I think it might have stopped.' She releases her grip slowly and dabs at Archie's nose, inspecting the tissue. 'No more fresh blood.'

'What do you say to Jenny for helping?' I prompt Archie.

'Thank you,' he says grudgingly.

'I'll get back now,' she says. 'As you say, we can catch up another time.'

'Hang on, Jenny.' I hand Archie some fresh paper towel. 'Just hold that to your nose, poppet, while I see Jenny out.'

We walk to the door together.

'I didn't mean to sound as if I'm prying,' I say gently. 'I know we've just met, but we seem to get on well and I've been a bit worried about you.'

'Have you?' She blinks. 'Why's that?'

'I didn't like to say, but for a while now I've heard a lot of banging upstairs… and shouting.' She shuffles closer to the door. 'And do you put your phone on the floor when you go to bed?'

Her mouth drops open. She must be wondering if I've got a camera trained on her up there.

'The reason I ask is because often, in the middle of the night, there's what sounds like a phone buzzing, constantly. Again and again, all through the early hours sometimes.'

'You can hear that down here?' She looks up at the ceiling.

'Really clearly.' I nod. 'It must be something to do with the vibration against the floor. I can hear that clearer than anything else… apart from when it sounds like things are being thrown around. Obviously that can be quite loud.'

Two red spots appear on her cheeks.

'I had no idea. I'm sorry. I…'

'I didn't mention it to complain. I just want to make sure you're OK.' I open the door and expect her to bolt out of the flat. But she doesn't.

'Sometimes Mark gets angry.' She's whispering, and I have to lean forward so I can hear. 'He doesn't believe me when I say I'm home, you see. So on the nights he isn't here, he constantly rings at odd hours to try and catch me out.'

I close the door and turn to her. 'You'd better come back through,' I say.

CHAPTER 53

'At first it was flattering, but now he scares me.'

'Let's go and sit in here,' I say gently, and guide her into the living room. 'Please, Jenny, sit down. I'll just sort Archie out.'

A few minutes later, Archie is sitting in front of his Xbox with biscuits and pop, shameful auntie that I am after criticising Louise for doing the same thing.

'When is she going?' he growls. He's so antisocial; no wonder he struggles to make friends at school.

'Soon,' I say, peering at his nose.

Thankfully, he looks OK for now. Apart from the smears of blood on his cheeks.

I sit on the sofa next to Jenny.

'Does Mark hurt you?' I ask.

'No! He's never touched me. Admittedly, he gets angry, throws stuff around, but he's… he's lovely underneath. I think I've got this way of pressing his buttons and he—'

'Oh, please. Don't tell me you've fallen for that one.'

'But it *must* be me. He was so lovely when I met him, so caring. I make him angry because I keep going on about…'

'Yes?'

'About him leaving his wife.'

'I see.'

'Please don't judge me,' she begs. 'I didn't set out to have an affair with him, it just sort of happened. He's a personal trainer at my gym, you see, and about ten years older than me. He just seemed so much more mature than the younger guys... Alice?'

'Sorry, I'm listening. I'm just... thinking about what you've said.'

I feel sick. Martyn's face flashes in my mind. The gym, his temper, the way he used to control my sister... and then I think about the note pushed through my door. He said he'd bide his time and make me pay.

I know I'm being illogical, but it feels like I'm stranded on quicksand.

'He's protective, you see, that's what it is,' Jenny continues. 'He admits it and that's why he went wild when I told him about James finding out where I lived.'

My breath catches in my throat when she says his name, even though I know it's him.

'You said Mark had "sorted" James. What did you mean by that?'

'He just said I wouldn't be having any more trouble from him, but not to ask him any questions about it.' She hangs her head. 'I haven't been looking out of the window so I don't even know if he's still coming past.'

I want to tell her that he isn't watching the flat from the tram any longer, and that I have his phone in my kitchen drawer, but I can't say any of that without going through everything that's happened.

'I'm not allowed to talk about Mark to anyone. He... he wouldn't even like it if he knew I'd come down here for a chat. He doesn't like me having any friends, but I feel so lonely sometimes.'

I try and process this.

'I know how bad it sounds,' Jenny says sadly. 'I know I must seem like a complete idiot to you, but things will get better soon. I just know it.'

'I wouldn't bank on it,' I say. 'He might not physically beat you, but he's controlling you in lots of other ways. Stopping you going out, telling you who you can and can't see, scaring you into silence and insisting you behave as he wants you too. Bet you have to run what you wear past him too, right?'

She looks at her hands.

Bullets fly as Archie pummels his controls and the screen splatters with digitised blood. My mind starts drifting.

Twenty years earlier

That day… the way Mum spun around like a ballerina so that the tasselled red dress flipped out and fluttered prettily around her slim pale legs.

'That one, Mum!' I called out in delight. 'Wear that one tonight.'

Mum's laughter tinkled like a silver bell.

'Yes… definitely that one!' Louise added, dancing around her. 'You look so—'

The bedroom door flew open and we all fell quiet.

'There's an awful din coming from in here,' Dad said, stepping into the room. 'Can I join in the fun?'

Mum stopped spinning.

'Paul… you're home early,' she said faintly.

'Mum's choosing the prettiest dress.' I beamed at him.

'I thought we'd agreed you'd wear the beige maxi dress, darling,' Dad said evenly, loosening his tie.

'Mum says beige is dull and boring,' Louise grumbled. 'But everyone knows that red is bright and exciting!'

'Red is cheap and nasty,' Dad said softly, walking closer. He stared at Mum for a moment. 'Everyone knows that red means available.'

Mum had stopped smiling now and she began to slip the red dress from her shoulders.

'She can wear the red dress this time, though, can't she, Dad?' Louise tried to appeal to him. 'She looks so pretty in it!'

Dad didn't answer. He stared at our mother as if he were in some kind of trance… like a horrid witch had put a spell on him.

'Dad's right,' Mum said quietly. 'I should never have got carried away, trying on all these different outfits. It was silly of me.'

'So why not get your dresses out now, all of them?' Dad said. 'You can try on every single one and we'll tell you which ones you ought to keep and which ones to bin.'

'Oh no, I—'

'Yes, Mum, it'll be just like a fashion show!' Louise exclaimed. So that was what she did.

She tried on every single dress and Dad played the judge and we were the jury, but it was the judge who had the final say each time.

At the end of the afternoon, when Mum was exhausted, Dad had a big bag full of dresses that he took down to the bin, including lots of pretty ones that we loved but he and Mum didn't.

'So which one are you going to wear tonight?' Louise scowled when Mum's favourite red dress was added to the rubbish bag.

'The lovely beige one, as Dad suggested.' Mum smiled at us but her eyes shone with sadness and her voice sounded thin, like it did on the morning she told us Benjy Bunny had died. 'Dad's always right about these things.'

Present day

Jenny coughs.

I look up to find her watching me with a faint frown.

'Sorry…' I try to smile. 'I got caught up in the past for a moment.'

I need to chill out a bit.

She nods. 'I don't want you to get the idea he doesn't love me. It's because he cares that—'

'There's a name for what he's doing to you, Jenny. It's called coercive control and I've seen two people I love caught up in it.'

'Like I say, things will change soon.'

'How can you be so sure?'

She glances at Archie and then smiles, a bloom lighting up her face.

'Because I just found out I'm pregnant!'

CHAPTER 54

When Jenny has left, and before I go back through to Archie in the lounge, I stand at the kitchen window, trying to get my thoughts in order.

Why am I so troubled about the fate of a man who didn't even know I existed until I introduced myself to him in a coffee shop?

I'm making a big drama out of a throwaway comment that some thug – Jenny's boyfriend, Mark – has 'sorted' him. He probably simply threatened him and James has stopped getting the tram, that's all. Not my business.

But why was he visiting a criminal law solicitor in the city? Why did he look afraid in the coffee shop when he was being bombarded by phone calls?

I take James's phone out of the drawer. There's still some charge left on there, but it seems nobody has called or texted him since I turned it back on. He hasn't rung the phone himself to try and trace it, and he hasn't been back to the coffee shop to ask if anyone has handed it in.

Doesn't tell me anything in itself, but put together, it just feels odd. It doesn't sound like normal behaviour.

I can hear Archie shouting at the screen in the lounge, so I gauge I still have a few minutes. I click into the call log again and reach for a piece of paper. When I dial the answerphone, the robotic voice tells me there is one message waiting, dated two days ago. I shiver when I realise the time matches up exactly with when James and I were in the coffee shop. The phone kept ringing and he kept ignoring it, getting jumpier by the second.

I click play to listen to the message and a gruff, rasping voice fills my ear.

'*Last warning. Stay away from her or you're a dead man.*'

There's a click as the call ends. No more messages.

'Auntie Alice,' Archie calls. 'Is tea ready yet?'

My hands are shaking as I shove the phone back in the drawer. Maybe it was an empty threat; people say all sorts of things when they're fired up. I really can't think about this right now. I have to choose where to put my energies: a man I don't even know, or my nephew, who needs me to look out for him.

I turn on the oven and slide a couple of slices of frozen pizza in there. Not the ideal choice for a growing boy, but I forgot Louise was bringing him over this evening so I didn't think about tea. It just occurs to me she didn't even say whether he's staying over or whether she'll pick him up later.

'Tea's on, Archie,' I say as I walk into the lounge. 'Can we pause the game, just for a minute?'

A request like that would have had him kicking off big style just a week ago. Now, it merits a little huff before he presses the pause button and lays down his controls.

'How's the nose?' I say, peering at his face when he sits down next to me.

'It's OK.'

'So, what happened last night? How come you hurt your head?'

He pulls down the corners of his mouth. 'I wasn't playing football like you told that lady. I don't like her.'

'No, I guessed you weren't. But she doesn't need to know that. Why don't you like her?'

He doesn't elaborate, so I try another approach.

'Who was home when you hurt yourself?'

'Mum and Dad were both there, but they were in the other room, arguing.' His knee starts jiggling up and down.

I can hear my own breathing.

It feels like I'm prying, like I'm questioning my nephew in an underhand way that would make Louise hit the roof if she were here… But she's not here, and this is important.

While Louise and Darren have obviously got their own relationship problems that they're trying to sort out, someone needs to be looking out for Archie.

'Do you know what they were arguing about, your mum and dad?'

'I'm not sure,' he says quickly.

I put my finger under his chin until he turns to look at me. 'I'm your auntie, right?'

He grins. 'I know that, silly!'

'I *know* you know that.' I nudge him playfully. 'I also want you to know that your auntie will never get you into trouble. You can tell me anything, OK? You don't have to get through stuff alone. That's what I'm saying.'

He nods, but stays quiet.

'Archie, how did you hurt your head?'

He sniffs.

I wait.

'There was shouting and Mum got mad…' He shakes his head as if he's trying to stop the pictures from coming. 'Dad tried to…' He covers his ears with his hands and closes his eyes, and his voice becomes quiet. 'Mum pushed me hard and I fell over.' He touches his right temple.

'And that's when you hit your head?'

He nods. 'On the side of the worktop. My nose was OK at first, but then it started to bleed.'

I part his hair gently in a few places but he doesn't seem to be cut.

'And then she told you not to mention it to your teacher this morning?'

He looks at the frozen television screen, his fingers fidgeting against each other. 'She said they might try and take me away.'

I swallow down the rising fury clogging up my throat.

'All right then. Well, have ten more minutes on your game and then I've recorded us a programme about the Egyptian pyramids to watch, if you fancy that?'

'Cool!' He beams.

I stand up to go and check on the pizza and he grabs my hand.

'They were arguing about stuff and Mum said if he didn't stop, she was going to leave him and take me with her.'

His features look drawn and pale.

'And what did your dad say to that?' I ask him softly.

'Nothing.' Archie looks away. 'He just sat and cried.'

'I'm sorry you had to witness that, Archie.'

I sit back down and hold him in my arms, but he doesn't get upset, he just sits there stiffly as if he's enduring my affection.

'I can't tell you any more,' he whispers so faintly I almost miss it.

'There's more?' I sit back, my hands on his shoulders, and look at him. He shakes his head.

'That's everything.' He's looking not *at* me but *through* me, lost in his own thoughts. 'Apart from the secret. And I can't tell anybody that.'

CHAPTER 55

Three years earlier

I took a few tentative steps down the corridor towards Jim. His forehead patterned with a frown and his mouth was opening and closing, but all I could hear were my own tortured thoughts.

I have to do this. My career will never recover if I let them down. It's just an hour… that's all. Nothing is going to change in an hour.

I took a deep breath, threw my shoulders back and stopped biting down on my back teeth. Jim smiled faintly as relief flooded his face and the frown dissolved.

I can do this. I have to do this for myself and for Jack. I've worked so hard to get here.

But when the gap between us was no more than three or four feet, I stopped walking, and Mum's face flashed into my mind.

Darren called to take her shopping and found her on the kitchen floor. They think it's a heart attack.

For a moment, I saw her, prostrate and alone on the floor in her enormous dated kitchen with its free-standing cooker and the same scratched oak table we sat at as kids.

They've taken her to the Trent Cardiology Centre at the City Hospital. 'I'm sorry, Jim.' I coughed as the words caught in my throat. 'I have to go.'

'What? I knew it!' Jim's face flushed scarlet. 'I could see there was something wrong, you standing here in the corridor like this.'

'I'm sorry, Jim. It's my mum… she's… not well. I have to…'

He stepped closer to me and placed his hands on my upper arms.

'Alice, please. Just stop and listen for a moment. Breathe, that's it.' He squeezed my arms lightly. 'I'm sorry to hear your mum isn't well, I really am. But this is your career, it's about the rest of your life. Finn thinks a lot of you, and if you do a good job in there, your progression in the company is secured. I know you want this.'

Jim had spent hours talking me into believing I could do the job, that I was more than capable. He'd been brilliant and selfless with his time, and now, the guilt I felt about disappointing him entwined with my overwhelming guilt about choosing the job above Mum.

'I do want this, I really do,' I whispered. 'But I couldn't live with myself if something happened to Mum and I wasn't there… She's all alone in the hospital; they think she might have had a heart attack.'

A tear trickled down my cheek and I left it to carve a neat trail in the perfect make-up I'd applied earlier.

'What about your sister?'

I shook my head. 'I've just tried to reason with her on the phone, but she can't get out of an important work meeting.'

Jim's mouth set in a grim line.

'Yet she expects you to walk away from what is potentially the most important interview in your career so far?'

'You know Louise.' I shrugged.

He didn't know Louise personally, of course. But he knew she worked for the PR company and her name had frequently come up when Jim had counselled me about nurturing confidence in my abilities at work.

In one conversation just a few weeks earlier, he had asked who it was who'd done such a good job of undermining me all these years, and I'd replied that nobody had. I told him my parents had been supportive; that they had always encouraged me to believe I could achieve anything if I put my mind to it.

But Jim hadn't been fooled. He'd kept prodding, foraging for more.

'What about siblings… have you any other brothers or sisters?'

'Just Louise,' I'd replied faintly, and just like that, a memory I'd turned my back on long ago surfaced with a vengeance.

I'd openly shrugged it away; it was just a silly childhood remnant that had no business coming back in a work situation. But there was no fooling Jim.

'Tell me about it,' he'd urged me.

Reluctantly, I'd relayed the story of the school Christmas nativity when I was just seven years old.

'Mum and Dad were so proud when the class teacher, Mrs Jephson, chose me to play Mary. It was a pretty big deal back then!'

I beamed and then caught myself. What an idiot Jim must think me.

'Sounds great. You know, it's exactly those kinds of achievements and milestones that have made me and Jean proudest of our kids over the years. Definitely a big deal.'

'Well, that was until Louise convinced me I would make a dreadful mess of it, embarrassing myself and our parents.'

'And how exactly did she convince you of this?'

I thought for a moment, surprising myself with the sudden clarity of the realisation.

'You know, looking back, I guess she kind of worked at it. Conjuring up terrible, believable scenes where I'd forget my lines against a backdrop of disapproving silence and Mum's mortified face in the front row. Or I might fall off stage to the raucous laughter of the audience and the whole school would be there to witness it.' I shuddered. 'She'd run through the awful possibilities every night before bed and as soon as we woke up each morning.'

'From the look on your face, she did a very good job. You still seem haunted by the story even now.'

'I've never thought of it like that, but I think I might be.' I nodded vaguely and then shook myself, laughing. 'Anyway, how did we even get onto this nonsense?'

'One more question.' Jim raised an index finger. 'Louise is three years older than you, right?' I nodded. 'So, had she been a roaring success on the school stage before you? Is that how she got to be such an expert?'

'That's just it, she wasn't! She would have loved to act in a lead role, but despite being a confident girl, as soon as she got on stage, her legs always turned to jelly. So the teachers stopped giving her decent roles. Her jealousy didn't make any sense.'

Jim smiled. 'I think, if you mull our conversation over in a quiet moment, you'll find it makes perfect sense. Even today.'

'Alice?' Jim waved a hand in front of me now and I snapped back to the awful reality and the choice I had to make.

Mum was alone in hospital and a panel of extremely senior investors were sitting just feet away from where Jim and I now stood, with the power to hand me the job of my dreams.

I swallowed hard. 'I'm sorry, Jim. You've been so supportive, but I have to go and see my mum.'

Jim's lined face looked strained, pale. 'I give you my word, the second the interview is over, I'll drive you back to Nottingham myself. You'll be there no later than…' he consulted his watch, 'twelve thirty, one o'clock tops. Your mum is in the best hands; they've probably sedated her, so she'll be none the wiser that you're not there. What do you say?'

I looked at this man who'd put himself on the line to back me against the opinion of the board, who probably didn't believe I was experienced enough.

And then I thought about my poor mum, lying in a hospital bed, afraid and alone. Wondering why nobody in her own family cared enough to be there for her.

'Sorry, Jim,' I said, turning around to head in the opposite direction. 'I've no choice but to go.'

CHAPTER 56

Three years earlier

I tore off my jacket, threw it onto the back seat and jumped into the car.

I was boiling hot but I couldn't stop shaking. Driving out of the car park, I called Jack on hands-free. No answer.

I pulled over and texted him instead.

Call me when you can. Mum's been taken into hospital. On my way back to Nottm xx

How could everything turn upside down in a matter of minutes?

I felt sick with worry. I couldn't believe Darren hadn't gone to the hospital with her, at least until someone else could take over. Whether Archie was there or not, we all owed Mum, and it broke my heart that she was there alone right now.

I couldn't even bring myself to think about Louise. At that precise moment I felt like I could happily never set eyes on her again. Accusing me of being heartless in putting work before family and then merrily skipping off to her own job while Mum was possibly in a critical condition.

The M1 was predictably busy, but the car was still moving and for that I felt grateful. I was on my way and that was what mattered.

I drove in a kind of focused trance. All I could think about was being there for Mum when she woke up.

The speaker blared out with Jack's return call and tipped me into the moment again.

'Alice? I just got your text. What the hell happened?'

'Mum had a fall.' I suppressed a sob. 'Louise rang and said I had to come back to be with her at the hospital.'

'So you didn't have your interview? You were about to go in when we last texted.'

'No. Louise refused to hold the fort until I could get there. I had to leave the panel hanging.'

I heard Jack mutter something angrily under his breath.

'OK, give me the ward details and I'll meet you at the hospital.'

I breathed out with relief at the realisation that I didn't have to face this alone and gave him the details of where Mum had been taken.

'I'm about halfway back now, so I should be there in around thirty minutes or so.' I sniffed.

'I'll meet you outside the ward,' he said. 'And Alice?'

'Yes?'

'I love you.'

'Love you too,' I croaked before ending the call and dissolving into a pit of grief.

I felt like I'd never stop the tears, but I dabbed my eyes with a tissue and forced myself to focus on the road. I knew I needed to keep my wits about me or there could be another one of us in hospital.

I parked up at the hospital and rushed inside.

Jack was waiting as promised. I fell into his arms, sobbing.

'I tried to find out how she was, but they won't tell me anything as I'm not family,' Jack said.

Jim was right. Mum was heavily sedated and hadn't a clue that she'd been alone.

'We'll keep her that way a while longer,' the doctor said. 'The best thing you can do is go home and get some rest. Someone will call you when your mother is awake.'

I wouldn't go. I couldn't. We sat there for hours. A couple of times I fell asleep on Jack's shoulder but jerked awake again the second there was a nearby noise. The lack of sleep the night before my interview was taking its toll.

After four hours of waiting, I finally took Jack's advice to go home.

'You're too tired to drive,' he said. 'Leave the car here and we'll get a cab back to yours.'

'I'm fine,' I said stubbornly. 'I want the car so I can come straight away if they call.'

Jack hadn't passed his driving test. We'd talked about me showing him the basics but hadn't got around to it yet.

'Alice, seriously. You look whacked.'

'I am tired, but it's only a fifteen-minute drive. Stop fussing.'

After ensuring the doctor had the correct phone numbers, I allowed Jack to lead me out to the car.

It was quite a walk back to the car park, and I felt so exhausted, I could have happily lain down on the grass verge and nodded off. But I kept putting one foot in front of the other and eventually the car came into view.

'Last chance,' Jack said cautiously, as if I might snap his head off. 'There's a cab with its light on over there, look.'

I followed his eyes to a green Hackney cab, the driver looking hopeful we might hail him.

'I'm fine,' I said again, and the car's sidelights flashed as I unlocked it.

And that was it. The worst decision in my life had been made.

CHAPTER 57

Three years earlier

Jack knew I wasn't quite right. He kept talking to me, telling me everything was going to be just fine.

But I wasn't listening.

And I wasn't focusing on the road.

I took my eyes off it just for a second or two… and that was when it happened.

A car coming the other way, appearing out of nowhere… I swerved to avoid it and we hit a tree.

Jack died at the scene and I suffered concussion and lower back injuries.

Two seconds.

That was all it took.

CHAPTER 58

I haven't got kids, have never worked with kids, don't hang around with friends who have kids. So I guess it follows that I probably don't know that much about kids.

Yet the moment Archie mentioned a secret, I instinctively knew that, instead of interrogating him, I needed to bite down on my tongue and give him space.

Trying to force a kid to tell something they've been specifically told *not* to is probably the worst thing you can do in terms of risking them internalising it and maybe even blaming themselves for whatever it is that's happening in their life.

I won't go down that path, but I can't just ignore it either.

I call Louise's phone, but it's turned off.

So I call Darren. It rings for so long without cutting to answerphone that I'm about to end the call, but at last he answers.

'Hi, Alice. How are you? To what do I owe this honour?' he jokes.

I briefly explain what's happened.

'You have Archie there? I thought Louise was taking him to football practice tonight.'

Football practice? He seems to have no clue about what's happening with Archie and Louise when he's out of the house. It seems she's deliberately misleading him.

'I'll come over,' he offers right away. 'I literally just walked in from work, though, so give me half an hour to get changed and grab a sandwich.'

I end the call and put Archie's pizza slices on a plate with a sliced tomato and a few carrot batons.

'What's that?' He pokes at the carrot.

'It's called a *carrot*, Archie. It grows in the ground.'

He laughs.

'Seriously, you need some fresh food in your life, not just takeaway crap. There's some fruit salad for pudding.'

'Whoopee,' he says, without enthusiasm.

'And… just so you know, your dad will be over later.'

He puts down the slice of pizza he's holding and looks at me.

'Nothing for you to worry about. I just want to make sure he takes you to the doctor's to check out your head.'

'You promised you wouldn't say anything.' He forces the words out from between clenched teeth. 'You *promised*.'

'I'm not going to repeat what you told me, Archie. I gave you my word and I meant it, but there are certain things we can't ignore. Now, eat your pizza.'

He pushes the plate away. 'I'm not hungry any more.'

Darren arrives within the hour.

He kisses me on the cheek and then rushes straight through to the lounge.

'Are you OK, mate? Auntie Alice says you had another nosebleed.'

'I'm fine,' Archie says, keeping his eyes on the television. 'I kept telling her I'm fine.'

'I told you, you're not in any trouble, Archie,' I say from behind Darren. 'We just need to make sure your head is OK, that's all.'

'That's right, champ. How are you feeling?'

'Fine,' Archie says. 'Auntie Alice is just making a fuss, Dad.'

'There was quite a lot of blood, Archie!' I defend myself before speaking again to Darren. 'And my upstairs neighbour was here, so when Archie said he'd hit his head but hadn't been to the doctor's, I felt a bit—'

'I didn't tell her anything, Dad,' Archie says, his voice quivering.

Is he referring to me or to Jenny? The fear on his face tears me apart inside.

'Hey.' Darren walks over to him, sits beside him and puts his arm around his shoulders. 'What am I always telling you, eh? You're not in any trouble. This is not your fault, so chill out, right?'

'Right.' Archie nods and Darren affectionately presses the boy's head to his shoulder before standing up and looking at me meaningfully, tucking his T-shirt into his jeans.

'Got a minute?'

'Let's go in the kitchen,' I say.

Once we're in there and he's out of Archie's eyesight, Darren seems to deflate like a balloon. Over coffee, he enlightens me about a situation far worse than I imagined.

'Louise has lost the plot and I don't know what to do about it.' He hangs his head and worry lines pool around his features. 'She seems to get angrier by the day, often with Archie. And her drinking is out of control. I caught her pouring vodka into her lunchtime water bottle the other day.'

I don't mention the bottle of vodka I found in her bag.

'This can't go on.' I give him a pained look. 'Archie is a nervous wreck, you can see it in his face.'

Darren nods gravely. 'And as if all this isn't enough, yesterday I found out something else that tops it all. It came to a head last night and that's why she kicked off big time.'

'She's having an affair as you suspected?'

Darren shakes his head. 'I still suspect that, but this is more damaging in its own way because of its potential to threaten our livelihood, our home. She's got badly in debt, signed loans on our property. Worse still, she faked my signature.'

'Why would she do that?' I gasp. 'What does she need the money for?'

'I asked her exactly that, but she was so angry with me I couldn't get a word of sense out of her. I confess I'd searched her desk drawer in the home office and I'm not proud of that – but I was desperate, Alice. I've known for some time that things were going badly wrong, but so far she's refused to discuss it with me.'

'Do you think she's amassing funds to start a new life?' I say, feeling disloyal to Louise, despite the worsening situation.

'Maybe that's it, I don't know.' He sounds defeated. 'I never wanted the big house, the SUV, the exotic holidays, but I stretched our finances and worked extra hours to get it all so Louise was happy. Now every penny of what we earn is accounted for but she's already tired of what we have.'

'So she refused to talk about the loans?'

Darren nodded. 'She just blew up, threatened to leave and take Archie with her. You know that would kill me, right?'

'I'm sorry, Darren. It must have felt awful to hear her say that.'

He falls silent. Archie told me how upset his dad had been. I could throttle Louise for what she's doing to them both.

'Archie said… Louise pushed him and he fell over and hit his head.'

I feel like I know too much about their private lives. It's awkward, to say the least, but it needs raising.

'She did.' Darren is clearly devastated. 'I'm his dad and I just stood there while she made him promise not to breathe a word to anyone. What kind of a man does that make me?'

'A confused one. A very worried one, and there's no shame in that.' I lay my hand on his arm. 'Don't blame yourself for this, Darren, but you know you can't let it go on.'

'I know,' he whispers. 'People are going to start noticing… sounds like your neighbour has already heard more than she should. If school get wind of problems at home, we could end up losing Archie. I…' His voice cracks and he covers his face with his hands.

'Thankfully it hasn't got to that stage yet. We can try and sort it all out now before there are serious implications. Don't worry about Jenny upstairs: she's OK, and she's busy with her own problems anyway. She's probably already forgotten about it. But people at school are bound to start drawing conclusions if Archie's disruptive home life continues.'

He hesitates before speaking.

'I wondered if… I thought… Oh, forget it. It's a stupid idea and you don't need the hassle.'

'Go on,' I urge him. 'If I can help, I will, you know that.'

'I wondered if *you* could have a word with Louise.' He holds up a hand when he sees my face drop. 'Just test the water, see if you can make a bit of headway, because she sure as hell won't listen to a word I say.'

I think about Louise's legendary temper, her scathing put-downs and the fact that I'm getting closer to my nephew. I don't want that contact cut off. At the same time, I have to put Archie first.

'All I can do is try,' I tell him.

CHAPTER 59

I fire off a text to Louise to ask if Archie is staying over or if she'll be picking him up later.

The curt reply comes about ten minutes after Darren has left. *Will pick him up about 9. L*

Darren left it to me to ask Archie not to mention that his dad was here. I feel awful asking him not to say anything; it seems almost as bad as Louise telling him not to mention his head injury and nosebleed to his teacher.

I desperately wanted to ask Darren about the 'secret' Archie had mentioned to me, but it was a fine line I was trying to tread, trying to protect my nephew without getting him into trouble. Kids are kids and it's possible it's not a worrying kind of secret at all.

Still, I have more things to fret about now. I glance at the clock and see that I've got about an hour before Louise arrives.

'Can we watch the Egyptian programme now, Auntie Alice?' Archie asks me.

My heart sinks. I'd forgotten about that, but it only lasts for half an hour and I suppose I can just zone out while it's on instead of pacing up and down waiting for Louise to get here.

It sounds as if her temper has reached a whole new level now, and that's got to be addressed, especially if she's taking it out on Archie.

She's always been a bit snappy, even when she was really young, and she has a habit of speaking before she thinks, but

I've been able to deal with that by reminding myself what she's been through.

Ten years earlier

When she fell pregnant with Archie within three months of meeting Martyn, I sat down with her to tell Mum.

If Dad had still been alive, Louise would really have had something to worry about, but after he died, nothing much seemed to faze Mum any more. In fact, when we got home after his funeral, I remember her standing in the middle of the kitchen, closing her eyes and just exhaling for what seemed like an age.

Then she walked over to the worktop and emptied out the contents of her handbag, before turning the tap on full, allowing water to spatter everywhere.

Louise and I had exchanged glances.

When Mum opened the cupboard doors and mussed up all the tidy front-facing tins, I spoke up.

'Mum, why are you doing all this? Are you feeling OK?'

She turned to us both then and smiled. She looked as though someone had rubbed a wrinkle eraser around her eyes and mouth. Her skin was brighter. She looked ten years younger.

'I'm feeling great and I'm doing it for the best reason on earth,' she replied. '*Because I can.*'

Then, on the day she had buried her husband and our father, she threw her head back and laughed.

So when Louise broke the news that she was pregnant, Mum simply shook her head.

'Of all the men out there, you chose him to father your child?' She looked sad.

'I want you to be happy for us, Mum.' Louise started crying and I sat there feeling hopeless, unable to help the two people I cared most about in the world.

'You grew up watching how your father behaved,' Mum said softly as she reached for my sister's hand. 'I didn't want the same for you, darling.'

But her words inflamed Louise. 'Martyn is a good man, Mum. He loves me… loves our baby. He'll be a wonderful father.'

She aimed a warning glance at me and I duly bit down on my tongue. Mum wouldn't hear the awful truth from me about Martyn's reaction to the baby news, that was for my sister to tell her. It was still early days in terms of the baby – Louise was only eight weeks gone – but the more pregnant she became, the more Martyn's lack of interest in her became evident.

I'd been doing a bit of digging on him, and to say that the stuff I'd found out was worrying was an understatement.

I couldn't decide what to do about it. Stress Louise out while she was pregnant or let her continue in this fictitious world of Martyn's that she believed unquestioningly?

If I told Mum, she'd worry herself sick and blurt it out at the first opportunity.

One evening, Mum felt unwell for no apparent reason and had already gone up to bed. We didn't know at the time, but it was probably an early sign of what was to come.

Louise had said there was some kind of problem at their flat, and she and Martyn had decided to stay at ours for the night. I said goodnight and left them watching television, retiring early for the evening myself.

The stuff I had found out about him without really trying too hard at all – details that Louise could have readily discovered for herself had she had the curiosity and the inclination – prevented me from sitting in the same room as him, forced to buy the verbal diarrhoea that spewed so effortlessly from his mouth.

But I had an annoying tickly cough that disturbed my reading, and so after about twenty minutes, I padded downstairs barefoot for a glass of water.

I froze at the bottom of the stairs at the sound of Martyn's vicious words.

'I'll tell you one final time. Get rid of it or I'm out of here.'

I heard Louise stifle a sob.

'It's our baby. *Ours.*' Her voice sounded thin and tortured. 'I can't just—'

'You *can* and you've got no choice. If you care about us at all, that is.'

When Louise spoke next, I knew she'd gathered some of her gumption again.

'It's my body and my choice, Martyn. Don't try and bully me into doing this, because I'll go ahead and have the baby alone if I need to.'

My bare feet shifted uneasily on the cool wooden floor outside the living room. There were a few moments of silence when nobody spoke but the air held a kind of dreadful weight, even out here.

Then I heard Louise gasp and give a soft cry of pain.

I didn't think about it; I just pushed open the door and stormed into the room.

'Leave her alone!'

He was bent over her, his fingers digging into the soft flesh of her wrist, and he'd twisted her arm round the wrong way.

He immediately let go, the element of surprise catching him out.

'Get away from her!'

'Alice… it's fine. Go back to bed,' Louise pleaded.

'Yeah, and mind your own business,' Martyn snapped.

Every nerve ending in my body was on red alert. My fear and wish to avoid confrontation melted away in the white heat that burned when I saw how he was treating my sister.

'Mind my own business? I wish I had, but it's too late for that now, Martyn. I know some things about you that Louise might be very interested in.'

'What? Shut your filthy mouth. You know *nothing* about me.'

'Really? I know that your fancy duplex apartment never belonged to you at all but to the man you rent your gym building from.'

That had been a stroke of luck. I'd visited the apartment building after Louise had willingly given me the address early in their relationship to show that Martyn was a man of means. I'd waited until someone left the building and held the door open for me, and then I'd gone up to the fourth-floor apartment and waited.

It was my lucky day. When a tall, well-dressed man came out and I said I was looking for Martyn Hardy, the person who lived here, he'd laughed.

'He stayed here one night while I was away, wanted to impress a woman, he said.' He looked at me. 'That was before he fell behind with his rent on the gym. You seem like a nice girl. My advice is to stay away from him. He's bad news.'

'Don't listen to her.' Martyn sat down next to Louise and reached for her hand.

'I googled your name and got an online newspaper report about your bankruptcy hearing. It was that easy.'

'The online stuff is all lies!' Louise glared at me. 'It's not true, is it, Martyn? You wouldn't do that… Dad's inheritance… I—'

'Of course it's not true. She's jealous… pure poison.'

'You've given him your half of Dad's money? He's been tried twice for fraud, Louise. For cheating people out of their savings. The second time, he was convicted.'

Martyn shot me a look of undiluted hatred and then stood up, all six-foot-something of him, towering over a cowering Louise, his face puce with rage.

'You stupid bitch, you've ruined everything.' He raised his index finger and pointed at me.

'Martyn…' Louise's voice was scarcely more than a whisper. 'Tell me it's not true. Tell me Alice is mistaken. You said they'd lied, that—'

'There's no mistake, Louise,' I said sadly. 'There are no investors, no franchise deal. Your fiancé is stony broke.'

Louise touched his arm and he turned and raised his hand to her.

'Leave her alone,' I hissed, stepping forward and looking as fearsome as I possibly could in the hope he wouldn't see me shaking. 'I'll help Louise, she doesn't need *you*. And when the baby is born, I'll help her come after you for maintenance. This baby wasn't just her mistake; you had a part in it too.'

His nose wrinkled as he tried in vain to mask his fury.

'Now you listen to me.' He looked straight at me as he issued his chilling threat. 'I will make you pay for ruining our relationship. It might not be now, or next week, or next year. But one day it will happen, of that you can be certain.'

Then he turned and thundered out of the house, slamming the front door so hard, one of the two opaque panes of glass cracked from top to bottom.

My sister sat shaking and crying. Terrified of him but wanting him to come back and tell her everything was going to be OK.

It was just like watching Mum with Dad all over again.

What I never expected, years later, was for Louise herself to exhibit those very same traits with her own husband and son.

CHAPTER 60

Louise

Ten years earlier

The months after Martyn left felt like a wilderness to Louise.

The initial three-month tenancy agreement had lapsed on their flat and so she moved back home. Her mother and sister were waiting at the door to welcome her back, but that only served to make her feel even more of a failure.

For the first few weeks she was convinced that Martyn would come to his senses, realise what he'd lost. In her dreams, they would reconcile and find a way to sweep up the fractured pieces of their lives together.

Every time there was a knock at the door, every time the phone rang or a strange car parked outside the house, her heart leapt thinking it might be him.

But it never was. He never contacted her again and that was the thing Louise found hardest to bear.

She asked Alice to drop by the gym, see if he was around.

'It was all shut up, no notice of closure or anything,' Alice told her when she got back.

One day, in a weak moment, she texted him.

Can we talk? L x

But the text never delivered. She tried ringing him, but a detached robotic voice informed her the number had been discontinued.

'Good riddance to him,' her mother said when she found Louise crying over old photographs on her phone. 'You should thank your lucky stars. I expect he'll have found some other gullible fool to pay his bills by now.'

'Mum, honestly!' Alice sat down next to her and slid her arm around Louise's shoulders. 'It will get better. And you've got a wonderful thing happening in your life soon. Try and focus on that.'

But when Louise looked down at her bump, the pain in her heart increased threefold.

Nine years earlier

The day Archie was born, she fought exhaustion and forced herself to stay awake for hours, just in case Martyn had somehow heard he had a son and turned up at the hospital.

But there was no sign of him.

She lay on the maternity ward and looked at her son in the Perspex cot next to her. So tiny, defenceless and utterly perfect.

'I'll look after you, Archie,' she told him, her face swollen and wet with tears. 'We'll make a life together, just you and me.'

Once she'd made the vow, she felt stronger.

Meeting Martyn Hardy and believing his lies had been the biggest mistake of her life, but all was not lost. Louise had learned a valuable lesson.

She felt different, as if some of the warmth inside her had turned to impenetrable ice.

She would never make the same mistake again.

The last thing she needed in her life was a man. She was done with them.

CHAPTER 61

Alice

Archie bounces up and down, infected with enthusiasm from the programme about Ancient Egypt we just watched together. There's no evidence he feels unwell from the bump to his head or the nosebleeds.

I didn't see much of the programme. I was too busy thinking through what I was going to say to my sister. But I put on a good show and Archie is under the impression I've enjoyed it too.

'Our alphabet has twenty-six letters and the Egyptian alphabet had more than SEVEN HUNDRED hieroglyphs!' Archie grips his temples dramatically with the enormity of the idea.

'Yes, so spare a thought for schoolboys back then trying to learn to write,' I laugh.

Magnus saunters in and Archie bows low in front of him. 'Cats were sacred animals to the Ancient Egyptians. Sorry I pulled your tail, Pharaoh Magnus.'

The cat brushes against his legs and Archie strokes his head. They've come to some kind of truce over the last couple of weeks.

'And can you remember how long the bandages of an Egyptian mummy would stretch for if you laid them out?' I quiz him on the one fact I did manage to retain during the programme.

'Erm… I think it's a very long way!'

'Correct. One point six kilometres, to be precise.'

I glance at the wall clock. Louise will be here soon.

Archie grabs his school scarf from the arm of the chair and rolls up his sleeve.

'I'm going to be an Egyptian mummy,' he declares.

I leave him to it, tidying up plates and cups around him. Anything to keep busy.

'Have you got any more scarves, Auntie Alice?' he asks. 'Or bandages perhaps? Then I could do my whole body.'

I look over at him. The school scarf is wrapped around his forearm and he has rolled his jumper further up so more arm is exposed.

He turns around, and that's when I see them.

A row of perfect fingertip-shaped bruises that encircle his upper arm.

By the time Louise arrives, I've taken pictures of Archie's arm on my phone and also called Darren.

He offered to come over so we could speak to Louise together, but he sounded so baffled and shocked about the bruising, I said I was happy to do it.

'I can't believe I haven't seen it,' he kept saying. 'I feel like I've failed him.'

I assured him they are easy marks to cover up with a sleeve, but it does concern me that Darren is out of touch with his son. He was under the impression Archie had been football training, after all. Anyone who remotely knows Archie would be aware of his aversion to football. Darren obviously needs to step up the time they spend together.

I didn't say any of that on the phone. There are far more important issues at stake.

Archie sits on the sofa now, subdued and staring at the television screen. Soon as he realised I'd seen the marks, he pulled down his sleeve and clamped his mouth shut.

When I insisted, he allowed me to take the photographs, but he wouldn't answer any of my questions about who had hurt him.

'Do you want a drink or a biscuit?' I ask him, but he just shakes his head.

The door entry buzzer sounds and Archie jumps. He wraps his arms around himself and backs into the corner of the seat as if he's trying to make himself smaller.

I open the door and she sweeps past me without saying hello.

'Lift dead AGAIN!' She kicks off her four-inch heels and shrinks to my own height. 'This bloody place drives me nuts.'

She looks frazzled. Hair less styled, lipstick worn off, eyes a bit wild.

It feels strange to look at her not as my sister, who I know inside out, but as someone who I'm not sure I trust any more.

'Why are you looking at me like that?'

'Come through to the kitchen,' I say.

When the door buzzer sounded, I turned the television back on for Archie and reassured him nothing bad would happen, I just needed to talk to his mum in the kitchen when she arrived.

He looked relieved more than concerned and stretched out on the sofa to watch a replay of a Harry Hill comedy show.

'Where's Archie?'

'He's in the lounge, Louise, he's fine. But I need to speak to you before you go in there.'

'What's up?' She punches her hands onto her hips and glares at me.

But I'm not going to be silenced. Not tonight.

'Someone is hurting Archie,' I say.

'Rubbish! Don't start all this again. Listen—'

'No… you listen! He's got a ring of bruises on the top of his arm.'

It's hard to tell with her make-up but she looks to have paled.

'He's probably done it at school.'

'*He* hasn't done anything. Someone has grabbed him hard enough to bruise his flesh.'

'Another kid, then.'

'Maybe. Although kids tend to thump or kick, don't they? It seems more of an adult thing to me.'

'Who then… a teacher?'

She's trying hard to cast doubt on my suspicions, but I'm not having it.

'You know, I'm finding it unsettling to hear you speak about your son in such a casual way.'

'Don't you—' She catches herself as her voice starts to rise. 'Don't you get all Miss High and Mighty with me, Alice. He's my son, so you can keep your nose out.'

'I've no intention of keeping my nose out. Especially when you pushed him hard enough so that he fell and hit his head last night. And he had his second nosebleed here, in front of my neighbour.'

'It was an accident.' She sits on a stool. 'Darren and I, we had an argument and… It was just an accident.'

'Then why did you tell him to keep it quiet from his teacher? And why hasn't he been checked out at the doctor's?'

She stares at me, but not in a challenging way. Her usually straight shoulders are sagging a little and she's digging her nails into her palms.

When she speaks, her voice is calm, measured.

'Alice, there are things you don't know. Things happening you don't want to know about, trust me.'

If only she knew that I'm more than aware of what's been happening.

'I have something to ask you. Something utterly enormous that I've hinted at, but now the time has come to say it outright.'

This knocks me off guard.

Is she going to ask me for help? To look after Archie for a while because she can't cope?

'What is it?'

'It's about this place.'

I'm struggling to believe that in the middle of discussing her son's injuries, she chooses to even attempt to discuss money.

I was Mum's carer for the two years she was virtually bedridden. Rightly or wrongly, we never discussed money, but I was aware that Mum had bought the flat outright when she sold our family home. Most of the surplus went on home care and medical bills.

When she died, as expected she left the flat equally to us both, but neither of us had expected the provision that, in acknowledgement of my care of her, it would only be sold as and when I wanted to move out. She'd also left me a modest sum to compensate for not working.

'Don't move out on our account,' Louise said airily at the time. 'We don't need the money.'

I could tell she was miffed but I felt relieved she'd accepted Mum's wishes.

'The selling price of this hole has rocketed, although I can't imagine why,' she says now. 'A two-bedroom went last month for two hundred grand, so this three-bed will get even more.'

'But I've got to live somewhere,' I say. 'And I'm not ready to move for the foreseeable. I feel... safe here.'

'We could find you somewhere else just as nice, better, in fact. I'd go with you to view. What do you say?'

'Sorry.' I find something to do at the sink. 'It's not an option right now.'

'Arrrggh!'

She smashes her hands down on the worktop. Her face is bright red and her eyes wide.

'For goodness' sake,' I rush over. 'Calm down! You're going to have a heart attack at this rate.'

'I'm under so much pressure, you would not believe it.' Her voice is low. Dangerous. 'I need you to do this. If you knew what was happening behind the scenes, you'd agree to it like a shot.'

But I do know what is happening behind the scenes. Darren has discovered her fraudulent loan applications and she's been caught out. And now, instead of taking accountability and being a fit wife and mother, she is pressuring *me* to get her out of a mess.

'Know what I think? I think you're a selfish, uncaring person who's only interested in herself.' She opens her mouth to defend herself, but I carry on. 'I really wanted to give you the benefit of the doubt, do you know that? But now I know. You're not a fit mother to that boy.'

'No! You're wrong. Alice, please…'

'I've heard enough,' I say. 'You can leave now, but I want you to know I'll be going to see Archie's teacher first thing in the morning to tell her what I know. I have no choice.'

CHAPTER 62

Louise

She never stopped missing Martyn, but in the years that followed, she rekindled her interest in digging into his past, discovering undisputable evidence that he was a cheat, a crook and an outright liar.

She often looked at her son and wondered how she'd tell him one day. Thank goodness, that day was a long time in the future yet.

If only she'd listened to that voice in her head a little longer when they were together. If only she had delved a little deeper… It was all there for the finding in the search results she'd printed off and the subsequent pages online.

If only she'd listened to her mum and sister's concerns, she'd never have lost all her dad's inheritance to Martyn Hardy's empty promises.

If only… if only… if only. It was the soundtrack to her life.

Five years earlier

The magazines and women's fiction Louise read seemed solely concerned with how to meet the ideal man.

Despite her promise to herself that she was done with men, she was desperately lonely.

Online dating, shopping at the supermarket after work, trying new hobbies… the list of ways to meet a partner that the magazines recommended went on. Louise had heard it all and largely ignored it.

It wasn't her idea of fun to go out actively hunting.

'I'll just have to resign myself to growing old alone and taking in stray cats or something,' she'd giggled with the girls in the office, but when they'd gone back to their own desks, her smile had faded.

So when her fifteen-year-old Ford broke down on her way to a conference in the middle of Derbyshire, the last person she expected to meet was her future husband.

The car had spluttered to a stop on a country lane. There was a field with cows on one side and a dry-stone wall that formed a boundary on a sparse patch of woodland on the other.

'Damn it!' Louise cursed, banging the steering wheel with the heels of her hands.

The car had been exhibiting signs for the last week that all wasn't well. The engine had been hiccuping and stalling from time to time, while the temperature gauge, although not sky high, had crept up above what it usually read.

She had ignored all this, mindful of the fact that she was still ten days away from payday and her credit card had been maxed out for months.

She turned the key in the ignition a few times, but it sounded hoarse, like Archie last month when he'd picked up a chest infection from nursery school.

She grabbed her phone and let out a groan when she looked at the screen. No service.

Opening the car door, she stepped out in her tight skirt and high heels and tottered to the front of the car. There was a lever under here somewhere to… She abandoned her search and jumped back when tendrils of steam began to seep from the edge of the bonnet.

She grabbed her handbag and moved away from the vehicle in case it exploded or something. As it began to spot with rain, she stood under the overhanging branches of a large oak tree and raked her fingers through her hair, clueless as to what to do.

A sudden movement up ahead had her running into the road, waving her arms above her head like someone possessed.

'Hey! Please… stop!'

The black BMW slowed to a complete halt in front of her and the driver's door opened.

A well-built man with a kind face and a willing smile emerged.

That was the first time she set eyes on Darren Thorne.

Fourteen months after that day, Louise stood by the lounge door and watched as Darren and Archie pieced together Lego.

Her husband and her son, forming a wonderful bond, the sort she'd feared Archie would never know.

The adoption papers had been completed, their family counselling interviews had been successful and the solicitor said they could expect to hear that Darren was legally Archie's father any day now.

The core of ice in Louise's heart had melted some time ago. She felt a warmth and optimism she'd never felt in her life before. It had never been like this with Martyn, even though she'd truly believed she couldn't live without him at the time.

Life had a funny way of knowing what was best, even if it took some time to get around to actually doing it.

CHAPTER 63

Alice

I don't know how, but by some miracle, I sleep OK. When I wake up, I have a conviction about what I need to do. First things first.

I use James's phone because I know, from buying credit online, it's an unregistered pay-as-you-go contract. Nobody is aware that it belongs to him.

I dial non-emergency 101 to speak to Nottinghamshire Police. It feels like the right thing to do. I don't feel comfortable doing nothing at all, because I have certain information that James might be in danger, and he has disappeared, after all.

'I wanted to know if someone has reported a man missing,' I begin, already worrying that what I've said sounds random.

'Can I ask the name of the man?' the operator asks and I imagine her rolling her eyes to a colleague to signify she's got a crackpot on the line.

'His name is James Wilson. He's about six foot tall with brown hair and—'

'Do you actually know this person?

'Yes. Well, no, not really. I spoke to him once but he always came past my place on the tram and then one day he disappeared and…'

I stop talking. I nearly mentioned having the phone.

'And… you were saying?'

'And the girl upstairs said he used to be her boyfriend and I think her *new* boyfriend might have done something bad to him.'

Silence on the end of the phone.

'Hello?' I say.

'Yes. Just looking at what we've got here and I'm afraid it's not enough, it's too vague. We'd need full contact details at least. Do you think you can get his phone number and an address?'

'I'll try,' I say dully before ending the call. I can't blame her for not taking me seriously. I've just made a complete and utter fool of myself.

I decide to call upstairs at Jenny's, to try and find out a bit more about James.

It's the last thing I can do, I think. If this doesn't work, then I might just let it rest. I don't really have any choice.

She opens the door and I immediately notice the dark shadows under her eyes and her dishevelled appearance.

'Are you feeling OK?' I ask her. 'You look really tired.'

'Didn't sleep much. Come in.'

She offers me coffee and I accept a cup. She doesn't use her new-fangled machine but just makes instant with boiling water.

We take our drinks through to the lounge and I walk over to the window, noticing the blind has been raised again now.

'Seen anything else of your admirer lately?' I look down at the tram stop, imagining myself sitting directly underneath smiling like an idiot at a man who hadn't even noticed I was there.

'No,' she says curtly. 'I told you, it's been sorted.'

That chilling phrase again. She obviously isn't at all keen on talking about it.

'Did you just call for a chat, or did you want something?' Her voice is flat and I immediately feel caught out.

'Just a chat. I wanted to see how you were, how you were feeling after your news.'

I smile and glance at her stomach, but she doesn't respond.

'Have you had the chance to tell your boyfriend the good news yet?'

She slams her mug down and her eyes overspill at the same time.

'He called me stupid, told me to get rid of it,' she says. 'Can you believe it?'

'Oh no! I'm so sorry, Jenny.'

I feel so bad for her. Not least because I can remember how awful it was for poor Louise when Martyn told her virtually the same thing.

'Yeah, I know. Apparently he does want us to have kids but only when the time's right, and guess what? Now is not the right time.'

I shiver at the similarity of what was said to Louise. Are all men the same?

'He might come round a bit, it's probably been a shock.' Why I'm defending a selfish, controlling thug I've never met, I don't know. Although it's got something to do with trying to make Jenny feel better.

'Maybe,' she mumbles.

'But you know, this isn't just his baby, is it? You have a choice in the matter, it's your body. If you want to, you could bring the baby up alone. Plenty of people do.'

She looks at me, shocked at first, but then her eyes brighten a little. Whoever this man is, he's done a sterling job of convincing her she needs him in order to survive.

'They do, don't they? I could do that, I don't have to do something awful to my baby.'

She rubs her stomach.

'Thanks, Alice.'

I reach over and squeeze her hand and for some reason choose this moment to ask my question.

'Jenny, what's the name of that guy on the tram? James…'

I just need to hear her say it. So I can be sure.

'What the hell is wrong with you? Are you mental?' she yells. 'Why are you asking questions about someone you've never even set eyes on?'

She's wild and unpredictable. I've got to try and calm her down before people hear the commotion.

'I have… set eyes on him, I mean. I've seen him from my window too.'

'What?' She frowns, trying to understand what I'm saying.

'I have breakfast by the window and I'd see him every morning, smiling and waving up.'

She stares at me, and my stupid burning cheeks give me away.

'You thought… he was waving at you!' Her hand flies to her mouth, but she isn't shocked. She's trying not to laugh.

I feel a sudden shiver of dislike for her.

'No! Well, not exactly. It was more that I didn't know he was waving at *you*.'

'I can't believe it! Although at a bit of a distance I suppose you wouldn't be able to tell where he was focusing,' she concedes. '*Now* I understand why you're so interested. The truth is, I don't really know anything, but I hope he's OK. I should have never have told Mark that he had found out where I lived. James was all right really, although a bit intense… obsessed, my mum called it. I tried to make it work for four years, but we just sort of grew apart. He was devastated when I left.'

My mouth is dry and I'm finding it difficult to focus, but Jenny is finally opening up a bit and I can't waste that chance.

'Look, Jenny, I hope you know you can trust me. I'm worried about your situation and yesterday I meant to give you my mobile number. Can I put it in your phone now so you've got it?'

'I'll be OK, honestly, but that's kind of you, thanks.' She tossed her phone over to me. 'There's no lock on it; Mark says we shouldn't have any secrets from each other.'

'Have you thought about visiting your doctor? He'll get you in the system for scans and stuff.'

Her face brightens and she starts talking about all the things she's been reading about early pregnancy. I nod and grunt in what I hope are the right places, keeping one eye on the call list I've just opened.

Her incoming call log is the same number repeated numerous times. I recognise it. It's the one that filled the call log on James's phone; the number of the man who left the death threat message on his answerphone.

The strange thing is that there's no name, it's just the number, as it is if someone who isn't in your address book calls you. Still, I'm convinced enough that I know I need to tell Jenny everything for her own safety, as well as James's.

'And I think they do the second scan at—'

'Jenny, I'm sorry, but there's something really important I need to tell you.'

She stops talking immediately, her eyes wide, and I tell her. I tell her everything.

CHAPTER 64

'I don't know what to say.'

She's remained silent the whole time I've been speaking. All through telling her about the coffee shop, picking up James's phone, the stuff that was on it and finally my call to the police this morning, she's never said a word.

'So let me get this straight. You didn't want my phone because you were worried about me; you wanted to check my boyfriend's number.'

She holds out her hand and I place her phone in it.

'Sorry,' I say, chastened. 'But you'd never have willingly given it to me, would you? You're too afraid of him.'

'How dare you?' she snaps. 'You're treating me like I'm a child who can't make her own judgements, just like *he* does. You're no better than him!'

'At least I'm not the one hassling someone with phone calls and leaving threatening messages. You owe it to James to find out if Mark has done something terrible.'

I think about the note I received… Who sent it?

Her phone beeps and she glances at it.

'You'd better go,' she says, swallowing hard. 'Mark will be coming over soon.'

I stand up and follow her to the door.

'I'm just asking you to find out if James is OK, that's all,' I say. 'Mark can't just hurt people when the mood takes him. What kind of a father will he make?'

She opens the door and I step into the corridor.

'Alice?' I turn round. 'I think it's best if you don't come up any more.'

And with that, she closes the door.

Once I'm back in the apartment, I take a stool and sit by the kitchen window with my phone. This is my chance to see the mystery man, Mark, and take some photos if I can.

Within a short time, my back and legs are throbbing, but I can't take any more painkillers until tonight. It's mind over matter, I tell myself.

I need to keep my eyes on the car park, so I can't read to pass the time. Movement catches my attention, but it's just an elderly man I've seen before who I think lives on the ground floor. A couple of minutes later, a young woman drives into the car park, unstraps a baby from a car seat and walks towards the building.

And that's how it goes, getting busier as the afternoon wears on.

I've been sitting there an hour and I'm finally thinking I need to move before my joints seize up again when I hear a loud thump from upstairs in Jenny's flat. Raised voices follow.

I seem to hear better here in the kitchen; maybe it's the shared pipework or something. I can't hear actual words, of course, but I can hear a man shouting and he sounds very, very angry. There's another loud bang, and then everything goes quiet for a while.

I hold the worktop and lean forward, stretching my aching back.

Now I know more about the type of person Jenny is involved with, should I call the police? What if that final bang was Jenny hitting the floor because she's dared to have a visitor up there? Maybe she's told him about my concerns over James and he's gone crazy. I'll feel so bad if I'm to blame for making things worse for her.

Then I remember her words earlier today: *I think it's best if you don't come up any more.* I'm not her keeper. She's made it clear she wants me to butt out of her affairs.

My stomach feels a bit delicate. I walk into the hallway just to make sure I locked the door, which of course I did. I can't seem to stop Martyn's face flashing in my mind.

I nearly jump out of my skin when the doorbell rings. My feet freeze to the floor and I hardly dare breathe.

'Alice? It's me, Jenny!' The bell rings again. 'Alice? I know you're in there… please let me in. I need your help.'

She sounds desperate… scared, even.

I don't move.

Now she's knocking on the door, banging. 'Alice, I beg you, please… open the door!'

I can't stand it any more. I can't just leave her there. I unbolt and unlock the door and she's there, head hanging.

'You look terrible,' I say. 'I heard all the noise and—'

She literally flies into me, knocking me to the floor and pressing a vile-smelling cloth to my face. I cry out as pain pulses through my body, so strong I think I'm going to pass out. I feel myself being flipped over and someone gripping me like iron, then something is being stuffed in my mouth. As I hear the door slam closed, I start to feel sick and drowsy…

When I open my eyes, it's dark.

I remember the cloth against my face and claw at it with one hand, but my nails scratch my mouth because there is no cloth there.

My throat feels so sore, as if someone has scraped it with sandpaper. I try to cry out, but sound won't come. I have to move… but that's easier said than done.

My right hip actually feels dislocated. I can't sit up, so I crawl forward on my belly, like a snake, until I reach the kitchen door.

After a short rest, I roll over onto my back and bend my knees. My head, back and legs are throbbing but I'm slowly managing to move. Using my legs as leverage, I inch my shoulders and upper back against the wall next to the kitchen door.

The lights from the car park are providing a little illumination to the kitchen and hallway, but not much. At last I'm in a seated position and I close my eyes and allow myself a few deep breaths.

I remember Jenny shouting outside the door. I can't recall her exact words, but it was enough to make me think I should let her in after the noises I'd heard upstairs.

When she flew at me, her face was pained, like mine when she hit me. She looked… odd… as if she was hurting too.

I don't remember anything much after that, just the feeling of darkness and losing control… and then I woke up. I haven't a clue how much time has passed; I'm not wearing my watch.

I open my eyes again and slowly, painfully, using the door frame as support, get myself up to standing.

I head for the sink. Desperate for water, I down two glasses and fill a third. As I turn to walk away, I see a silver glint on the worktop. James's phone.

I snap on the light and look at it. I don't remember leaving it out, but I'm glad Jenny didn't take it.

My head is banging, banging, the pain almost unbearable.

And then the doorbell rings.

I nearly collapse with fear. What if Jenny is back? She assaulted me, she's crazy.

It rings again and I step into the hallway. The bolts are off, of course, but it looks as though the catch is on, so it must have locked when she left.

'Miss Fisher?' A loud male voice. 'Police. Open up, please.'

I don't know why, but I don't doubt the voice. I slide the chain on and open the door. Two plain-clothes officers stand there, holding ID.

'I'm DI Peters,' the first one says. 'And this is DS Khan. We'd like to come in, please, to discuss an allegation with you.'

I glance at the ID and I'm satisfied it's genuine. I open the door.

'What's all this about?' I say, my voice croaky. 'I've just been assaulted in my own home.'

The detectives glance at each other.

'Really? Have you reported it?'

'No. I've just… I've only just come to.' I know I'm not making any sense, so I decide to shut up for now. 'Please, come through.' Maybe one of the neighbours has reported a fracas; I don't know if I shouted out or not, but perhaps someone heard something.

I'm still holding my glass of water when we sit down in the lounge, but I don't offer the detectives a drink. I don't feel steady enough on my feet.

'Miss Fisher, can you tell us if you know a man called James Wilson?'

'Oh my goodness, have you found him? Is he OK?' They look at me stony-faced.

'Just answer the question, please.' DS Khan frowns. 'Do you know him?'

'I didn't know him very well… I haven't seen him for a while.'

'Do you mind if I take a look around?' DS Khan asks.

'I suppose…' I follow her with my eyes as she circles the room, picking things up, studying them.

'We've had a missing person report filed this morning for a James Wilson by his father,' DI Peters explains. 'And we've reason to believe you may know of his whereabouts.'

'I told you, I haven't seen him for a while,' I say, distracted by DS Khan leaving the room. 'Where's she going?'

'She's just taking a look around the rest of the flat.'

'Well he's not here, if that's what you think!'

'No, I don't expect he is.' DS Khan appears in the doorway again, holding something up. 'But I believe this might be his phone.'

CHAPTER 65

Louise

After Alice's arrest in connection with James's disappearance, the detectives took her to the station. While she sat in that small, cold holding cell, so confused she'd forgotten what day it was, Louise sprang into action.

She had a spare key for Alice's apartment that her sister had given her years ago, in case there was an emergency with their mother. She'd never used it, always preferring to ring the bell for speed, but it had lived at the back of the kitchen drawer at home, where she occasionally set eyes on it. She retrieved it and drove to the flat with Archie in tow.

'We need to look for clues about what happened so we can help Auntie Alice,' she told him.

'I'm brilliant at finding clues, Mum,' Archie said. 'I might be a forensic investigator when I grow up.'

When they arrived, a couple of scene-of-crime officers were already in there.

'This is my sister's flat,' Louise told the police officer at the door. 'We've come to get her some spare clothing.'

'Sorry, madam. This apartment has been declared a crime scene. You can gain entry when they've finished.'

They were standing there in the corridor, not knowing whether to wait or come back later, when eagle-eyed Archie grabbed Louise's arm.

'Mum!' he hissed. 'I've just seen Jenny walk upstairs. She lives above Auntie Alice. She might know something.'

Louise realised that the unreliable lifts she'd always hated had probably forced Alice's neighbour to walk up to her apartment.

They climbed the stairs and knocked at Jenny's door.

There was no answer at first, so Louise knocked again. After a few seconds, the door opened and Jenny's face appeared, complete with guarded expression.

She looked down and smiled when she saw Archie.

'Hi, it's Jenny, isn't it?' Louise held out her hand. 'I'm Alice's sister. Could I come in, just for a minute or two?'

She wondered if it was her imagination or if Jenny's face had hardened when she introduced herself.

'How's your nose now, Archie?' Jenny asked pointedly.

'Fine.' He shrugged and turned to his mother. 'She helped me when I had the nosebleed.'

'You'd better come through,' Jenny said, turning to walk down the short hallway that was a carbon copy of Alice's. 'My boyfriend Mark is here and we were just wondering what had happened.'

Louise and Archie followed her towards the lounge and both stopped dead at the door, both their faces frozen in horror.

'What the…'

Darren jumped up from the sofa.

'What the hell are you two doing here?' he yelled.

'I could ask you the same question,' Louise said faintly, trying to keep her legs from buckling beneath her.

'What's wrong… Can someone please tell me what's happening?' Jenny said, her eyes wide and confused.

'Your boyfriend is also my husband.' Louise stared, the sound of her own voice surreal in her ears. 'Except his name is Darren. Mark is his middle name.'

'What?' Jenny looked at him, her eyes wide and accusing. 'Mark?'

'You knew I was married,' he frowned, 'so don't go acting all shocked now.'

'Yes, but I didn't know Archie was your *son*! I didn't know we were having an affair above your own sister-in-law's bedroom!'

Archie began to shake.

Louise placed her hands on his shoulders and watched as he began to cry inconsolably, his eyes never leaving Darren's. Her racing heart felt as if it would split any second.

'You lied to me,' Jenny whispered, her face drawn and pale. 'You told me you were separated from your wife and you'd got no kids.'

'Archie is his adopted son,' Louise told her. She looked at Darren. 'Forcing me to try and get Alice out of the flat to pay the debts you've run up... Threatening that you'll get custody of Archie—'

'That's enough!' Darren clenched his fists and stared at Jenny. 'You'd better keep your mouth shut, bitch. You know what I'm talking about.'

Archie stepped forward and spoke between sobs.

'Auntie Alice says you should never be afraid to talk to someone, Jenny.'

'Shut it, champ,' Darren snapped.

'I'm not your champ.' Archie pulled up his sleeves. 'He told me to keep a secret too, Mum.'

Louise cried out at the bruises on Archie's upper arm.

'You little...' Darren took a few strides forward and Archie yelped in fear as he ducked around his mother and ran from the flat.

Darren grabbed hold of Louise's arm.

'Don't touch me,' she cried. 'Let go!'

'Get out you lying, cheating . . .' Jenny picked up a lamp and cracked him hard on the back of the head with it. He roared, clutching his skull, then turned and pushed her so hard she flew across the room.

Louise turned to run, but he grabbed her by the hair.

'Get off me!' she screamed. 'I have to find Archie.'

Suddenly the police officer from downstairs appeared with Archie at his side.

Darren let go of Louise and backed off to the other side of the room.

'You two, please take the child and wait outside the flat. Additional officers are on their way.'

Louise and Jenny ran past him, Louise pulling Archie by the hand.

'You did amazingly, Archie,' she said breathlessly. 'Now tell me, what did your dad ask you to keep a secret?'

CHAPTER 66

Archie

Me, Mum and Auntie Alice sit in the living room of her flat.

The forensic officers have finished in here now. They were looking for evidence that James Wilson was here, but Auntie Alice says they won't find any because he has never been to her home.

They both sit staring into space and they don't even drink the coffee that Mum has made for them. They look a bit dazed, like they've been near an explosion. If this was a computer game, it would be very boring and nobody would buy it.

'How's Archie?' Auntie Alice says like Archie is another boy who is sitting right next to me.

I don't answer and Mum says, 'I was so proud of him, finding the courage to speak out like he did.'

They both turn and smile at me.

'Mrs Booth says nobody has the right to keep anyone else silent if they want to share something… a secret,' I say.

'Mrs Booth is right,' Auntie Alice says, looking at Mum. 'I'm sorry, Louise, I thought *you* were the one hurting him, controlling him. Darren told me things, said your behaviour was erratic, that you couldn't be trusted.'

'All lies.' Mum shakes her head sadly. 'It's OK, Archie, you can tell Auntie Alice what happened now.'

They both look at me, their eyes boring into me like lasers. Maybe they can see inside my head and read my thoughts. Maybe they know that I—

'Archie?' Mum says.

'When Mum was at a work conference, I saw Dad and Jenny kissing in his car,' I say, looking away from them at the window. 'I tried to sneak away but Dad saw me and came in the house after me.'

'You hated Jenny on sight,' Auntie Alice whispers. 'But when she came to the flat, she didn't seem to know who *you* were.'

'Only Dad saw me watching that day.' I shrug. 'I ran back inside before she could see me.'

'Tell Auntie Alice what your dad said,' Mum says.

'He said I had to keep quiet or he'd hurt me.'

'Poor Archie.' Tears spring into Auntie Alice's eyes. 'The burden he's had to bear on his own. I can't stand thinking about it.'

Mum nods.

'And the bruises I saw that day, Archie, who did that?'

'Tell her,' Mum says.

'Dad,' I whisper. 'When I asked him if he was still seeing Jenny, he grabbed me really hard. Said that's what he'd do to Mum if I said another word about it.'

Mum clears her throat and smiles, but I can see she feels like crying.

'School are aware and they say he's like a different boy,' she tells Auntie Alice. 'Happier, friendlier to the other kids. He's been under so much pressure and I blame myself for never realising it was connected to his dad.'

'And Jenny… thank goodness she spoke out!' Auntie Alice clutches her throat.

'Why did you care so much about that man Dad hurt?' I look at her. 'You didn't really know him, he wasn't *your* boyfriend. He just went past on the tram each day.'

'That's true,' Auntie Alice says. 'But people can't just go around hurting others, Archie. If you saw someone being hurt in the street, would you turn away and go about your business because you didn't know them, or would you run for help? In certain situations, we all have a moral responsibility to do the right thing.'

I turn her words over in my head for a moment.

What she said feels true deep inside me, in the place that *just knows* if things are right or wrong.

'Jenny was so angry,' Mum says. 'So, so angry that she was pregnant and Darren had lied through his teeth about everything. When the police got here, she just blurted it all out. Told them how Darren had strangled James to death and had attacked you here, in your own flat.'

They both look at me then, like I've heard too much. But I'm not a baby. I've always known more than they think.

'And they arrested him there and then, when Jenny told them the truth?'

Mum nods again. 'Predictably, he didn't go quietly, but he's got his comeuppance now, at least.'

'And all those times you were trying to get me to sell the flat, it was for my benefit, not your own?'

'He threatened to hurt you, and now I know he hurt Archie. He told me if I could persuade you to sell, he'd give me thirty grand of my share and a divorce. But if not, he'd never let us go.' Mum glances at me and drops her voice as if I might not hear her. 'He'd already tried to convince our neighbours to think of me as a drunk, a fraudster. He led friends and family to believe I was hurting Archie and had got us deep in debt…'

'When it was him all the time,' Auntie Alice adds.

'From the moment we married, he was keen to formally adopt Archie. He wanted to prove that he thought of him as his real son.' Mum looks at me and her face is sad. 'I thought it was a sign of love, but it was the ultimate form of control. Soon as the official adoption papers came through, he ruled me with a rod of iron and threatened to get custody from me at every turn.'

Tears roll down her face and I can't help staring. It's the first time I've seen Mum cry in years.

'Archie used to sometimes refer to the secret in passing but I thought it was just kid's stuff. I had so much on my mind, I stopped listening, and I feel so guilty now. Turns out his secret was real enough.' Mum looks at me. 'Sorry, pumpkin.'

I try to smile and tell her it's OK, but I can't do it. Because this isn't the only secret I've been keeping.

There is another secret. One that is far, far worse.

CHAPTER 67

Eighteen months earlier

The door opposite the bathroom in Auntie Alice's flat is ajar and I hear a noise coming from behind it. A sort of puffing, scratching sound.

I take a couple of steps closer and peer through the crack.

For a moment, it feels like I'm still in the game world. Where things aren't real, where nothing that's in front of your eyes makes any sense.

Before I can stop it, my breath catches in his throat. My hand flies up to my mouth but it's too late. The gasp is already out and I know I have been heard.

I turns to run, but I hear shouting and I feel a hand on my shoulder.

'I won't tell,' I cry out. 'I promise, I won't tell.'

'It's not what you think,' Mum says. 'She was in pain and I was just helping her, do you understand?'

'Yes,' I gasp.

I try not to look, but my eyes dart past her and I can see Granny lying on her back in the bed. Her eyes are wide open and her arm is hanging over the side. Her thrashing legs are still and the pillow Mum was holding to her face is on the floor.

Mum crouches down and holds my shoulders tightly. She presses her face close and I can see tiny red veins in the whites of her big round eyes. Her breath smells of coffee.

'They could put me in prison and you'd have to go and live in a children's home. Do you hear me?' Her voice sounds shaky and high and she's pinching my shoulders too tight.

'I know,' I say. My throat feels sore and swollen, even though I haven't got a cold. 'I promise I won't say anything, Mum.'

'It might have looked like I was hurting her, Archie, but I wasn't. I was *helping* her.' Mum looks behind me in the hallway. 'Auntie Alice will be back from the shop soon and it's really important we're upset about Gran. She must never know. Do you understand?'

'Yes,' I say. 'I do.'

'Good boy. This is our secret, OK? Just between you and me.'

'Yes,' I say, and Mum watches as I swallow the secret down like a big, hard nut.

CHAPTER 68

Alice

The flat is up for sale now, and for the time being, until I find something else, I'm living with Louise and Archie. It just feels better to be amongst family.

I think I'm slowly starting to feel better. Yesterday, I even got my paints and brushes out for the first time in years.

I've learned a lot about myself in recent weeks. That I'm a people-pleaser, that I've stayed quiet when I should have spoken up.

I don't know how I'm going to deal with what's coming, but I will. I'll find a way.

You see, there were never equal shares for myself and my sister in Mum's will. Mum left everything to me.

I was executor of the will, and the day I went to the solicitor's, Louise was ill and couldn't attend.

'Don't worry,' I told her. 'I'll sort everything out.'

The content of the will was a surprise to me. I gave Louise half of what was in Mum's bank account, though it wasn't much.

'She left us half of the flat each, but the will states I am the one who decides when to sell it.'

'So I can't force you out, you mean.'

I shrugged. 'There's no rush, is there?'

Her lips sealed together in a tight line, but she didn't say anything.

I couldn't face telling her about the flat that day, couldn't put up with the drama. I fully intended telling her soon, though. Then time just started racing on. A few weeks passed, a few months... I nearly told her when she started badgering me to sell. But I didn't. The time still wasn't right.

And here we are now, and it's twenty months after Mum died.

Darren is in prison, Jenny is serving a suspended sentence and has left the area, and Louise is going to have to sell the house. But even that won't cover all her debts.

Louise is not showy with her emotions, but I know that underneath it all she loved Mum. She was devastated when she died.

And that's why I've decided I will never tell her the painful truth. She will never know that Mum left her nothing at all. I won't break her heart.

When the flat is sold, I'll give half of the proceeds to my sister.

I smile to myself, enjoying the warm glow that comes when you know you've made the right decision.

'Auntie Alice?'

My nephew peers around the door.

'Come in, Archie, no need to hide back there.' I pat the seat cushion next to me.

Archie is staying with me tonight. Louise is leaving early tomorrow to visit Darren in HMP Wakefield. She got in touch with him a few weeks after he wrote to her apologising and professing his undying love.

I watch with concern as my nephew walks across the room. His face is pale, and although I was concerned about him piling weight on, he looks like he's lost quite a bit, and quickly. It's left him looking drawn and insubstantial.

He sits down next to me on the settee.

'If Mum couldn't look after me any more, would I have to go and live in a children's home?'

'What? Where's that come from?' I laugh softly and put my arm around him, pulling him closer to me. 'I don't know where this is going, but the answer is no, of course not. If there's some reason your mum couldn't look after you, you'd come and live with me.'

'Because we're family.'

'Too right.' I grin. 'And after everything we've been through, we want no more secrets ever, right?'

'Right,' Archie says faintly. 'Even terrible ones.'

'*Especially* terrible ones.' I nudge him playfully.

And then he pulls away from my hug, looks me in the eye and Archie tells me his secret.

CHAPTER 69

I don't sleep. I sit in bed staring at Mum's death certificate.

Cause of death: *heart failure*.

Except a death certificate cannot and does not say what happened leading up to a soul's final breath. And now I know.

I never suspected a thing. Even though Mum seemed to be stable and appeared to be coping well according to her regular hospital tests, I'd always known the end could be cruelly sudden, as was her first heart attack.

When I got back from the shops that day, Louise was distraught. The ambulance pulled up at the same time I reached the door of the apartment building. I heard the paramedics say my own apartment number as they grabbed the stretcher and equipment.

Louise had to attend to Archie, who was vomiting and near hysterical.

'Take him home,' I told her through tears. 'I'll sort everything out here.'

Good old dependable Alice.

Stupid, gullible Alice.

So what do I do?

Do I go to the police? Expect them to be interested in evidence presented by a child who was six years old at the time of the offence? Would they exhume the body and carry out macabre tests on Mum's body… Could they even tell if heart failure had been brought on by trauma beforehand?

If they put Louise in prison too, where would that leave Archie, who is already receiving counselling thanks to ongoing support from Mrs Booth at school?

I bury my face in my hands for the hundredth time.

What do I do?

The next morning, I take Archie to school and then text Louise to tell her I need to speak to her urgently. She agrees grudgingly, keen to set off to see Darren.

'What is it?' she says, glancing at her watch. 'I've got ten minutes max before I have to leave for visiting. The traffic is mad at this time, I—'

'Shut up and listen,' I say.

Her mouth falls open and her brows knit together. But she's not the one in control any more.

I hand her Mum's death certificate.

'What's this for?' She frowns and shakes her head, and then I see it. The dawning of realisation, the hard swallow and her cheeks draining of colour.

'I know, Louise,' I tell her. 'And I can see the truth on your face as if you've told me yourself.'

'Archie,' she whispers.

'To do that to Mum… and then burden your son with the knowledge, even trying to get him diagnosed with ADHD to shut him up.'

'I… You don't understand—'

'I understand perfectly, and you sicken me.' She opens her mouth to speak and I hold up a hand. 'I've listened to you for years, put up with your criticism and your judgemental attitude. Well that time is over. No more, Louise.'

'I didn't kill her!' She shakes the certificate in my face. 'It says here she died of heart failure.'

'You and I both know that was almost certainly brought on by you trying to suffocate her.' I snatch the certificate back. 'This piece of paper might have the final cause of death on it, but you hastened it.'

'It was… a moment of madness. I was tired of seeing her suffering, I—'

'Save it!' I wipe my wet cheeks with the back of my hand. 'You didn't see her suffering, you were never around enough to witness it. You just wanted her money.'

'You don't know the financial pressure we were under.' She spits the words out, backing away from me. 'You've never known hardship, pampered by Mum all these years. She'd have bailed you out, but Darren and I… we were left to sort out our problems alone.'

'The problems you had inflicted on *yourselves!*' I shake my head, incredulous. 'And you've never learned. I can't believe you've forgiven Darren everything after what he's done to Archie.'

'Everyone deserves a second chance,' she states tartly, suddenly recovering from her self-pity. 'With good behaviour, Darren's sentence could be halved, and we've already discussed what we'll do. If I file for bankruptcy and put Mum's inheritance in his name, the creditors won't be able to get their hands on the money. When he gets out, we'll have the means to start again.'

I shake my head. 'What planet are you on? You do realise, you're damaged. You need help.'

She throws back her head and laughs. A coarse, hacking sound that chills me.

'*I* need help? That's rich coming from you. The woman without a life.'

'Seeing Dad's behaviour all those years has had an effect on you, Louise. I've always thought you were like him, but underneath you're as much of a victim as Mum was. You bounce from one controlling relationship to another without even realising it.'

'I'm not that dumb that I'd take relationship advice from *you*!'

'Fine,' I say quietly.

'What are you going to do?' she says after a pause.

Her first thought, as always, for herself.

'I'm going to tell you something I should have told you nearly two years ago.'

She waits.

'Mum left you nothing. Your name doesn't appear in the will. She left every single thing she owned to me.'

'Liar!' Her cheeks inflame, her eyes wild and dangerous. 'The will… it says—'

'I told you that because I felt bad, because I was scared of your reaction.'

'I never saw the will,' she says faintly. 'I took your word for it.'

I nod. 'I intended splitting the proceeds of this place anyway. But now I know what I know, I can assure you that I won't be giving you… or Darren… a single penny, though I'll be putting some money in trust for Archie for when he reaches twenty-one.'

'You…' She takes a step towards me, her fists balled and her face a mask of pure hatred. I don't budge an inch.

'I want to play a big part in my nephew's life. If you try and stop me seeing him, I'll have no hesitation in going to the police about what you did.'

'I'll deny it!' Her face lights up. 'They couldn't prove anything. Not now.'

'I think you'll find forensic science has moved on quite a bit, Louise. You'd be surprised what they can tell when they exhume a body.' Her face pales and I keep my poker face, hoping she swallows my bluster. 'Besides, you need to ask yourself if you really want a police inquiry on top of all your other problems.'

She turns then and leaves the flat without another word.

I lock the front door and return to the living room, sitting down in the chair where Mum used to spend time watching her birds.

I reach for her photograph from the coffee table.

'I'm so sorry, Mum. I'm sorry I left her in charge that day.' A fat tear rolls from my cheek onto the glass. 'But I'll do right by Archie and I'll never forget you.'

I kiss the photograph and replace it on the table.

Then I stand up and head for the empty packing boxes.

I've a new life to start living, and it begins right now.

A LETTER FROM KIM

I do hope you have enjoyed reading *The Secret*, my sixth psychological thriller.

Reviews are massively important to authors. So if you did, and could spare just a few minutes to write a short review to say so, I would really appreciate that. You can also connect with me via my website, on Facebook, Goodreads or Twitter. Please do sign up to my email list below to be sure of getting the very latest news, hot off the press!

www.bookouture.com/kl-slater

I've always been fascinated how the truth just has this way of emerging, sometimes after years of remaining hidden. Despite efforts to keep it buried, it manages to rise to the top and show itself.

People don't always choose to keep a secret. Sometimes they stumble upon one, and as we know, some things are so dramatic, so shocking, once revealed they simply cannot be unseen.

Likewise, a chance sighting of a stranger can open doors you might wish had remained closed. Chance can put a fascinating spin on the most pedestrian of lives and lead to excitement – or a nightmare scenario.

Put a chilling secret and a chance encounter together and you might just have a problem.

It's not always easy to do the right thing… It's not always easy to even decide what the right thing is.

And what if a secret isn't your own? What should you do to help if you see a loved one sinking in a quicksand of guilt and doubt but they won't or can't confide in you?

I tend to briefly outline a book before beginning to write. There might be some key scenes or themes that I have in my head and it helps to get them down and give my editor some idea of how the finished book might turn out. But I usually know much less than I'd like. I just have to start writing and go with it.

The characters often have this way of misbehaving and turning into people I didn't expect at all. So it was in *The Secret*, when the character of little Archie started to develop and he suddenly wanted a bigger storyline!

The book is set in Nottinghamshire, the place I was born and have lived all my life. Local readers should be aware I sometimes take the liberty of changing street names or geographical details to suit the story.

As I say goodbye to the characters of *The Secret*, I say hello to the cast of Book 7, which I'm already excited to write!

Best wishes,
Kim x

 KimLSlaterAuthor/

 @KimLSlater

 www.KLSlaterAuthor.com

ACKNOWLEDGEMENTS

Huge thanks to my editor, Lydia Vassar-Smith, who has been a massive support every step of the way and whose ideas and advice have, as always, made the finished book so much better.

Thanks to Camilla Wray at Darley Anderson, who is taking such good care of me and giving great advice and support while my agent Clare Wallace is on maternity leave. By the time *The Secret* is published, Clare's adorable newborn son Vince will be nearly four months old!

Thanks also to the rest of the hard-working team at Darley Anderson Literary, TV and Film Agency, especially Mary Darby and Emma Winter, and to Roya Sarrafi-Gohar, Kristina Egan and Rosanna Bellingham.

Thanks to *all* the Bookouture team for everything they do, especially to Lauren Finger, Leodora Darlington and Kim Nash.

Thanks to Angela Marsons, such a good friend for many years now. I couldn't wish for a better writing buddy and partner in crime on my writing journey.

Massive thanks as always go to my husband, Mac, for his love and support and for taking care of everything so I have the time to write. To my family, especially my daughter, Francesca, and to my mama, who are always there to support and encourage me in my writing.

Special thanks must also go to Henry Steadman, who has again designed such an apt and eye-catching cover that I loved on sight and to Jane Selley and Becca Allen for their eagle-eyed copyediting skills.

Thank you to the bloggers and reviewers who have done so much to help make my thrillers a success. Thank you to everyone who has taken the time to post a positive review online or has taken part in my blog tour. It is always noticed and much appreciated.

Last but not least, thank you *so* much to my amazing readers. I love receiving all the wonderful comments and messages and I am truly grateful for each and every reader's support.